Golden Handcuffs Review

Golden Handcuffs Review Publications

Seattle, Washington

Golden Handcuffs Review Publications

☆

Editor

Lou Rowan

Contributing Editors

Andrea Augé
Nancy Gaffield
Stacey Levine
Rick Moody
Toby Olson
Jerome Rothenberg
Scott Thurston
Carol Watts

Guiding Intelligence

David Antin

LAYOUT MANAGEMENT BY PURE ENERGY PUBLISHING, SEATTLE

PUREENERGYPUB.WORDPRESS.COM

Libraries: *this is Volume II, #26.*

Information about subscriptions, donations, advertising at:
www.goldenhandcuffsreview.com

Or write to: Editor, Golden Handcuffs Review Publications
1825 NE 58th Street, Seattle, WA 98105-2440

Contents

Essays

RESPONSE

Disarticulated Fragments from *The Shenanigans*

☆

Brian Marley

You may be wondering why, from a cohort of nearly one hundred inductees, only six of you have been asked to attend this session. A tap on the shoulder, a whispered invitation, am I right? — I thought so. It's the modus operandi of the security services. That's how our headhunters in Personnel do things, too. Strictly hush-hush. Akin to being groomed, minus the sexual element. If you noticed it happening, you were probably flattered, slightly puzzled, but definitely intrigued. It's what we expect of you. Your special qualities have been noted, your potential duly assessed. I'll wager fifty chocolate ducats wrapped in edible gold foil that the headhunters know you better than your family knows you; better even than you know yourself.

You've been deemed top-drawer material, compared to which the other inductees are, not to put too fine a point on it, makeweights, cannon fodder, destined to occupy an enquiry desk in a Jobcentre in a bleak Northern town from which all hope has fled. Unless, against your better judgment, you choose to visit Wigan or Keighley or British West Hartlepool, you're unlikely to bump into any of them again.

Let me make my intentions perfectly clear:

The keynote I was asked to deliver today – bland, sickly sweet, and given the seal of approval by my line-toeing line-manager Jesus Rodriguez – has been binned, or, more accurately, shredded. If I'd read it aloud my teeth would have rotted down to blackened stumps. So what you're about to receive (and may the Lord make you truly thankful, as Rodriguez doubtless would say) is the unauthorised version.

Rodriguez is on unpaid leave at the moment, but were he here he'd do what his fellow managers always do after lunch: make themselves scarce. They're probably in a meeting of some kind or finding some other way to kill time meaninglessly, confident that they've left the running of this session in the hands of a trusted subordinate.

Their confidence is misplaced. Now that I no longer see the world as they do, I'm not to be trusted.

But rather than dwell on diagnosis and prognosis, let's crack on. The sooner I finish the sooner we get to go home.

≈≈≈

Those who toil in the bowels of this building have to sign the Official Secrets Act on their first day at work. Standard procedure. It's what all civil servants have had to do for a century or more. But U12 goes one step further: we swear a solemn oath – not to the Civil Service, but to U12 exclusively. We also expect new recruits to undergo a brief initiation ceremony which, I admit, may cause a certain amount of physical discomfort and psychological stress. It's not a hazing ritual per se, despite superficial similarities, such as the possibility that you'll sustain injuries, minor ones, usually nothing worse than a few abrasions and bruises. However, in the spirit of full disclosure, I should tell you that once, in the late 1980s, in the heat of the moment, things got a bit out of hand and someone's teeth were knocked out – three, as I recall, one of which was already badly chipped from (allegedly) levering the tops off beer bottles in a display of drunken bravado. A young initiate by the name of Muat, who has since become our keenest initiator. Again, I'm honour bound to tell you that he's a waterboarding enthusiast, though that's a technique we no longer practise at U12, much to his disappointment, Guantanamo having brought it into disrepute. Pushing small boys' heads down toilets was his favourite pastime at school, and waterboarding is, as he puts it, 'just an adult version of that – pure nostalgia, really'. He's acknowledged by one and all to lack self-restraint. Muat acknowledges it too, shamelessly, with a smile. Needless to say, we paid the full whack for his restorative dentistry, so no lasting harm was done.

Please don't get me wrong: humiliation is not the ceremony's principal aim. That said, a complete absence of humiliation cannot be guaranteed.

Nor, with intimidating body language, collective parade ground barks, madhouse shrieks, and sewer-fed streams of vile invective, do we wish to break your spirit and remould you in our image. If, however, you're particularly susceptible to influence of that kind – which, by the way, I wouldn't go so far as to call bullying, though I appreciate many do – you could be eligible for the *U12er of the Year* award, of which I'm a three-times winner. The gold buttons on my blazer are actually winner's medals. Impressive aren't they? And what's mine could so easily be yours if you're shown to be made of the right stuff. Think of it, at the very least, as a character-building exercise.

Nor do we seek to emulate our Japanese cousins, the yakuza, who we admire for their extraordinary self-discipline. Yakuzas willingly chop off the first joint of their pinkie (left hand if they're right-handed, and vice versa) to show fealty and atone for misdeeds past, present and, if naked ambition outstrips caution, as it nearly always does, future.

All we ask is that, for identificationary purposes, you agree to have a small black dot, indistinguishable from a mole, tattooed on a specific part of your body. If you're particularly dark-skinned, a negus-like red dot may be substituted. Surely that's not unreasonable, now, is it?

So, with the yakuza in mind, the point of placement we've chosen for the tattoo is the topside of the webspace between pinkie and ring finger. Can't quite visualise where that is? Between the two most outlying digits. In the connective tissue at the base of both, knuckle side up. The tattoo you'll receive is a dot no bigger than a tardigrade. Still can't visualise it? Here, take a look at mine and you'll see what I mean.

Unless, like I just did, you splay your fingers – an uncommon gesture in the UK, used almost exclusively by stage magicians when they're doing the abracadabra – it won't be noticed by anyone but a fellow U12er, and if someone else does notice it, no matter, they won't know what it signifies.

Look, the initiation ceremony is really no big deal, but I appreciate that's not how everyone sees it. If you find the idea worrying, by which I mean distressing, and don't wish to continue, feel free to join the other inductees in the lecture theatre ... far end of the hallway ... near the main entrance. Or, if you prefer, you can sail through the entrance and out into the street with, as they say, nary a backward glance. No-one will try to stop you or consider you in any way deficient if that's what you decide to do. Your choice entirely.

[...]

Okay, so we're one inductee down. Notice how he crept out of the room, eyes downcast, shoulders slumped, as if ashamed. As indeed he should be. His parents will be mortified – even his father, an armed robber currently serving eight to ten in HMP Belmarsh. He'd hoped for better things for his son, and those hopes have now been crushed like a jailhouse bedbug. Ah well.

I confess, from the moment I read the transcript of his job interview I had doubts about the lad.

By the way, just so you know: there is no initiation ceremony. Never has been nor will be. It was a ploy to test your staying power – a test you've passed with flying colours. Well done!

But ... there really is an oath.

Though incredibly wordy and wholly immemorable, it boils down to this:

Thou Shalt Not Steal.

If, after hearing what I have to say, you decide to take up a post in our department – *as indeed you should* – I warn you: temptation will be your shadowman, dogging every step you take.

Most of us are, to some degree, light-fingered. No, don't shake your head like that, you're shedding a veritable snowstorm of dandruff. What I've just said is true. About light-fingeredness, I mean. If that's your inclination, or, even worse, your tendency, the odds in U12 are heavily stacked against you, more so than in any other Civil Service department. We're fastidious about such things, and for good reason. Any department wishing to test the financial probity of any other department has to be seen by the Central Accounts

Committee to be scrupulous to a fault. Every ballpoint pen and staple in U12 has been fully accounted for. Paper is doled out by the sheet rather than the ream.

Sorely tempted you may be, that's understandable, acquisitiveness is a fundamental part of human nature, encoded in our DNA. But no matter how weak your resolve, remember:

Thou Shalt Not Steal.

≈≈≈

It's time I gave you a flavour of what we in U12 actually do. Although the case file I've chosen is far from typical, it's much more revealing than the everyday Holmesian gradgrinding we engage in. I'll let you draw your own conclusion as to whether I handled it correctly.

Please bear in mind that my liaison oppo at the Met, Sergeant Richard Aerosmith, has a quirky sense of humour. Every now and then he sends me a conundrum, something he expects me to try to make sense of, if I can. This is done as, I think, a joke, though sometimes, because I have an insufficiently developed sense of humour (so I've been told, by – who else? – Muat), I fail to get the joke. But not always.

That worries me less than the feeling that subtle attempts at one-upmanship are being made. Not by Aerosmith. Not directly. That's not the kind of man he is, nor the kind of thing he'd do. I have no evidence to back this up, but I suspect he's being leant on by his immediate superior, Inspector Rickets, who holds U12 in contempt. It's worth noting that Aerosmith thinks the same about Rickets.

In a nutshell, I think Aerosmith has been ordered by Rickets to put me to the test. If I fail the test, which he hopes I will, that small-scale failure will be flagged up as typical large-scale incompetence at U12. During negotiations for the scant resources that are shared between the Met and U12, the Met will then have the upper hand.

I may be wrong, of course. But how would I know, one way or the other?

Perhaps it's a conundrum you can solve on my behalf.

ITEM: *71424/DEP.c/WBag*

A prosthetic limb. A leg, to be precise. One of extraordinary length.

The average human femur is, from the medial condyle to the greater trochanter, 47cm in length, the shaft circumference 9cm. The lost limb differed considerably from that: length 79cm, circumference 8cm. The small circumference of the prosthesis relative to its length was made possible, one assumes, because of the material from which it was manufactured: carbon fibre, stronger than bone.

It was found at low tide near Wapping, lying on a bed of rotting seaweed. The foot was encased in a battered, salt-bleached shoe, a man's shoe of enormous size, similar to those worn by circus clowns. The style: brogue. Red leather. Handmade but without the benefit of a maker mark. Because of the state the shoe was in, it was probable that the prosthesis had been in the water for some time.

Obviously it must have belonged to someone very tall, a veritable giant. Assuming that all his limbs were in proportion, and this one, though artificial, was indicative, he would've had to be more than eight feet tall, perhaps as tall as Robert Pershing Wadlow (1918-40), who to this day, at just over eight feet eleven, is on record as the world's tallest man. Wadlow's coffin was more than ten feet in length and it jutted out of the rear door of the hearse. It's said that twelve strong pallbearers were required to carry it from hearse to graveside.

Having established that no-one of exceptional height and minus a left leg had been reported missing, and having no reason to believe a crime had been committed, Aerosmith forwarded the prosthesis to me.

As I was inspecting it, I felt hot breath on my left ear, accompanied by a waft of garlic mayonnaise. That spineless snoop Muat, who has the office next to mine, had entered the room like a sneak thief and was peering over my shoulder. He'd taken off his shoes so he could slink around without making a sound. Not that his approach could ever be totally silent. Had I not been paying such close attention to the prosthesis, I would have heard the crackling, distant thunderstorm of static that had built up between his cheap nylon socks and the needle felt flooring. But on this occasion ...
He pointed out something that Aerosmith had apparently failed to notice. Arrogant as ever, he assumed I had, too. There was, he said, no means by which the prosthesis could be attached to the human body.

I'd just that moment noted in my official report that there was, quote: *no implant connector, no flexible inner socket or laminated frame, no fleece- or gel-lined stump holster, no straps or couplings.*

I shot Muat a withering glance and showed him what I'd written. The keenness of my observation seemed to stun him. Or was he faking it? — *Of course he was!* He always is. "Well, Bagley, old son," he said. "Looks like you're not such a knucklehead after all."

Irony laced with venom and delivered with a smile.

As he turned to leave I couldn't restrain myself: "Goodbye, good luck, go take a flying fuck! In other words, *don't come back!*" He chuckled, as if it were a joke, though he knew it wasn't. We've toiled in this department for many a year, working side by side, separated by only a thin partition wall, but we've never shared a joke and never will.

It's frustrating. No matter what I say, or how often I say it, I know that during my next comfort break he'll be in my office doing something he shouldn't. How he manages to gain entry I've no idea. I've added an extra lock to the door (at my own expense; the standard model supplied by Estates Management wouldn't have kept a criminally inclined toddler at bay) and I always double-lock the door behind me, even if I'm only going to the water cooler, barely a hop, skip and jump away.

While walking to the cooler, the door to my room is out of sight for perhaps eight or nine seconds, fewer than that if I run, though for health and safety reasons running in the corridors is forbidden. But that's all the time it takes for mischief to take place. I've been told it can happen in the blink of an eye, so I try my damnedest not to blink. Easier said than done. My left eye twitches when I'm tired or feeling stressed, and attempting to control it by will power alone seems, if anything, to make matters worse.

Cameroonians and Hawaiians both believe that a left eye twitch means someone will visit your house unexpectedly.

It's also a sign of ill omen.

Sometimes I hold the eyelid in place, in the open position, while walking backwards to the cooler, so the door to my room remains visible at all times. If my antics cause my fellow toilers to raise a collective eyebrow, so be it. Let them snigger. Or sneer, if that's their preference. At least I can congratulate myself on having taken every possible precaution. Yet when I return to my desk, flimsy blue plastic disposable cup in hand, brimful with chilled water, I find my papers in disarray and words inserted or deleted from the computer files I'd been working on. Sometimes I discover live folders inside dead ones that earlier in the day I'd consigned to the trash. There's really no accounting for it, but I'm sure Muat is to blame.

It has to be him. Chubby Emtek in Security is the only other keyholder: the official key custodian of our basement kingdom, the so-called King of Keys. He's a loyal employee on the cusp of retirement, and I know he wouldn't under any circumstances put his well-earned reputation and pension at risk. I trust him implicitly. Added to which, he hates Muat almost as much as I do.

No favours there, then.

Perhaps Muat oozes under the door like the slug he is.

As for the prosthesis ... that problem was more easily solved. It was a prototype. An exhibit. Lost by British Airways two years earlier while in transit to a conference of prosthetics manufacturers in Antwerp. How it ended up in the Thames is something of a mystery.

When I made enquiries at the Intellectual Property Office, I was told that the rights to that particular design were held by a Mr Michael Meikle, managing director of Stand Proud Prosthetics, Stroud. It seemed reasonable to assume that he was the prototype's owner. If not, he'd know who was. But when I gave him a call, our conversation didn't go according to plan – neither my plan nor, I should imagine, his.

Most people are gushingly grateful when you identify yourself and say you've found something they've lost, particularly if that something is, as with the item in question, rather special. Not him. After a slight pause, he said, "The shoe is still attached, I hope." Brusque. Not a murmur of thanks. That's what made me suspicious. What was so special about a knackered old shoe? Surely the prosthesis itself was the principal item of value, the shoe a mere accessory. But no, he kept banging on and on about the shoe. "It hasn't fallen apart, has it? None of the seams have split?" Quite the worrywart, Mr Meikle. He was rushing his words then hesitating, as though trying to work out whether what he'd said was what he should be saying. He seemed, if anything, more troubled than pleased.

After several minutes of being bombarded with questions, I managed to squeeze in one of my own. "If you don't mind me asking, Mr Meikle, why is the shoe so important?"

"*Oh for Heaven's sake!*" he said. "I don't believe I'm hearing this. Surely it's obvious! Even someone in a persistent vegetative state could work it out."

I bit my tongue and let him continue. Not that I could have stopped him, even if I'd tried.

"Cast off your petty-bureaucratic bean-counter mindset, Mr Bradley –"

"Bagley."

"If you say so."

"It's my name."

"Well, it's immemorable. Ditch it and choose something better, as I have done. To get on in life you need a memorable name and a mind like a vacuum cleaner. Do you consider yourself a man of advanced sensibility, Mr Bradley, attuned not only to the extreme registers of the human condition but beyond, into other realms of consciousness and states of being? — Well, do you? Then show some humanity."

Shoemanity came to mind and I stifled a laugh.

"Empathise with that poor, badly injured shoe, Mr Bradley – or whatever your name is. Consider its plight. Surely that's not beyond even a witless office drone such as yourself. — But to answer your question as unequivocally as possible: the shoe's sibling is in my workshop waiting to be reunited with its twin. For business purposes I need both of them. But my needs are, and always will be, secondary to theirs. For emotional support and spiritual comfort they need each other."

As crackpot explanations go, that wasn't likely to be topped; not soon, anyway. But because he'd annoyed me, and, to be honest, for entertainment value, I decided to string him along.

"You do understand, Mr Meikle ... the shoe, though holding together, is in poor condition. Very poor. There's a strong possibility its sibling won't even recognise it, or on recognising it will become distraught. It's been pounded on the rocks, nibbled by fish, and become so swollen and softened by sea water I'm sure I could strip the leather from the prosthesis as easily as peeling a ripe banana."

"*No, please, I beg of you, please don't do that!*"

Whoa ...

Touched a raw nerve, that, didn't it?

I confess, I had no intention of doing anything of the sort until he begged me not to. That's what swung it. He really should have kept his emotions in check.

As you're bound to be unfamiliar with our procedures, let me explain. We're permitted to dismantle an item only if it *will* or (wiggle-room word) *may* help us to identify its owner. For example, the serial number etched on the inner case of a watch from the luxury end of the market (Rolex, TAG Heuer, Cartier, Lange Sohne, Richard Mille, etc.) might enable us to track the watch from manufacturer to retailer to customer, and the customer might, just might, be the person who lost it. But there's an important caveat: the item has to be capable of being dismantled and reassembled without damaging it cosmetically or causing it to malfunction. Removing and replacing the back of a watch is standard procedure, a doddle, I could do it in my sleep and on occasion have actually done so. But the shoe ...

While I was talking to Meikle, I began to prod it with the tip of a biro, pushing the pen gently between the outsole and the upper (the vamp, I think it's called), seeing how much it would give. My banana analogy was correct: the glue and the stitching had lost all integrity. I slid the pen along from instep to toe at a depth of approximately one inch, meeting little or no resistance. But when the barrel of the pen reached the toecap, it struck something hard, unyielding. Was the toecap steel reinforced, like a workman's boot? That seemed unnecessary, therefore unlikely. I tried to winkle it out, whatever it was, first with the pen then with a pinkie, but I couldn't quite hook my finger round it. Wedging the receiver between my shoulder and ear, and kicking the office door shut so what I was doing wouldn't be observed, I placed one hand on the toecap, fingers slightly spread, and another, likewise, on the outsole. Then I gripped both tightly and, with a violent jerk, pulled them apart.

It was a reckless thing to do and I regretted it immediately. There was also a wet tearing sound, which Meikle overheard.

"What was that?" he said. "Was that what I think it was?" The register of his voice was creeping up and up, edging towards hysteria.

"Nothing, Mr Meikle. Nothing to worry about. Just the death rattle of the coffee machine in the corner of the room. I made a good, strong brew half an hour ago and drank it soon afterwards, just before I rang you, but the appliance doesn't always complete its task until some time later. Its memory chip has developed the electronic equivalent of Alzheimer's disease, and, Sod's law, the guarantee recently expired. But I'm sure my consumer woes are of absolutely no interest to you. — I thought not. — No, but — Of course. — Yes, I realise your time is extremely valuable, Mr Meikle. As you say, much more valuable than mine. So let's not waste a second more of it, eh? When — Yes, the business world is, from what I gather, cut-throat, and every second counts. — So — So when would — When — When would you like to pick up the prosthesis? — Yes, of course, the shoe. Prosthesis and shoe, neither one without the other. — And some identification, driving license and/or — I quite agree. As you say, only a congenital idiot would fail to realise that identification of some sort would be required."

That last comment seemed to placate him. He managed an almost sincere "Thank you" before ending the call.

Out in the corridor footsteps were fast approaching. I leapt to the door and slid the bolt to. In the nick of time, as the thriller writers say, hoping to add zest to a flagging narrative. The handle was jerked down once, twice, the second time more violently than the first – then a bomb went off. The door shuddered and jumped on its hinges. Someone had given it an almighty kick, a proper toe-breaker. Thwarted, the kicker stomped back along the corridor to his own or someone else's room, some distance hence. Too far away for me to tell who it was, though I had my suspicions.

It was imperative that neither Muat nor any of my fellow toilers were able to barge in, as they tend to do, favouring the element of surprise, even though I have a Do Not Disturb sign hooked over the door handle. The shoe was ruined, and if they saw what I'd done to it, I would be, too. Upper and sole had parted company, but not cleanly. Parts of the upper were torn, ragged-edged, and still attached to the sole. Also, my thumb had gone through the leather, leaving, as one might expect, a thumb-sized hole. No amount of effort with stapler, glue stick and sellotape, the only tools at my disposal, would enable me to make a workmanlike repair.

Oh, but this was bad.

Really really bad.

What I'd done amounted to an act of gross misconduct that was bound to result in a stern reprimand. It might even ruin my career, which is, I freely admit, my life, my whole life, *without which I would be as nothing.* I'm sure you know the feeling, or think you do. It's all theory at your age, isn't it? You haven't had sufficient experience of life to acquire the lines of bitterness that start at the corners of the mouth and descend chinward. Nor the disgruntlement that results in deep vertical creases from mid-brow to bridge of nose, pulling one's eyebrows closer together and drawing out one's increasingly elephantine ears, African rather than Indian.

While frantically trying to work out what to do for the best, I reached into the toe of the shoe and yanked out the obstruction. Not a steel toecap: a semi-transparent plastic box with rounded corners, its lid welded shut. The box contained what looked like grubby pebbles embedded in a block of polystyrene.

Pebbles?

Surely not.

But if not ...?

There was only one way to find out, and that involved a further act of destruction.

Taking the Swiss army knife from the top drawer of my desk, I selected my favourite tool, the marlin spike, and plunged it into the side of the box. I twisted the spike round and around, making the hole bigger, levering upward, putting as much force into it as I could, trying to get the lid to separate from the base. Suddenly the box shattered and flew out of my hand. The stones skittered and bounced across the desk. One fell with a soft plop into the wastepaper basket. When I stooped to retrieve it, I still wasn't sure what it was. But when I held it up to the light ...

These were, I realised, very valuable pebbles indeed.

Diamonds.

Uncut diamonds.

Blood diamonds, in all probability. Mined in Angola, Ivory Coast or Sierra Leone.

I rang Aerosmith, explained what I'd found, and was told that Meikle would be apprehended when he came to retrieve the prosthesis. If the situation was as I said it was (which, I assured him, it most certainly was), Meikle would be arrested on suspicion of diamond trafficking. I then sent a carefully worded email to Rodriguez, scrupulously avoiding any mention of the damage I'd done to the shoe. He'd assume the police, a notoriously heavy-handed bunch, were responsible. At least, I hoped so.

Seconds later an *Out of Office* message pinged back.

Good.

No. Better than that: perfect.

It was common knowledge that when Rodriguez was away from his desk he rarely, if ever, accessed his work email. What he did when he wasn't at work only the snoops in Personnel knew ... though often I pictured him on his knees, in prayer, or mortifying the flesh to remind himself (as if he'd need reminding) of his irredeemable sin, depravity and vileness in the eyes of the Lord his God. A particularly hard taskmaster, God, never satisfied with his human playthings, especially the more gullible ones.

No matter.

It gave me valuable time in which to consider my options and, indeed, prospects. The latter were, I have to say, all things considered, looking up. Was I just imagining it, or had victory been snatched decisively from the jaws of defeat? Suddenly there was every reason to believe that, were Meikle to be arrested and charged, I'd be given a much prized acrylic display frame containing a commendation certificate signed by the head of the Civil Service, Sir Jeremy Heywood – something to place prominently on a shelf in my office, to be admired and envied by all.

Perhaps there'd even be a promotion in the offing.

Actually, the more I thought about it, the more promotion seemed not only possible but ... probable.

Don't get your hopes up, Bagley, I thought.

And yet ... and yet ...

This sudden reversal of fortune was dizzying. Many things triggered dizzy episodes in those days – still do, for that matter – but in its ferocity this one was without precedent. I slid to the floor and stared up at the ceiling, at the naked bulb revolving without apparent volition at the end of its cord, until, after half an hour or so, my internal gyroscope steadied.

By then I'd decided how best to deal with my fellow toilers:

Avoid them at all cost. (Business as usual, in other words.)

When that wasn't possible, be meek and modest. 'All in a day's toil,' I'd say. 'Frankly, I got lucky.'

Congratulations (patently insincere, spoken through gritted teeth) I'd acknowledge with a shrug and a sheepish grin.

Sheepish.

Not smug.

Definitely not smug!

I made a mental note to practise that distinction in the mirror when I got home.

≈≈≈

Did I happen to mention tardigrades a little while back? Sometimes known as moss piglets or water bears? I did, didn't I? If not, I should have. They're extremely hardy creatures. Tiny but tough. Much tougher than you and I, that's for sure. But as luck would have it they do us no harm. If you accidentally drank several hundred of them in a glass of water, trust me, you'd be fine.

Another thing worth noting: we don't seem to impinge on tardi consciousness. They act as though they're oblivious to us. Presumably we're too big to be seen clearly, just as they're too small. (Analogous to the gulf between Whitehall mandarins and lowly clerical assistants.) But if, in retaliation for having been snubbed and humiliated by tardigrades, we humans – not all of us, just those with rampant paranoia and genocidal tendencies – set about trying to eradicate them, we, or rather they, the paranoids, would fail. Come the apocalypse – and come it most certainly will, and soon, if John of Patmos and his fanatical fanboy Jesus Rodriguez are to be believed – tardigrades will outsurvive us. They and that inveterate landlubber the cockroach.

About cockroaches, least said the better. Ugly, disgusting creatures. Tardigrades, by comparison, are cute and wholesome. If only they were a tiny bit bigger (average length less than a millimetre, a mere dot) they'd be quite cuddly. They're appealing nonetheless, though you have to use a magnifying lens or suchlike to see what the little scamps are doing.

Could there be a pet more suitable for people like me who don't like other people knowing they have pets?

I adopted my tardigrades by accident, and all because of Michael Meikle's misplaced shoe. When, in a moment of madness, I ripped the sole from the upper and revealed the box containing the blood diamonds, a surprisingly large quantity of water that had been trapped in the toecap trickled out and pooled on the desk. Using the flat of my hand as a squeegee, I swept the water into an empty drinking glass. Needless to say, I had no intention of drinking from the glass, not until it had been thoroughly washed. That meant going to the lavatory, rinsing it in the washbasin, drying it under the roarer (the automatic hand dryer) and refilling it en route to my office from the dribbler (the malfunctioning water cooler, its nipper valve behaving like an eighty-year-old's prostate).

As mentioned earlier, I was unsettled (to put it mildly) by having discovered the blood diamonds. And the explosive kick at my office door did nothing to soothe jangling nerves. I knew I had to dispose of the evidence of my misdeed, and pronto. I was in a blind panic. If not that, I really don't know what possessed me. Before placing the glass on a nearby shelf, I bottoms-upped the sandy, salty water it contained.

For the rest of the day I hid in my office, studiously ignoring the phone's intermittent bleat. The door remained locked – strictly against the rules. But, in my experience, once you've broken one rule, no matter how trivial, there's really no going back; rule after rule gets broken, or shunted aside irrespective of the consequences, which are, more often than not, dire. Yes, dire. But not always. Sometimes, before you know it, you're experiencing something you'd previously been denied, something you hadn't thought possible. Which, truly, I hadn't. Not only was I breathing deeply, I could feel my ribcage flex with every breath. That hadn't happened in a good, long while.

Imagine what it must feel like to be laced into an iron corset. Hard, I know, but give it a try. — Dear oh dear, is that the best you can do? Screwing your face up like that suggests concentration but fools no-one. You might just as well place an elbow on your knee and knuckle your neanderthal brow.

Anyway, because of a childhood trauma (the details of which I won't go into; let's just say that the man I was instructed to call Daddy played musical beds and applied the rod vigorously), and the lightning strike I mentioned earlier (a wild-eyed horse trying to trample me underhoof, its mane and flanks ablaze, smoke and flames streaming out behind it like rocket exhaust), I began to suffer from sleep terrors. They arrived tumultuously, night after night, and still do to this day.

Because of that, or rather those, and other traumas too numerous to mention, that's precisely how I felt: corseted.

Nevermore.

And all because I broke a rule, breathed deeply and busted my stays. Blood was oxygenated, brain stimulated. Eureka! – a moment of revelation, though probably not the kind Rodriguez would approve of.

As if I care a hoot what he thinks.

All my life I'd been a conformist. I simply did what others did and thought nothing of it. But thinking wasn't really my strong suit. Because of chronic sleep deprivation I stumbled around in a permanent fog of bewilderment. If I'd been raised in a family of safe-crackers, in a community in which safe-cracking was considered as good and honorable a way to earn a living as any, I'm sure I too would have become a safe-cracker.

Hang on, that reminds me ...

Something Muat said that might, for once, be pertinent.

He said the Korowai say ... now what was it? — "Among cannibals one eats like a cannibal." And and and ... something else. Yes: "Cannibals eat missionaries even though they taste horrible." I suspect that's a rough translation from whatever language the Korowai speak; though not by Muat, he's no linguist. But that's what he said they said. He also said the Korowai say: "What spoils missionary meat, even the choicest cuts, is a surfeit of Christianity. The more fervent the belief, the greater the spoilage." Also: "Drowned sailors taste salty, sometimes too salty, and only those who've drowned that day provide good eating."

I mean ... it's nonsense, isn't it? Typical Muat nonsense. Though I suspect he's so deluded he believes every word.

The facts are these:

The Korowai live a long way inland, almost a hundred miles from the coast, and they haven't practised cannibalism for decades. Moreover, even the most zealous members of the Mission of the Reformed Churches eventually (late 1970s or thereabouts) gave up trying to convert them, thus avoiding the risk, negligible though it was, of being pot boiled or, more traditionally, spit roasted.

Pah! Enough about Muat. Let's stick to the topic under discussion: Unthinkingly doing what others do, i.e. conformism.

My parents were career civil servants, so, surprise surprise, here I am, a career civil servant. Other careers were dangled enticingly before me, but I took the easy option, the path of least resistance – precisely what a muzzy-headed, white, middle-class suburbanite lacking pluck and ambition would be expected to choose. Don't get me wrong, I love my job, it's more than what I do, it's what I am, my raison d'être, but ... I've come to realise how restrictive it is and how jaded I've become.

What can I say that hasn't been said before by millions of dead-eyed workers shuffling zombie-like towards retirement? Routine gradually wears you down. The familiarity that once proved comforting causes stress and, eventually, distress, something a luxury spa break in the Cotswolds or a month spent chanting OM in Dharamsala won't fix. And in my case, certain deep, dark yearnings came to light. After the conversation I had with Muat about the Korowai, I realised I had an overwhelming urge to taste human flesh, roast missionary in particular, rank taste notwithstanding. Or, better still, that of a certain born-again Christian of my acquaintance, currently driving a truck in an aid convoy in some strife-stricken dusty hellhole. Yum yum.

I can guess what you're thinking. What's that got to do with tardigrades and a locked office door?

Transgression, laddies – that's what.

When I gulped down that post-shoe sea water, it contained dozens, perhaps scores of marine tardigrades, not that I knew it at the time. Hours later I was lying on the floor, bent double, in pain, bladder full to bursting, in imminent danger of wetting myself. But I was reluctant to leave my office to visit the lavatory in case I bumped into one of my fellow toilers, snoops and snitches to a man. They'd be bound to ask why, strictly against the rules, I'd closed my office door and locked myself in. To which there was no satisfactory answer – not one that would do what I desperately wanted it to do: allay suspicion. And pretending to selective mutism wouldn't work; I'd used that excuse once too often.

There was nothing for it. I unzipped, snatched up the empty drinking glass, and after the first irrepressible gush, which made me moan with relief (handkerchief clamped over mouth to stifle the sound), I filled it, in trickly fits and starts, almost to the brim.

It was obvious at a glance that something was wrong. The urine I'd produced was as dark and murky as ditch water. It didn't have the usual golden hue that looks like liquid sunshine and brightens up a room (as any interior designer worth his salt will tell you); and I mean any room, not just lavatories, bathrooms and en-suites. I wondered whether this presaged a recurrence of the bladder infection that, several years earlier, ran spectacularly out of control and kept me hospitalised for almost a month, initially on life support. As my vital organs began to fail, not one by one, in an orderly fashion, queueing up politely as we Brits famously do, but all at once, pell-mell, in a race to extinction, I experienced what I later realised were hallucinations – an alligator prowling the corridors at night, nurses with two heads and many arms like Hindu gods, giggles rather than electronic beeps from the heart monitor – though at the time they seemed like aspects of everyday reality, perfectly normal.

Were the wiggly black specks in my urine a hallucination? At first I thought so. But when I sucked several of them up into an eye dropper, squirted them onto a glass slide, deftly inserted the slide under the eye of the microscope (one of the most important tools in our investigative arsenal) and twirled the knurled focusing knob, I saw them clearly, in extraordinary detail, and realised what they were.

Just that week I'd read an article about tardigrades: how they can survive for years trapped in sea ice, or, at the opposite extreme, remain unscathed by the boiling flux from hydrothermal vents; how they're able to fast for inordinate lengths of time; how they can withstand pressure of up to 6,000 atmospheres, more crushing than a car crusher operating at the bottom of the deepest ocean trench; how even the cold, irradiated vacuum of outer space probably cannot kill them. Scientists have speculated that if they manage to reach another planet on which there's liquid water, they'll survive and almost certainly thrive no matter how hostile the environment. Remarkable creatures. And, as all but the churls among us would agree, cute.

Apparently they have a primitive dorsal brain capable of thinking inscrutable tardi thoughts. Not complex thoughts; but that's true also of most humans. Are they blessed with distinct personalities? Do they form friendships with others of their kind? Having worked my way through the extant literature on tardigrades and given every scrap of evidence careful consideration, I'd say, on both counts, albeit tentatively, yes. In which case we're morally bound to act in accordance with their best interests and should treat them with the respect they deserve.

To that end, each of my tardigrades has been given a first

name, by which I mean a different one to that of its fellows, although, of course, as adopted family members they share my surname. I bought *The Really Big Book of Boys' Names* and have been working my way through it. I reached the Ds in less than a month, and I'm currently deep into the Ns. Once all the Ys and Zs have been exhausted, I'll go back to the beginning and start again.

When tardigrades are in an active rather than a tun (dehydrated, hibernatory) state they rarely live for more than a year, so a book as big as this should be capable of providing a name for each and every one of them without risk of duplication and, thereby, confusion. If, however, some of my tardis live longer than expected, or their numbers increase exponentially and I exhaust the alphabet without having named them all, then, when I start again at the beginning, I'll bestow on the newbies a middle name, usually the next one in the book. For example, if Aaden Bagley is still among the living, rather than give his name to another, probably younger tardigrade, the youngster will be dubbed Aaden Aaron Bagley. Likewise, the tardi elder known as Bailey Bagley will be joined in unholy namelock by Bailey Baldwin Bagley. You get the picture. One could, of course, use the suffixes snr and jr, but it isn't always possible to tell which tardigrade is the older of the two. There's also the numerical system our American cousins favour, whereby Cosmo Bagley's firstborn son would be known as Cosmo Bagley II, and the firstborn son of Bagley the second would be Cosmo Bagley III. A neat solution, if unimaginative. But what disqualifies it isn't that, or not principally that, it's that it doesn't chime with how we Brits have gone about naming our children for, well, forever. Otherwise known as tradition. Such things matter, to me if not you.

You're probably wondering whether it's hard for even an experienced surrogate parent such as myself to tell the members of his tardi brood apart. Am I right? 'Betcha phat ass, bub!' as one of the callow Cosmo Bagleys might say. And monitoring tardi breeding habits is harder still. Although they'll all eventually be granted a name – male, as stated – I'm aware that some of them will undoubtedly but unidentifiably be female. Every evening for hours on end I watch them, eyes glued to the microscope (yes, I also have one at home, a scanning electron jobbie bought at knockdown price in a forensics lab yard sale), but I can't say I've witnessed a single instance of sexual congress. Not one. Nor even a suggestion of courtship or foreplay. Yet still the births outnumber the deaths by a ratio of 3:1.

You may also be wondering whether I have a favourite tardigrade. Actually, I do. I know it's wrong to play favourites, but one quirky specimen immediately caught my eye. Because of his antics I can pick him out of a crowd without any trouble at all. Quite honestly, were I to be reincarnated in tardi form (which I really wouldn't mind, I'd consider it an upgrade) he's the one I'd most like to be like. There's a bond between us, indefinable on his part, but there, I'm sure, nonetheless. You'll just have to take my word for it. It may amount to nothing more than a faint awareness of being observed (known to those in the know as the Hawthorne effect), of being singled out, i.e. favoured (if he's an optimist, as I think by nature most tardigrades are), instigating a series of unconscious behavioural shifts in a blind search for more of the same (the feelgood factor). But it works both ways. Whenever I see or even just think of him, I experience an endorphin rush. A warm glow swells in my chest and filters through to my extremities. In that moment I feel more alive than I've ever felt. It's love, I suppose. That's why I gave him the benefit of my own name: Buster Bagley.

What? — What's that you're mumbling? — *Everyone knows that tardigrades can't survive passage through the human digestive tract. The acid in our gut would kill them.*

You're wrong, young man. About that and, presumably, many other things.

The arrogance of youth.

Sopping wet behind the ears.

What could you possibly know about anything at your tender age, you're barely out of nappies?

What's your name, son?

Michael Santos, eh?

Oh, *Miguel* Santos. *Miguel.* My apologies.

Well, Señor Smartypants, let me tell you – gut acid weakens tardigrades somewhat, but only somewhat. Survive they most certainly do. No matter what you and the pointy heads in the scientific community say about tardi gut deaths, my thriving colony of tardigrades proves you're wrong. Although tardigrades are unable to bear witness, and probably wouldn't wish to do so even if they could, preferring to maintain a dignified silence, *a strategy you should consider adopting,* the facts speak for themselves.

Actually, when I say colony, that's misleading. There are two colonies, one at home, the other at work. Hence I'm *doubly transgressive*. The home colony consists of Buster and those of his fellow tardis whose names run the gamut from A to M. The Ns onward are housed in a small perspex tank in my office, tucked away on a high shelf behind a row of ancient lever arch folders. The folders themselves contain nothing of interest to anyone now living; and the dead, for whom such things once mattered, are beyond caring. Of all the folders in my office, those are the only ones that never get touched, except with a half-hearted flick from a feather duster.

It comforts me to know that my tardigrades are safe from harmful scrutiny. By which I mean, of course, Oaf – have I mentioned him? Principally Oaf, because he's there in my office nearly all the time, spying on me. But Muat, too, who's almost as bad.

Speaking of the Hawthorne effect: that's probably what Rodriguez is suffering from. The poor deluded fool thinks God is watching over him 24/7, giving him the kind of gimlet-eyed scrutiny that would, in any other circumstance, be considered not just invasive but downright creepy. Stalkers aspire to that kind of thing but, by dint of occasionally having to sleep, they fall short of their own high expectations.

Quoth Rodriguez:

"Since that miraculous day when, with God's blessing and under His close personal supervision, I was – *Praise the Lord!* – born again, planes have crashed and ships have sunk in greater numbers than ever before. Not to mention workmen falling off ladders or electrocuting themselves or both. Car crashes. Accidental overdoses. Trips, slips and spills. A million different ways to die a million times a day. In the last year alone the loss of life has been heavier than at any time since the First World War dovetailed with the Spanish flu pandemic of 1918, and" – his voice cracked piteously on a sob – "*and it's all my fault!*"

That's what he said. Deadly serious. No hint of irony. He said he'd been keeping tabs on things, especially merchant shipping in the so-called Bermuda Triangle. Also in another large maritime area, the absurdly titled New Bermuda Triangle, which he described as a 'psychic dead zone in the East China Sea'.

"And something similar is happening just off the Isles of

Scilly. Small scale by comparison, as you'd expect in that part of the world. Devourer of rowboats, pedalos, jet skis, and most recently a blind canoeist who paddled in circles for nearly a week before, dehydrated, exhausted and frustrated to the point of tears, tears which wouldn't come, he died. His sonic compass was giving him scrambled instructions because of the zone's powerful magnetic ambivalence."

Powerful ambivalence, eh? That's a first.

"The canoeist story was all over social media a couple of weeks ago, but within hours the posts had mysteriously been taken down."

Hmm.

Anyone of sound mind and rational thought will conclude that divine scrutiny, no matter how loving, is all but indistinguishable from divine punishment.

I think Rodriguez, though unsound as a cracked bell, was beginning to realise that, too.

"I feel a burning sense of guilt for all those deaths," he wailed (yes, wailed, that's no exaggeration). "Lives lost because, during the time I was being adored — which was, basically, all the time, even while I slept — God was neglecting his other duties. And I wallowed in it, *actually wallowed*, as if in a warm, soothing bath enriched not with aromatic oils or crystals but love, unconditional love. *Oh, the shame! How can I ever forgive myself?*"

I confess: I laughed in his face. A heartless cackle. Come on, admit it, you'd have done the same thing, too. But Rodriguez looked stunned. He'd solicited sympathy — not much, just a quantum — from an old colleague. And what did he get? What he richly deserved, in my opinion. Drenched with Godly love as he was, or thought he was, he seemed to have forgotten that I hate him, have done so since the moment we met, and he in turn has always hated me. We not only hate each other, we also hate our fellow toilers. That's how it is in workplaces; all of them, not just branches of the Civil Service. Which is why, in the USA, there are so many workplace shootings by disgruntled employees, current or ex. Easy access to guns is a contributory factor. But even in the UK guns can be procured without too much trouble, especially here in London. Adolescents with parents-in-crime or weekend and holiday gang connections waltz them through the school gates, wrapped in their gym kit, and swap them for shoplifted Xbox shoot-'em-ups, Nike trainers and iPhones. There's one in my briefcase right now. You don't believe me? No? Because I have a mischievous twinkle in my eye? — Oh, but you should.

We'll come back to that in a moment.

Hatred, not love, is what binds us together. Without it, society would collapse. It's super-concentrated in prisons because of the inability of inmates to get, in stir crazy parlance, 'the fuck away' from each other, but the death toll remains low because combatants have to rely on makeshift weapons.

As for politics: the electorate hate MPs of all parties, and the MPs hate each other and, to an almost pathological degree, the electorate.

Hatred makes the world go round in an eccentric orbit that swings us nearer to Mars than Venus.

So I laughed long and loud, without the slightest hint of mirth, and the self-pitying look on Rodriguez's face was replaced by something baleful. That, I thought, is the Rodriguez of old, the pre-rebirth version, as unlikable a man as any I'd met but infinitely preferable to the one he'd become. His born-again manner was treaclesome and odious. It, therefore he, reeked of insincerity. He'd even taken to smiling now and then, if you can call it that. Cold, cold eyes and a baring of teeth. What TV reality stars and apes do when all the warning signs have been ignored and they're about to launch a vicious attack.

Much better to get hatred out in the open.

Like now, with you.

I could tell Rodriguez was thinking ugly, unChristian thoughts – perhaps of roasting me alive and tearing into my flesh with his remarkably vulpine teeth. Even if I tasted like the kind of person he thought I was: vile.

Or if you prefer your letters lightly shuffled: evil.

But it gave me pause. The way God looks at Rodriguez (according to Rodriguez) is similar to how I look at Buster – and I'm no god, not by a long chalk, unless there's a god of schadenfreude.

Perhaps there is.

If not, perhaps there should be.

Seaside Story

☆

Lori Baker

You come here every year, before things have really gotten started:
before it gets expensive, before the tourists come: during what they
call the "shoulder season". Shoulder means you might be able
to take your low-slung folding chair out to your favorite beach: the
same silvery new moon of sand that you remembered, green fringe
of salt marsh behind, dense forest of pitch pines behind that; ahead
the ocean like a luminous blue mirror stretching out toward the
glimmering sand bar, with always, so it seems, the same delicate
pink ribbon of cloud above it, the same skein of seabirds heading out
to sea. Or else, because it is the shoulder season, it might rain and
you'll have to stay indoors; in which case you'll take up your book
and a place by the fire; or maybe a place by the window: looking
out at everything, it's all smudged, there's fog perhaps, the edges of
everything softened, indistinct: grey water, grey sun, grey sky, pitch
pines bent low in the wind. You don't mind, you're just happy to be
here. This is your place. Sometimes you think you like it better grey
and soft, *contrary to popular opinion.* Grey and soft, everything with
a pearly sheen, the beach with nobody on it is like a secret, your
secret. There's an inn you like to stay at, this is like a secret too. It's
called The Grey Ghost and it perches there, softly, above the sea,

grey as its name, the color of sea mist, so much so that sometimes it almost seems to disappear into a solid mist or a fog. That's why they always leave a light on. It beckons, on a foggy night: *Here I am, over here - The Grey Ghost!*

You have a favorite room here - the one with the window seat with the blue cushion, overlooking the sea. You also like the mirror in the bathroom, made to look like a porthole, though recognizing there's something silly about this: opening up a porthole, putting your toothbrush on the little shelf inside it, closing up the porthole again. This silliness gives you joy; so, too, the painting on the wall beside the bed, of ducks taking flight above a lush green marshland. These things help you to feel at home. When you arrive you always check, anxiously, to make sure they are still there: the porthole mirror, the ducks flying, the window seat with the blue cushion. Once you've seen them, and the ocean outside the window, you can relax.

There's always a smell of the sea in your favorite room, and a little grittiness underfoot - as if there's sand on the floor - though of course there isn't, The Grey Ghost is always immaculate. It's almost always empty, too, or nearly so, during the shoulder season. It doesn't bother you, that's part of the beauty of it: the emptiness. At night the whole place creaks and groans in the wind, the lights flicker, the shades clatter in the windows, and you imagine the other, empty rooms: the neatly made beds, the unused metal hangers jangling in the abandoned closets, doilies tentatively reclining on the arms of uneasy chairs, The Grey Ghost's original, eponymous tenants taking shelter in the folds of the curtains: above the door jambs: in the drawers of empty bureaus: between the neatly folded sheets and the comforters: behind the exotic elephant's foot footstool topped with a vase of peacock feathers, on the third floor landing, front stairs. Once you even thought you saw one, a ghost that is: it was in the early morning, soft watery not-quite-light filtering in between the blinds, you awoke with a start and saw her there, at the window, looking out, looking out, she was half-turned away from you: seen in profile therefore: white cheek, dark curling hair, an expression of infinite sadness or maybe it was boredom: you sat up in bed, rubbing your eyes, thinking *what an odd time for the landlady to be bringing fresh towels!*, and at once she was gone: only then did you realize. You felt badly, you had scared her away, a strange reversal this: and afterwards you watched for her, in the hallway, in the bath, on the turning of the stairs, in the dining room with its gleaming mahogany sideboard: you tried to maintain a welcoming attitude: thinking this might draw her back to you: once or twice you thought you heard or rather perhaps felt a footstep behind you when nobody was there: but you never saw her again: and now you think: *maybe it was only a dream. Maybe it was myself in the mirror that I saw...*

Nonetheless the sense of disappointment lingers, it has attached itself to your room, your favorite room, though you know this is silly, sillier even than the joy of putting your toothbrush inside the porthole in the bathroom: because you should be afraid of ghosts: the absence of ghosts is relief, reality, reassurance: the everyday world running trustingly along its well-trod track: or is it?

You wish the ghost were like a chickadee that you could lure into your palm with a handful of seeds. Even a sign of her would be welcome: the clothes in your closet rearranged, or the items on the surface of the dresser: or the bookmark removed, a passage, containing a message, mysteriously underlined in whatever book it is you are currently reading. But no. No.

You are alone.

And you are lucky: arriving in this your favorite place on a clear blue day, cool but not cold, refreshing rather, breeze bearing with it a promising foretaste of summer: call of gulls: intoxicating scent of the sea. You take your book, your beach chair, your wide-brimmed floppy hat, nodding to the landlady who goes unobtrusively about her business, (dusting, rearranging), and to your fellow guest, a Grey Ghost regular, who sits at a table by the window, working on her jigsaw puzzle: an image of the sea: with pieces cut in sea shapes: fish, gulls, seahorse, mermaids, spirals of weed, branching coralline, the outline of an anemone or a snail, even the pinkish clouds are there, she at the table shifting these pieces around, moving them, dissatisfied, putting them back again, and again: rapt, while, just outside the window...

It is hard to understand this preference for the simulacrum: and yet she seems harmless enough, with her thick round glasses and white hair: always here: a resident rather than a guest: someone permanent, you see her every year though you don't know her name: while you, of course, are temporary. To make up for the lack you give her a name. Mrs. Crabbe, you think her.

With a pleasant nod to Mrs. Crabbe, you pass through the door. The Grey Ghost settles and sighs behind you.

You step out into something different.

This beach, your favorite beach, is bright and hard, kaleidoscopic, fractured into dazzling shards of blue and green and gold: dark tumult of wind-whipped hair, through which, in confusion, you descend: chair, hat, book: the ground shifting suddenly beneath your feet: through the sharp glitter of sea wrack and sea grass, sand-spackled bone-white fragments of shell, stones that have been taken and turned by the sea, taken and turned and smoothed by the sea, then spit out onto the shore.

It is, as often at this time of year, quite deserted.

You carry your chair along the curve of the crescent: not too far (you are lazy in this): about an eighth of the way: just far enough so that The Grey Ghost recedes behind you, and your confusion, too, recedes: the world falls into place, here it is, the thing you have waited for all year: the luminous blue mirror, the sand bar, the delicate pink ribbon of cloud, the line of seabirds rising, falling, breaking apart, descending into the sea: or skimming along just above the surface: held aloft by some strange alchemy of motion and feather and wind. They are a kind of hieroglyphic, there is a message in those bodies that rise and fall, if only you could read it. But you can't. Instead you open your chair, your book, put on your hat, remove your shoes, sink a bit, yourself, into the sand. You are absorbed into the day, you feel yourself loosen, somewhere a net opens and the grains of worry, of stress, sift through: the office, or that particular face or voice, loving or angry or ambiguous, you can't tell which, the expensive scarf that you bought and lost and you don't know where, the calls you never returned, the unpaid bills, that closet that really needs cleaning, all these sift through and are lost in the infinity of glittering grains of sand. And then other things, memories, rise unbidden: the hiss of bicycle tires in the cemetery at dusk; the scent and sound of the fallen leaves you walked through as a child on your way to the library: yellow they were, not yet brittle, scent of wood smoke in the air; that rock you turned over in the woods, and the little animal that came out from beneath, salamander or newt (you still aren't sure which - and what's the difference?), brown with a red stripe along its back, and those tiny, rubbery, precisely-formed toes; waiting for fireworks on the Fourth of July, sitting with your transistor radio on a blanket in the dark; the brown and white sea shell, brought by your cousins from Florida, resting on a kitchen counter near a sink; even, strangely, the angle of sunlight on the auto teller machine where you went to take out cash when you were working your first job, the one that you hated: these things rise, pass through your mind, they too fall through the net, and are lost.

Opening one eye you see a white sail moving slowly, left to right, across the ultramarine horizon.

It is possible that you sleep: have slept.

You come to yourself suddenly with a sense that something has changed: the angle of the sun is lower, shadows have lengthened, the color of the ocean is different, darker, the ribbon of cloud above it turned to purple, and something else, you don't know what: this felt rather than seen. The book in your lap is still open to the same unread page, and yet...

Then you know, suddenly, that you are no longer alone. You feel yourself watched. Surreptitiously from beneath the wide brim of the hat you scan the beach, seeking the other. At first it seems no one is there; but you can feel it: that persistent sense of being watched. Someone is looking, observing, taking note of you. Your presence has been registered by the other, some other whom you cannot see but whose gaze, penetrating, inquisitive, you can feel as surely as if it were the touch of a hand on your shoulder...

And then you see that someone *is* there: far up the beach, an eighth of the way from the opposite end, where the silver crescent terminates in a breakwater not unlike the one in front of The Grey Ghost, someone is sitting in a low chair, facing the sea. It is impossible to tell, from this distance, whether the other is watching. Certainly you feel yourself watched, but the face, from this distance, is just a smudge. You cannot see the eyes, the direction of the gaze. You can see the other's jacket though, dark blue, shapeless, flapping in the wind, which has risen off the sea and which now also lifts, coldly, firmly, insistently, the brim of your hat, your hair: now rifles, like a thief, the pages of the book in your lap, which you have, until now, neglected and ignored... And you think, *how strange that someone is here, in this place, at this season, the shoulder season.* And more: there is no access to the beach at that end, through the pitch pine forest which is, you've always heard, utterly impenetrable. Though you've never tried it. Never tried: a failing on your part. Still... *how?* You feel a sudden chill: attribute this to the rising wind, the dampness of the sand, the dimming of that blue mirror, the sea. Hurriedly taking up book and chair you turn back toward The Grey Ghost, your comforting familiar. At first you cannot see it, but you are sure it is there. And it does reappear as you climb: the chimneys first, all four of them; then the weathervane in the shape of a running fox that always amuses and charms you; then the steep, shingled gables; the windows, facing east, reflecting the sea; and finally the capacious porch: still there. You are reassured. Mounting upwards, you hear, from the darkening fringe of the salt marsh, the sea sparrow's valedictory song...

Later, though, you berate yourself for it: for running away. For being afraid. Afraid of what? This is unclear. It is a puzzle. You are a puzzle to yourself, in this. You ruminate over the puzzle all evening. That smudge of a face. The blue jacket with the flapping sleeves. Your fear. At least, you think, nobody saw you running away: or if they saw (if, for example, Mrs. Crabbe, at her table by the window, saw) it would not have been obvious that you were running. Merely that it was late: the shadows were growing longer: the wind had risen: it was getting cold: time to come in. You take comfort from this thought, but then you have to amend it. The sea sparrow saw you run.

And the other.

This disturbs; and so you take the thoughts to bed with you, ridiculous as they are, and you lie awake, listening to the wind rattling the window panes as if it is trying to get inside: trying first one window, then the other, prying tenaciously at the screens. All night long it tries, and fails, and tries again. For a long time you lie awake, listening, thinking. You worry that this place, your favorite place, has been spoiled for you. Behind the wind you can hear the sound of waves, dark, imagined though unseen, lashing the shore. And then at last you sleep.

Despite the tumult of the night, it's another clear blue morning. The wind has left no trace on the sea or the shore. At breakfast, attempting to speak casually over your plate of eggs and toast with jam, you ask the landlady about the new development: isn't there a new development, you ask, up there, at the other end of the beach? You try to keep the excitement out of your voice. *New houses*, you say, *up that way? Big grand houses.* That's what you have heard. You gesture, imprecisely, toward the north. *Such a shame*, you say.

The landlady, interrupted in the act of pouring your coffee, raises an eyebrow. She is a stern woman: not that she is mean, or angry: just firm, as granite is firm. Her hair, which she wears swept up into a sort of bun, is steely gray. After all these years you ought to remember her name: but you don't: so you name her, in your mind, Mrs. Buckle.

I don't know what you mean, says Mrs. Buckle, with some asperity, *there is no new development.* Her eyes, sharp and bright like sparrow's eyes, focus on you now in a way they didn't when she was just pouring your coffee, just setting down your plate. *That would never happen*, says Mrs. Buckle. *All the land around here is protected land.* There is perhaps a touch of self-satisfaction in the way she says this; and indeed she repeats it, as if particularly pleased with the phrase: *Protected land.*

But, you say, *certainly there is an access road, up there, somewhere?* Again you gesture vaguely towards the north.

There is not, says Mrs. Buckle, regarding you suspiciously with her berry-bright eye. *This is the only access point. This is it. Anybody goes out there, has to go past me.*

Ah, you say, *that's good. Very good. A relief.*

But this is insincere, and Mrs. Buckle knows it; with a final, penetrating glance, she purses her lips, takes her coffee pot, and goes away.

From your table you can look out, over your egg, at the silver crescent of beach, empty as ever, and the brilliant blue sea, innocently shining. Beckoning. But then you think there is an ominous cast in the relentless sunshine, in the unremitting blue of the ocean: so very blue that in its opacity it is nearly black. This is something you have never noticed before. And the waves - how cold they must be - gray-green, sharp as steel, or like the scales on the back of a monster that turns and rolls over and over in the soft silty bed of the sea. This image, once you have thought it, fills you with dismay, even dread: but you cannot dislodge it from your mind.

Nonetheless, you think it is important to behave as normally as possible; as if nothing is wrong: and so when you leave the breakfast room you nod and smile at Mrs. Crabbe who has set up with her puzzle: just like always. Indeed this is so normal, all of it, the breakfast room, the bright sky and the bright ocean beneath it, Mrs. Crabbe and her jigsaw puzzle, that you reprove yourself, inwardly, for having any doubts. Nonetheless you do doubt, and the doubt is very painful, and cannot be dismissed.

And so on this bright day, when you gather up your things (book, hat, sunglasses, low folding chair), you do not carry them out to the beach, as usual, but out to your car instead; glancing back over your shoulder at The Grey Ghost just in case anybody should be watching, though why should it matter? Who cares if Mrs. Buckle is watching, or even Mrs. Crabbe? And of course they aren't watching: Mrs. Crabbe is rapt over her puzzle, Mrs. Buckle has her books to balance, her breakfast dishes to clean: the windows on this side of the house are blank, the curtains undisturbed, none drawn aside by a surreptitious hand for the benefit of a prying eye. And yet you rush, loading your belongings into the boot of your car quickly with the prickling sense of being watched; and you do not feel at ease again until you have pulled out of the drive, heading north, and have put some distance between yourself and The Grey Ghost.

You drive along the coast, the silver beach to your right, though you see it more and more distantly, first across the brilliant green impediment of the salt marsh with its sharp grasses and silty wandering streams - then the marsh itself is hidden from you by undulating dunes punctuated with small wind-bent sidewinding trees - how do they hang on, you wonder? - and then the forest begins - pitch pines: blinding light above, inscrutable dark below: flash and spark of wings among a dense midnight of branches: a sense of something ancient, impenetrable: if you were to walk among them, you think: you long: and you cannot see the water anymore: though you know it is still there, because of the seagulls, circling in the updraft...

You want to stop, but you don't. You drive on, looking for the entry point: because there must be an entry point. The road loops around, narrows, turns back on itself, and now you are immersed, fully immersed, in the pitch pine forest. From either side of the road the branches reach out, arch above you, meet, forming a tunnel, a sort of winding nave along which you progress with suitable gravity. Brilliant shafts of sunlight descend from clerestories hidden high up among the branches. The road, which had been paved, becomes sandy. With growing anxiety you roll along a rutted track, narrower and narrower; branches knock against the car doors, the roof, the windshield, until, abruptly, it simply ends: you find yourself nose-first in a thicket. Switching off the engine, you sit for a moment staring at the pine branches squashed against the windshield, against the windows on either side: sense of choking, of being choked; of a small room with spiny walls. You have gone on too long, too far, too insistently; now you're wedged in tight. Even getting out of the car is difficult: you have to press hard against the branches which work actively against you, trying to push you back in. There seems a fearsome and willful intelligence behind this, though you know it is, at most, the illusion of an intelligence, the illusion of a *will*. Branches have no will, forests have no will. Nor have they any intelligence, that is what you think. You press your way out, then struggle for a few minutes to shake the twigs needles dirt pinecones beetles spider webs out of your hair, off your face, your clothes; you try to shake free everything that has gone down the neck of your shirt or up your sleeves, you feel smell and recognize your helplessness against the pungent sticky pine sap that nothing but hot water will remove. You've gotten this viscous stuff onto your hands, worse yet on the back of your neck, in your hair. What would Mrs. Buckle think.

After all this shimmying and shaking comes paralysis: you stand very still beneath the trees. This is a process of acclimation. It will take a moment to adjust, to assess your next move. It is dark, though patches of light fall through, glittering gemlike on the enigmatic boughs, illumining secret grottoes in the deeply-rooted clefts of the pitch pines. You move forward gingerly through the black fallen bodies and contorted limbs of the trees. You are sheltered by the trees, though you can see or sense wind moving far above, in the uppermost branches, as if in another world: one from which you have been excluded. Here, where you are, it is warm, strangely hushed; this forest, judged by you as lacking both in will and in intelligence, holds its breath: waits to see what you will do.

In the stillness small things move: slither, scratch, scrabble, flutter. Flash of something bright among the branches.

Turn to look and it is gone.

Quiver of witch hazel, of lady slipper.

You think: this is what I longed for.

Trembling.

This unsilent silence.

Listening always for the sound of the sea.

Despite all, you are still convinced there must be an access point, if only you can find it.

You cannot hear the sea though, in this place. There is a sort of vibration underfoot, an intimation of something that might be the collision of waves with shore. Moving towards it proves difficult: it surrounds, seems to contain you. This hushed forest of pitch pine is like a bubble beneath the waves; or a pearl perhaps, trapped in the smooth coil of a seashell: subsumed within yet separate always from that which has formed it: without which it could not exist.

You intuit this, but nonetheless you tell yourself: I will find the access to the sea. I will find the entry point. If only I keep looking I will find it, I'm certain...

So you go deeper. One last look: reflective glimpse of metallic red: your car, there in the thicket, devoured by pine. Then there is a sort of path that you follow, up a ridge slippery with fallen needles, across a brackish runnel where green things grow - jack-in-the-pulpit, lily of the valley, feathery bracken, creeper, emerald-green moss. The path is not a real path, you know that. It has been made by the trees. It is *the space between* the trees that you are following: and it will take you where the trees want you to go. This is a difficult lesson for you to learn, at first: you keep veering off, thinking, this way must be the sea! But the trees will not allow it; they gather thickly; they needle; they push you back with spiny branches into *the space between*. Finally you accept it: the trees have made a decision about you. There is a sort of restfulness in this. No further decisions are needed. From darkness you emerge suddenly into a sunny hollow populated by beeches, tall and slender, pearly green, nearly in leaf: booming rat-a-tat-tat of woodpecker; abrupt retreat of something red, tipped with white: and then you are back in the dark again, ducking under coiling pine boughs. You try to feel to listen for the vibration of the sea: realize with a sharp sadness that it has gone. You cannot feel it, cannot hear it. Where is the sea? Certainly it still exists - in this sense, your sadness is out of proportion. There is a sea; undoubtedly you will encounter it again, perhaps today. But not yet: the trees have other ideas. Abruptly you emerge onto a piney ledge above a small, still, round pond, deeply blue, in which a single cloudlet is reflected: you are uncertain, for a moment, whether what you are seeing is water or sky: sky in water: brilliant sapphire with a single occlusion. All around, it is fringed by reeds, and by dark trees that lean together, whispering… It is like a blue eye, you think: a single, dazzling blue eye at the heart of the pitch pine forest. In the hush you stand and stare, though it is almost too bright to look at: it repels observation: you have to draw back: catching as you do a glimpse of something someone moving on the opposite shore, among the reeds: drawing back…raising, perhaps, a valedictory hand…

This is hard to comprehend. You are uncertain what you have seen. You look again: see nothing. There is no movement on the opposite shore, no disturbance among the reeds, no trace of color (of a blue windbreaker, for example) among the pitch pines over there. *Over there*, you think: *Should I go over there and see? Should I finally get to the bottom of this?*

Then it occurs to you that you don't know what, if anything, you'd be *getting to the bottom of.*

You feel foolish just for thinking it.

Nonetheless you begin to circle the blue eye.

The trees are against this. As are the reeds, the undergrowth in general. There is more of it than you had anticipated. Once you descend the ledge there is no more *space between*: you have to fight your way. The ground beneath your feet is boggy, moist, uncertain, the branches and brambles so thick that you cannot see where you are stepping. Each step is a risk. You flail. You crash and career.

You have lost what might be called the "element of surprise": if you ever had it.

Eventually you find yourself *over there*: looking back across the blue eye toward the ledge. You can see the spot where you were standing. No one is there: a relief. You don't, for example, see yourself standing there, on the ledge. No one is here. No one, you think, could have receded silently from *this* shore.

It is alarming to think that you have imagined all this: or dreamed it.

You try to recede, yourself, and find it more difficult than expected. You have to fight your way through thick undergrowth, intertwined branches, climb over fallen logs, rocks, brambles, then claw climb your way up a dark ridge coated with slick pine needles in order to regain the pitch pine forest. Reentering the safety of the darkness, waiting for your eyes to adjust. Now you will begin again, traversing *the space between*: except that, by circling the blue pool, you have lost your bearings. Now you are on the opposite side, though of what, it is hard to say.

You think: I will never see the sea again.

This is a melodrama. It is also a loss.

All you can do is move forward. Or back. You aren't sure which.

Nonetheless you do move, almost mindlessly, picking your way through the pitch pines, negotiating *the space between*. You seem to go on forever, stumbling over exposed roots, rocks, slithering down hills and into hollows, scrabbling your way up other hills, ridges, sliding back down in the loose, sandy soil, you feel like Sisyphus, your self the rock. You hadn't planned for it, this business of getting lost. What will you do, you wonder. You make contingency plans: edible berries, mushrooms, fiddlehead ferns. You can dig a hollow in the sand, you think: cover yourself with a blanket of leaves. You imagine tough fibrous roots, biting ants, spiders, the dark dampness that lies beneath. So, a mossy spot perhaps. Or you could sleep up in a tree, make a nest in the crook of a branch… *maybe I could see the sea from there!*…Though in another sense you have forgotten all that: the sea, the entry point, the mysterious figure at the other end of the beach: irrelevant: now it is the exit you want. Just the exit.

It has gone on for quite some time, the scrabbling, the slipping, the ducking and winding, the spider web across the face, slither underfoot of the long sinuous secret hidden behind the fallen log, patches of dazzling light, windows of sky in which seagulls can be seen, then patches of inky dark; conversations with the birds - chickadee, cardinal, tufted titmouse - then silent hush, every snap of a twig beneath your foot an affront to something you cannot see but can only sense. Suddenly a flash of something up ahead - a reflection, glint of light. You imagine a snug house among the pines, sun reflected in its windows, or a forest ranger signaling to his colleague with a mirror. Your pace quickens. The trees, colluding together, try to slow you down at first; then you feel branches pressing at your back, hurrying you along. At the precipice of a hollow, you misstep: pitch forward, tumble, turn, slide down on your back, bumping and banging: landing at last, with a resonant thud, by the passenger-side door of your own car.

You were not wanted here after all: so it seems.

Back at The Grey Ghost you wash your humiliation down the drain, along with the dirt, pine needles, twigs, webs and pine sap that you picked up on your journey.

All the things that you like, the familiar things that give you comfort, are just the same as always: the mirror shaped like a port hole, the painting of ducks over a salt marsh, the blue window seat by the window overlooking the sea. You sense no irony in these things: they are not laughing at you: nonetheless, you feel your relation to them has changed.

Downstairs (because you must go downstairs - to remain in your room would, you feel, be to admit failure, humiliation, defeat) things are the same also: Mrs. Crabbe, at work on her puzzle, doesn't look up when you enter the room. Mrs. Buckle with her light feather duster moves, humming, from one precious shelf of bibelots to the next: and there may be irony, you think, in the look that she gives you as you exit The Grey Ghost once more with your low chair, your book, your hat, your sunglasses. She knows, does Mrs. Buckle, that you have looked for the access point and failed to find it. She may even be laughing, behind her feather duster. You look back surreptitiously over your shoulder as you exit: but Mrs. Buckle seems, in fact, the same as ever, as she turns the implicitly disapproving the gaze of her wire rimmed spectacles toward a row of Kashmiri papier mache boxes which have grown palpably dusty. She has picked up one box, gold and black, shaped like an owl, and frowns at it severely as she dislodges the dust. She isn't laughing: on the contrary: you've imagined this. And so, reassured, you pass through and out, onto the beach.

And this seems the same as well: the silvery crescent lit by the late afternoon sun; the luminous blue convexity of the sea, cormorants skimming over it in wavering, hieroglyphic lines; the distant sand bar; the pink skein of cloud, progressing now toward purple. Though it is still day, the moon has come up: a new moon, low and fragile on the horizon: and just above it, a single star that pulses like liquid quicksilver in the ultramarine sky...

You lean back in your chair, open your book, but the book is useless to you, just a prop, you do not read. Your narrowed eyes are focused instead on the horizon, on that distant, watery blue point where sea and sky meet, become indistinguishable...You think you would like to go there, row out in Mrs. Buckle's old rowboat, to find that place, the hinge where sea and sky come together, the fulcrum on which this world, your small world, turns. But you know very well that a horizon is an imaginary place: endlessly pursued, never obtained: it recedes before you...

There is peace in this, in watching the new moon tangled in the quivering net of the waves, just above the receding line of the horizon. But of course it doesn't last. Though you don't want to, you feel compelled to look to the left, up the beach. For some time you resist, as the moon rises, the sun sinks, the shadows grow longer. Everything, no matter how small, now casts a shadow - each piece of driftwood, every salt-matted tangle of dried seaweed, the dips and hollows in the sand. The sandcastle that somebody built, with its glittering ruined turrets, is turned into an entire shadow city. Your own shadow is long, it's immense, the shadow of a giant, stretching down to meet the waves. You think: I won't look. And for a while, you don't. The blue distance darkens, the waves are shot through with exciting shades of indigo and aquamarine that shrink, lengthen, form glassine tubes that burst open in sudden cascades of white and green. This absorbs you, for a while. But finally you can't resist: you look, and sure enough, the figure is there, the one you feared to see, at the other end of the beach, your secret sharer, indistinct face turned resolutely seaward, blue wind-breaker flapping...

You think of the pitch pine forest, those sharp-needled branches and how they pushed and pulled at you, the nauseating labyrinth of *the in between*: and you shudder. How...?

You feel, close upon you, the great weight of the impossible. Once again you must retreat to The Grey Ghost.

Now you find that new guests have arrived. A young couple is spooning on the couch in the parlor. In the hallway, Mrs. Buckle is engaged in what appears to be a complex negotiation with a dark-haired, heavy-faced man, accompanied by many cases. As you pass through, she introduces him to you as Desmond, a journalist. You realize that, indeed, one of his cases, the small one, might contain a typewriter of the old-fashioned variety. Desmond, evidently distracted, nods at you: you think that Mrs. Buckle smirks as you pass: though you can't be certain - the light is reflected off her glasses so that you can't tell whether she is looking at you, or at Desmond. They are disagreeing, strenuously, over the value of a room at The Grey Ghost. As you go up the stairs, you overhear Mrs. Buckle saying waspishly: *No, the ghosts are not included!*

But then you think you must have been mistaken.

The infiltration of strangers alters the atmosphere of The Grey Ghost. You hear, with unease, the movements of these others - in the hall, on the stairs, through the floor, the ceiling, the walls, even through the pipes, which hiss sympathetically every time a tap is turned on in another room. This is true despite the fact that the rooms in which the newcomers have been lodged are, perhaps, nowhere near your own: indeed, you know that Mrs. Buckle makes a practice of such separations - that she prides herself on giving her guests what she refers to as *their space*. The labyrinthine nature of the The Ghost has helped her in this: built over years through a series of additions, it is, in a sense, several different houses imperfectly wedded: with even (you know, having stayed here several times), staircases that end at blank walls, rooms that may be entered only from outside, etc. Despite this palimpsest nature of The Grey Ghost, you are exquisitely aware of every foreign creak, every whisper, every unfamiliar footstep. How oddly sound carries in the labyrinth! You've no doubt that if Desmond, the journalist, turns over in his bed at midnight, you'll hear him: but if you were to search for his room - even if Mrs. Buckle would give you his room number, which she wouldn't - you'd never find it, not if you wandered up and down the halls and staircases of The Grey Ghost for hours... Reflecting on this, suddenly you think that you might have to leave sooner than you had expected: given the hotel is now too busy: and this is a great disappointment.

Dinner that evening is altered by the presence of the newcomers, particularly by the young couple, who giggle together over the soup, make ludicrous facial expressions and eye movements during the fish course, touch surreptitiously (but noticeably) under the table, then afterwards retire for another spooning session on the couch in the parlor before finally, mercifully, disappearing entwined together up the front staircase. You are left in the parlor with Mrs. Buckle, assiduous at her knitting, Mrs. Crabbe, and the journalist, who sits in the corner, smoking a cigarette, moodily watching Mrs. Crabbe's struggles with her jigsaw puzzle. He stares openly, making no effort to disguise his interest: though the expression on his face appears to be one of brooding disdain - as if he despises what interests him, or despises himself, for being interested.

Though he doesn't speak, his presence fills the room with palpable unease that hovers over everything like a specter.

At last there is an attempted exorcism: Mrs. Buckle asks, *And what brings you here to Allswell Grove, Mr. Desmond?*

Her tone is much more genteel than it was when she haggled with him over the price of a room.

Desmond inclines his wide face, with its dark halo of leonine curls, in Mrs. Buckle's direction. He appears heavy-lidded, impassive. *I'm writing a book*, he says: and smiles unpleasantly by raising his lips to show his teeth clenched around the white cylinder of his cigarette.

Such a portentous announcement can't, of course, stand unmolested. *What is your book about?* mischievously cries Mrs. Crabbe.

The journalist is unperturbed.

It's a murder mystery, he says, *set in a house by the sea, and centering on a woman who does jigsaw puzzles...*

Hmph, snorts Mrs. Crabbe, *that's not very realistic!*

Desmond laughs. *Real, unreal, who can say? We make up our own reality as we go along, that's what I think. In itself reality doesn't exist. Though in my case, my book is completely realistic. It is based on an actual incident - just one that hasn't happened yet.*

What could be said, in the face of such obfuscation?

Mrs. Buckle, petting her ball of yarn and the long, complex skein emerging from it, attempts to make a joke of it: *And does it contain an old lady who likes to knit, this mystery of yours?*

Of course.

Then I guess we had better be careful, Mr. Desmond - otherwise who knows what you will make of us! How does your mystery turn out?

But the journalist, expressionless, only says: *I don't know.*

I know, says Mrs. Crabbe.

What does she know? How does she know it? She doesn't say; no one asks.

Desmond resumes brooding, his cigarette between his teeth: contemplating Mrs. Crabbe as if she were an open hearth, flames merrily leaping.

Shortly after, Mrs. Crabbe goes up: as do you: earlier than usual.

Though you suspect the journalist of lying, you hear his typewriter late into the night. It is impossible to tell from what direction the sound is coming - whether from above, below, next door, from the opposite side of the hotel entirely, or even from somewhere outside. For hours, the impassioned bursts of tapping alternate with long silences, during which you imagine the journalist seated at his desk in the pose of The Thinker...once or twice you almost drift into sleep...Later comes the wind, worrying at the eaves: you feel The Grey Ghost shift beneath you, dream yourself at sea in a small boat, rising and falling on the waves...

Morning, when it dawns, is a muffled thing, lacking definition: likewise your waking, which is, rather, a slow ascent from some deep place. It is possible you have lain in your bed for a long time in the twilight, not knowing you were awake, not knowing it was morning: until certain sounds began to rouse you - somewhere, a door opening and closing; a footstep in the hallway; voices, coming from far away; and likewise from outside - the mewling calls of the gulls, soft lip-lop of waves. The sounds seem simultaneously too close and too far away, isolated from each other, difficult to place. Rising, you draw back the curtains and see the fog outside your windows: packed close: so thick that the ocean has disappeared, and the beach, and the salt marsh: all gone. In their place you see only the swirling eddies of fog which form fantastical shapes outside your window.

You look around you at the familiar things that have given you comfort - the window seat with the blue cushion, the painting of ducks flying, the mirror shaped like a porthole. How unfamiliar they seem in this new, shadowless world!

You pack your cases quickly. It is always easier to pack when leaving: there are no choices to be made: there are only tasks, the balm of mindless routine. When you have finished, you descend. It is, you realize, later than you thought. The Grey Ghost appears abandoned. There is no one at the front desk: Mrs. Buckle's office is empty: door ajar, lights on. The parlor too is empty, and though it is cold, no one has bothered to make a fire: the hearth is black, ashy, untouched. In the breakfast room the dishes have already been cleared away. The windows, spattered with rain, look out onto a field of dense cotton wool. Unusually, there is no sign of Mrs. Crabbe or her jigsaw puzzle: instead, a small manual typewriter, in the old-fashioned style, perches on the table by the window, a sheet of paper protruding from the platen. Next to the typewriter, a cigarette smolders in an ashtray. Coming closer, you can see the long, pendulous ash no one has bothered to flick away. Surreptitiously you look about: left, right, behind. You are alone: except for a vague movement by the sideboard, which may be a fly buzzing, or the hand gesture of a ghost, sensed out the corner of your eye: looking straight on, no one is there. And so you will do it. This is the forbidden thing. You know you shouldn't, but you can't resist the temptation: you lean over, read what the journalist has written. Then, taking up your cases, you step out, and disappear into the fog.

Excerpts from *The Boghole and the Beldame*

☆

Joanna Ruocco

The Donkey and the Bear

I eat leeks with the beldame. I drink juice with the beldame, the juice of the leeks. When we finish, we sit on the stump without eating or drinking. I throw our bowls and cups into the boghole and the bearded bottoms of the leeks. A thief approaches the boghole. "Sometimes the night is full of sounds," says the beldame, "and there is no room for the sounds of a thief approaching. But tonight the night is empty of sounds and we may listen to the thief's approach." I listen. I hear the braying of a donkey and the growling of a bear. "The sounds of the thief approaching are stealthy sounds," says the beldame, "if attributed to the thief. Otherwise the sounds are common enough." I feel heat on the back of my neck, but I do not know to what I should attribute this heat: to the breath of donkey, bear, or thief. I turn my head to the side and the breath passes beneath my nose. The breath is redolent of leeks. "Yes," says the beldame. "Beyond the village of the shambles, I descended the dell. I came to a house. The light from the house spilled into the dell. I found the casements of the window thrown open, the crib pushed to the window, the child asleep in the crib." The night is silent. A lamp has floated to the top of the boghole. Fen-berries float in the light of the lamp.

The Valley of Josef

The valley of Josef is a narrow valley, the slopes too steep for sheep to graze peaceably. The grazing of sheep in the valley of Josef is a mighty feat, a feat of a mightiness not common to sheep. The sheep in the valley of Josef are prized for their mightiness, but they know no peace and their lives are short. The young men of the valley of Josef live among sheep. They wear robes, ungirt to reveal their thighs, which shine with the oils of the wool. Their feet are unshod. Their heels are hard as the hooves of sheep. One road runs through the valley of Josef. The road is the width of a dung-cart. If the drivers of the dung-carts wish to lie with the young men of the valley of Josef they stop their carts on the road. There are no trees to shade the road so it does not matter where on the road they stop. The road that runs through the valley of Josef is the same road in all of its parts; it has no features—no dips, bends, grades, ruts, growths—or rather, its features are everywhere the same features. Stopping the dung-carts on the road is no different from driving the dung-carts on the road. The drivers of the dung-carts might as well stop their carts to lie with the young men of the valley of Josef, even if at first it is not what they wish. Lying with the young men of the valley of Josef is the only difference between stopping and driving the dung-carts. Without this one difference, the drivers of the dung-carts would never know if they were leaving or remaining in the valley of Josef. The dung in their carts is intended for the orchards of the Fane. The drivers cannot discharge their duty by dunging the road that runs through the valley of Josef and so emptying their carts; they must continue towards the Fane. The dung in the carts does not burn the windborne seeds that settle. Lush grasses and fruit trees grow from the dung in the carts. Each cart contains an orchard. The valley of Josef does not differ from the Fane in any way. The road through each is the same. The orchards are the same. The valley of Josef cannot be confused with the Fane. The young men who live in the valley wear no sandals. They worship nothing but sheep.

Zucchini Flower

"The axe-head moon in the zucchini flower season," says the beldame, "brings the beldame." "The skin prickles in this season," I say, "but the blood is stagnant. The skin does not redden. The moonlight is long and yellow. The eyes film. The lips grow together at the corners so speech involves the tearing of the lips." "In sleep," says the beldame, "the beldame crouches on your chest. For every sleeper, a beldame, crouching." "On this stump," I say, "I am afraid to sleep. Asleep, I may roll into the boghole. I do not sleep," I say, "but you crouch upon me." "Only in speech do we tear apart," says the beldame, "but the tearing produces a glue, a serum that adheres us more closely." Beneath the smell of leeks, the yellow smell of this serum, thinner than the smell of rotting. It must be a thin smell, otherwise it would not fit between my body and the body of the beldame. Our skins are as the seam between lips.

The Girl and the Boy

I make a tube of hide and fit it with a lens. I train the tube across the boghole. There, on the other side of the boghole, a girl with a jar. "If her jar is made of optic glass," says the beldame, "and she holds it to her eye, she may see you motioning from the stump, but she will see you only as a figure of miasma, for everyone knows that miasma forms figures that beckon to young girls, coaxing them towards fever." The girl does not hold her jar to her eye. She dips her jar into the boghole. "In the village of the shambles they drink a certain tea," says the beldame, "cultured with liquid from the boghole. The girl comes to the boghole to gather liquid for this tea." I turn the tube and look away from the boghole across the stump. There, on the other side of the stump, a boy with a saw. "If he had arrived earlier," says the beldame, "he might have felled this tree and built a ship large enough to move his village across the sea, but he has arrived late and the tree has disappeared into the boghole. He will not build a ship to move his village and the villagers will die in the chasm that even now opens beneath the village." I throw hide and lens into the boghole and run from the beldame, across the stump, towards the boy. Soon I am back at the beldame, led to her by the rings of the stump.

Pancake Bell

Each villager is waiting her turn to climb the tower and ring the pancake bell, but not the mason and the cartwright. They are fishing in the river. The mason fishes with a peacock herl and the cartwright fishes with a peach flower. Both peacock herls and peach flowers ride the currents of the water. The mason believes that peacock herls are more toothsome to fish, and the cartwright believes that peach flowers are more toothsome to everything. The cartwright dips her hand often into her pouch of peach flowers and drops flowers into her mouth. "The rocks in the river have grown larger," says the mason. "It must be that the water is lower," says the cartwright. "Quantities of water may vary in a river, but rocks only dwindle. This is the way of rocks." The mason fishes. The cartwright fishes. Herl and flower ride the waters. "The fish are insensible to pleasure," says the cartwright. "They desire neither herl nor flower." The lines spool on and on, carried by the river. "The rocks may have displaced the fish," says the mason. "The capacities of rivers are limited and so the ratios of fish to rock relate inversely." "The peach flower has grounded on a rock," says the cartwright. "Earlier the rock did not break the surface of the water, but now the rock rises above the water, like an islet." The mason and the cartwright look about. The understory presses against both sides of the river. "When the water is low, two silver lines bank the river," says the mason, "the clay of the river-bottom silvering upon contact with the air." Ferns bend over the river and the long tops of wild onions and spotted lilies. "There are no silver lines," admits the cartwright. "The water runs high and sweet with the snowmelt. But it is a strange thing to encounter rocks that act contrary to their nature, growing instead of dwindling in the river." "It must be that the rocks are snails," says the mason. "Great snails from ages past who found their way into the river through tunnels in the earth." "They have eaten the fish," says the cartwright. "Yes," says the mason. "They grow fat on fish. This is the way of snails." "If we wade deeper in the river, we can use our arms as levers and lever out a snail," says the cartwright. The mason and the cartwright tie the ends of their lines to the hornbeam. The cartwright empties the pouch of peach flowers into her mouth. The mason and the cartwright enter the river. They crouch to lever the snail and the water runs over the tops of their shoulders and chills even the long chin of the cartwright. It smells faintly of peaches.

Figures of Miasma

How I do not block the wind. Yes, says the beldame. How water falls through my hands. Yes, says the beldame. How when I lie on your breast, I am the color of your breast, I am the shape of your breast, I am long and white like your breast. Yes, says the beldame. You are my breast. I am your breast. You are my breast, says the beldame, when you lie on my breast. When I lie on the stump, I am the stump. When I wade in the bog, I am the bog. Do not wade in the bog, says the beldame. She hangs her feet in the bog. Jars float in the bog. She unscrews the lid of a jar with her feet. The wind sings in the jar, says the beldame, the jar sings in the wind. How when I fill I will sink. I will sing, says the beldame. The night is too dark to hear. The skin is too close to touch. Yes, says the beldame, I feel your breath on my breast.

Cream of Lettuce

A man arrives at the village of hubbard. He is carrying a pot and has black whiskers on his face. When he reaches the center of the village, he bangs on his pot and the women of the village of hubbard come to greet him with kisses, but the man's black whiskers are stiff as wires and closely rooted in his cheeks; the women find no space for their lips to rest peaceably. The man lowers his brows, long and stiff as his whiskers, so the women fear to kiss even his nose. I search for the demon of kell, says the man. Where might you search for such a demon in our village? ask the women. In the village of kell, says the man, the demon dwelled in a red-thorn bush as tall as a tree. I might search for the demon in such a bush in your village. We have such a bush, say the women. We pruned the red-thorn branches after the dew dried, say the women, to make our red-thorn garlands. We did not find the demon of kell among the thorns. The man sees that red thorns garland the heads of the women. The demon of kell in the red-thorn bush did not look unlike many women, brown limbs, and above, red-thorns between long drapes of hair. The man overturns his pot and sits heavily upon its base. He looks up at the women. I search no more, he says. You must search a little more, say the women. It may be that your demon dwells in our lettuces, which grow just beyond those stones.

Jasper

The path, though green, is not grass but jasper. The river, though blue, is not water but lazuli. The sky, though clear, is not ether but quartzite. And the women, says the beldame, are they onyx or salt? Yellow fluids run from the scalls of the beldame. Between scalls, coarse grains of skin. I touch the coarse grains of the beldame. I say, salt. Yes, says the beldame. The women are salt. They were mined from the mountain. The miners marked the path to the river with women, one woman for every fork in the path. How many forks in the path to the river? I count the grains of the beldame. As many as grains. Yes, says the beldame. The women point the way to the river. You can't lose your way, says the beldame, but you will not reach the river. You will reach another woman pointing yet farther down the forking path.

Wheat Porridge

"Do not marry," says the beldame. "In the village of the Herm, they strew the bridegroom with fruits, but the bride they chase through fields, until she is treed and bayed and dragged to earth. They strip her. They lash her wrists and ankles around a pole and bear her to the Herm where she is laid upon an oiled stone and packed with hot wheat porridge. Before the porridge, she receives two reeds, one in either nostril, and her skin is cooled with flasks of river water; but even so," says the beldame, "the bride does not find the hours gladsome. She is held to the stone until the porridge dries and can be cut from her. She is given olives to eat. Her hair is perfumed and braided. The Herm is heavy stones. In the course of a day, the weight of the stones presses the earth like a grape so that the dusk flows from the earth, the dark, sweet dusk. It pools around the

Herm and slowly the fields darken, the trunks of the trees darken, the hills darken. The darkness crests the hills, and the sky darkens, and the bride begins to enjoy the dusk. She stands by the Herm and feels swift movements in the dark air: nighthawks, bats, moths, thick cinders from the fires. Beside her stands her likeness, a bride of porridge filled with fruits for the demon of the Herm," says the beldame. "And who do you think is more pleasing to the demon?" says the beldame, "the bride or her likeness? That is a question answered by the demon," says the beldame, "After the dusk has clotted but before the dusk has powdered, the demon decides which is pleasing. The bridegroom pours fresh oil upon the stones of the Herm to honor the choice."

The Valley of Josef

There is a story told in the valley of Josef. A man arrives in byrnie and helm. He holds a long-bearded axe. I am in search of a demon, says the man, the demon of kirk. He has no flesh on his bones so he wears a swaddle of fleece. His spine is bent so he walks on four feet. I have followed this beast to your valley, says the man, and so here I will seek, climbing the hillside with my axe aloft, though you like it not. We like it not, say the young men of the valley of Josef, and the man climbs the hillside with his black-hafted axe held to the sky, and the young men climb after. The man sees a beast grazing in the scree, grazing in the sliding, steeply pitched scree. It is our sheep, say the young men, but the man will not believe them. Such grazing is a feat too mighty for sheep, says the man, and he runs with the long-bearded axe, leaping from stone to stone up the slope, swinging the axe as he goes, preparing to strike the head from the sheep, but the stones slide from beneath his feet, and the man tumbles down the slope. His helm is loosed from his head and the young men see his pale curls darken with gore as he rolls to the base of the slope. When they reach him, his face is not the face of a man. The young men unbuckle his byrnie to hear if the heart beats yet in his chest. Beneath the byrnie, they find neither shirt nor skin. They find a cavity packed with damp fleece, and shank bones lodged therein, stinking. The young men buckle the byrnie. They cover the body with stones, small stones and sand. So formed the high sandy comb on the slope of the valley of Josef. It is a formation of fleece and shank, mail and stone and sand.

Pancake Bell

The cooper finds correspondence between her palms and the buttocks of the brewer. The ale-maker finds correspondence between her palms and the buttocks of the cooper. "It is not a subtle correspondence," says the cooper, inspecting her own palms as she bends to allow the alemaker's inspection of her buttocks. Bending, the cooper sees more clearly the buttocks of the brewer. The cooper holds apart her palms to make a frame and peers through the frame at the buttocks of the brewer. The ale-maker inspects the buttocks of the cooper. The ale-maker has small deep palms and the cooper has small conical buttocks. "It is not a subtle correspondence," says the ale-maker. The cooper sits on the palms of the ale-maker. The brewer sits on the palms of the cooper. The ale-maker is sustaining the weight of both the brewer and the cooper. "Even though we three have found correspondences between palms and buttocks," says the ale-maker, "and so might suppose that others in the village will also find correspondences between palms and buttocks, we cannot suppose that the correspondences of palms and buttocks will correspond to each person's capacity to sustain the weight of the owner of the buttocks that correspond to her palms." "Moreover," says the cooper, "we cannot suppose that the correspondences between palms and buttocks will correspond to each person's capacity to sustain the weight, not only of the owner of the buttocks that correspond to her palms, but also of the owner of the buttocks that correspond to the palms of the owner of the buttocks she sustains." The cooper is sweating beneath the weight of the brewer. The ale-maker is sweating beneath the weight of the brewer and the cooper. The brewer holds her palms up to the sky.

Bjartur's Dream

Before the end, he will come to great sorrow, and when at last, he finds himself dying, quite without strength of body, it is remarkable

that he cry out, surprised, for this is the way it is foretold and must
happen, and many other bright eyes will dim and gold hairs go
to dust without graying. Now it is time to begin. He is young but
imposing. His father is king of broad lands with warships that scull
well on the waters. The boy must leave these lands, though leaving
speed his death, to earn red gold and praises. He takes wise counsel
from the witch. Ride south, says the witch, when the butter melts,
there a serpent breathes fire. Pierce his heart with this spear and
eat his tongue of charred honey. That is a feat for a deedless man.
Later you will drink from a poisoned cup and run the length of the
hall, but poison is as fast as the fastest man and runs with him just
beneath the skin. Running you will fall with the foam in your mouth.
First ride, says the witch, while your blood is unmixed and your lips
show no lather. The boy takes his spear, a good horse, and the thrall
who has best cause to love him. He rides and when the butter melts
and the fire makes the death-lights shine on his helm, he fights the
serpent. He pierces the serpent, but how can he find the heart of
the serpent? In a man the heart lies at known distance between the
head and the foot. The boy knows nothing of a serpent's heart. It lies
behind scales, in deep coils upon coils. His white helm shines with
a terrible light. One scale in the serpent's breast winks like an eye.
The boy pierces the serpent's heart through this eye and eats of the
tongue. Soon he can speak the language of crows. When he sleeps
in the forest, the she-wolf brings a cloak in her jaws. The thrall she
devours. There is nothing for the boy to bury. The cloak is stitched
with red flames. Of the serpent's treasures, he has taken rings and
the reforged sword. He kills countless kings beneath their banners.
No man has done such deeds or married such a woman. He would
not tip chair and table to run past white faces, he would not raise that
cry that the walls send back, but what can he turn to fight? There is
nothing. There is green foam like the leeks. It is a hard thing to hear
your name on men's tongues grow faint and fainter. But the sorrow
is not smaller when the holdings taken are but sheepfold, croft, and
homefield. Fire's warmth is not warming. I have slept in the forest so
long my beard tangles with mosses. As the breath goes, it travels
through mosses and mimics the speech of no creature.

The Kirtle

"Do not marry," says the beldame. "At the feast, the horn of mead is passed around the table, and honeyed breads, and the meat is portioned hugely. The men each eat their portion, and the women too, and between the portions no difference is permitted. The bride and bridegroom must eat their equal portions. They must each drain the horn of mead as dry, and soon the bride dozes," says the beldame. "She dozes by the fire and her kinswomen carry her behind the arras to a cooler chamber. They stitch a woolen kirtle to her skin, a white woolen kirtle, thick enough so the blood does not spot the white wool of the kirtle. If the bride struggles," says the beldame, "they choke her wind until she dozes. They stitch her lips around a ball of wool. They carry the bride into the meadow. They shatter her ankles with a heavy stone. They apply white pepper to her lips and tasting white pepper, the bride awakens," says the beldame. "The bride awakens in the meadow. Her kinswomen have crept away and the bride sees only sheep. There are many sheep, white sheep. The bride crawls among the sheep. When the bridegroom is brought to the meadow, his kinsmen tie a linen strip around his eyes. They put the sharp knife into his hand. He stumbles among the sheep of the meadow. He catches hold of the sheep and cuts away their wool with his knife. He feels the skin of the sheep, the soft beating skin of the sheep, and he feels where the skin slopes and rises. He feels for the slopes and rises of the bride," says the beldame. "She sees him," says the beldame, "the bride sees the bridegroom. She sees him through the legs of the sheep, above the backs of the sheep, cutting away the wool of the sheep. The bridegroom must cut the bride's kirtle," says the beldame, "but the kirtle is sewn to the skin of the bride. Does the skin lie beneath the kirtle," says the beldame, "or is the kirtle the skin? The bridegroom stumbles between sheep in the meadow. He holds the sheep. He feels the slopes and the rises. White wool drifts through the meadow. The bride dozes in the drifts of wool. When the bridegroom thrusts his hands into the drifts," says the beldame, "he feels only the wool. No matter how deeply he cuts," says the beldame, "the slopes and rises of the bride are not revealed to his touch."

The Village of the Boghole

"The nettles are soaked and will not sting," says the beldame. "I soaked them in the boghole." She eats cold nettles close beside me on the stump. "I would dress the nettles with oil," says the beldame. "But I have no oil. I would press oil from the stump," says the beldame, "but I have no stone. I have no strength," says the beldame. "In the village of dock," says the beldame, "the women press oils from roots. They press the roots between boulders. In the village of logan," says the beldame, "the boulders move at a touch. The women of logan caress only the boulders," says the beldame. "Those who would touch them they crush with the boulders. To crush takes just a caress." I eat cold nettles with the beldame. The nettles sting my lips. They sting my tongue. They sting my throat. "Drink the water from the boghole," says the beldame. "The water is soothing." I put my lips to the boghole. I drink. The water coats my lips. It coats my tongue. It coats my throat. It is soothing. "In the village of the boghole," says the beldame. "I drank the water of the boghole. I filled my body with the water, the dark water of the boghole." Great cries come from the beldame. "My skin is stinging," says the beldame. "There is pitch in the water," says the beldame. "My scalls leak the pitch." I touch the black scalls of the beldame. "Your fingers will stick," says the beldame. "They will stick to my skin. Keep still," says the beldame, "you will tear the hairs from my skin." I keep still. I stand in great darkness. The darkness is thick. The darkness is as thick as the water from the boghole. It coats my lips. It coats my tongue. It coats my throat. "Am I breathing?" I ask the beldame. "The stump is sinking," says the beldame, "but we float on the water. We are filled with the water," says the beldame, "so we float. Hold me beneath the water of the boghole," says the beldame. She speaks in the voice of a sow, of a broken-toothed ewe. "Why can't I sink," says the beldame, "why can't I leave?" Great cries come from the beldame. "Yes, you are dying," says the beldame. "I will hold you," says the beldame. "I will hold you as I sink." I feel the cold that comes from the boghole. "It comes from my bones," says the beldame. "It comes from my teeth. Look up," says the beldame, "those stars are my teeth." I look at the darkness, the star-shaped dark in the darkness. "Are we deep in the boghole?" I ask the beldame. "Yes," says the beldame, "you are inside my bones. You are inside my teeth. I am diseased in my skin," says the beldame, "but you are deeper than skin." "I am cold," I say to the beldame. "I ache in my bones." "Yes," says the beldame, "Come close. I will hold you. I will hold you beneath the disease in my skin." "Do not hold me," I say, but she holds me. I weep upon the beldame's breasts. I can't lift my head. I can't see to leave. "There is nowhere to go," says the beldame. "There is no other village. There is this darkness," says the beldame, "a darkness without silence or peace."

The Bargeman

Beyond the boghole, a fern brake. A forest. A mountain. A plain. When you reach the corner of the plain, says the beldame, take the plain in your mouth. Take the corner of the plain in your mouth. The light will empty your mouth. We walk together on the stump, along the rim of the stump. It is dark. I hold the dark in my mouth. I hold the bog in my mouth. There is no way to reach the plain, the corner of the plain. The corner of the plain is a bright tongue; it fits in the groove of a mouth. My mouth has filled. It has filled with the dark of the boghole. Dark water flows from my mouth. How can I reach the plain? Each pipe of grass has three edges that reflect light. They shine into the dark of a mouth. The mouth is not my mouth. Dark water flows. It flows across the plain. Sunken in the boghole, a fern brake. A forest. A mountain. A plain. Bright pipes of grass. Who will have me? says the beldame. In the village of lichen, I was mistaken for lichen. In the village of lilies, I disfigured the lilies. I was the furze in the lilies. I was burnt like the furze. In the village of swards, I butchered my sow. I cupped the blood of my sow. I soaked my scalls in the blood of my sow. My scalls are deeper than the skin. They are filled with my blood. There is no room in my blood for the blood of my sow. The hairs on my scalls have turned white. I have no hairs on my head, says the beldame, but I have these white hairs on my scalls. We walk together on the stump. We come to a man, a crooked one, who leans over the rim of the stump. He is leaning on a pole, a pole that he thrusts into the boghole. He is poling the stump through the bog. From his pouch, he removes a bannock of oats. With one arm he poles. With the other arm, he eats of the bannock. You need strength, says the beldame. Yes, says the bargeman. The strength of the oat. That is why I eat these oats. I eat these oats so I can pole us strongly through the bog. His mouth is filled with oats. His arm shakes as he poles. I will take the pole, says the beldame. She takes the pole. She thrusts the pole into the boghole. It does not touch the bottom, says the beldame. No, says the bargeman. But we are moving through the bog. I know because I vomit oats.

Questions

☆

Marream Krollos

Well, I figure he was just a disturbed person. You know what I mean? I mean, I've had days where I just come home and I don't know what to do with myself. It isn't every single day that's that way, but I can imagine. Just last week I had such a bad day at work that I needed to go home, take my clothes off, get in bed and wait for it to end. Talking to my husband only makes things worse. My husband has a way of seeing how everything is my fault. But I at least have a husband, he may have had no one. So, maybe he came home one day and was upset because of something he had said or done and there was nobody there for him. Only with him that feeling never went away. That's how I explain it to myself at least. He knew his sadness was small, caused by something small, but he couldn't help feeling overwhelmed. Maybe that's how it happens to them. You know, people like him. He knew he was upset over nothing but couldn't stop rehashing the conversation that went wrong in his head, or couldn't stop thinking about how he wished he had done things differently. It was no big deal, whatever it was, but he felt worthless anyway. He came home upset one day and realized he just needed to take off his clothes and get into bed. He started with his shirt, looked at his arms and was repulsed by how hairy he was. It seemed to him like all that hair really didn't belong on his body. It didn't look like a human arm. It looked like a short pink snake with brown hair growing all over it. He took off his pants and saw his round belly. He thought it was strange that somebody with such a thin frame could have such a swollen belly. Like one of those starving children you see on television. I always saw him as half boy half man. Maybe that's part of the reason he was so drawn to them. His feet looked to him like dead toads that he had to keep lifting off the ground until he could hide them under the covers. He never told anybody this, so it stayed inside him and became something that he does. You know what I mean, this feeling became a reaction, an instinct. He kept asking himself why he had said what he said or did what he did. I don't know if you can relate to this, but sometimes all I want is for people to think good things about me, and all I can do is imagine all the horrible things they must think of me. It became easier for him to believe that people were unkind to him, that the world was unkind. All those little boys he was with were only going to become men that would be unkind to him, men who would misunderstand him, or judge him. So he kept doing it. Of course, it couldn't have been just one bad day that made him do all this, it would have to happen more than once, the bad day, I mean. Maybe this started from the time he was a little boy. He came home many times and thought of cutting his own skin to get his mind off of things. Sometimes I think just one little cut on my wrist would help ease my mind. I wouldn't tell my husband this, of course. What would be the point? But I can imagine that he would have wanted a part of his skin pinched so hard that all of what he was feeling would stay on that little patch of skin instead of inside him. All I can come up with as an explanation is that he hated himself, the way only a woman can hate herself, but he was not a woman. He knew he did not want women, and he didn't want to act like a woman either. He wanted to be a man who wanted women, a man who women wanted, a real man in his own eyes.

Question

No, I didn't know then. But I can't say I was surprised when I found out about what he had done. I guess, you can say I sensed it in him. I mean, I'm not the type of person who meddles in other people's business, so I left it alone. There was no way I could have really known, you understand. But there was this combination of cowardice and anger in him that was special, distinctive, to me. He would get angry at little old ladies who sold street food in Seoul and just start swearing at them. One time he threw a full beer bottle at a taxi driver who he thought overcharged us, but then ran off when the driver got out. There was a little old man driving. You would think somebody that angry could handle a little old man, wouldn't you? You see, he felt comfortable being angry but only around people he thought were weak, weaker than he thought he was at least. I am not trying to defend it, but he just probably didn't want to get hurt. He wanted somebody to take his anger in without complaining, or judging him. I have felt this same feeling before. Just a little while back my husband and I were on vacation, in Thailand, considering who we are talking about now, of all places, and I was just acting like a crazy person. I just wanted to be moody and upset and emotional and have him stay in that hotel room with me and take it. That is the only thing that would have made me feel loved at that time, and a little love was all I wanted from him. Of course, he didn't stay. He said I was acting like a child and stormed out of the hotel room. I realized then that I have never in my life felt like I could be bad and still be lovable. Do you know what I mean? Not even when I was a child did I feel that. I know it sounds silly. I mean, why would anybody be lovable when they are being bad? But that is what I wanted desperately right then and there, and I didn't get it. Now, I'm not going to go off and be with children because of it, but I can see how something in your mind could go wrong and that feeling could take over your whole life. I mean, I really can't say for sure that anybody loves me. My husband is the one person I am closest to in the whole world and I cannot say that I know with all my heart that he really loves me, loves me for who I am.

Question

Well, that's because when we first met I felt a kind of kinship with him. We were both young, living abroad, and alone. You could say I smelled my own. I could tell he hated himself though. He was not a good looking man by any stretch of the imagination. He was thin and funny looking. I mean, you know all this, I suppose. He wasn't comfortable moving his own body around. His mouth was shaped funny. He would laugh suddenly and too hard for people to not look at him funny. Right away I tried to be his friend. I tried to be open with him. I usually don't do this with people that I have just met, but I felt I could with him. It only made him get angry at me in the end. Although, I think he knew I understood him better than anybody else did. I remember getting a phone call from him at five in the morning once. This is after he had gotten into whatever he had gotten into, but I didn't know that at the time. He was crying hysterically talking about how he was an evil person. I asked him why he would say such things. I thought it was the prostitutes he'd said he had been with. I thought it was the women that he paid to be with, and all the mean things he would say about people sometimes. I had no idea that he was crying because he had been with little boys. I kept repeating you are a good person, you are a good person, and I gave him examples of all the ways that he was good.

Question

Well, you know at a time like that, when somebody calls you wailing hysterically, you have to feel something for them. I thought of all the ways he was unique. I talked about how smart he is, you know, his philosophy degree, his vocabulary, his sense of humor. And I meant all of it. I mean, he would say the funniest things sometimes. I remember once I was walking behind him up the stairs to his apartment and he passed gas. He turned around and said, oh, that was a little duck there on the stairs. You know, because it sounded sort of like a quack, I guess. Little things like that would really endear him to me. I told him that he was very easy going in a lot of ways. One day we were walking around a lake and I had a runny nose and no tissue. I was always sick then, I just couldn't get used to the air pollution there. I had to keep blowing my nose on my sleeve because I got tired of sniffing all that stuff back into my lungs. It really was disgusting. I had green and yellow mucus all over my sleeve. He just made fun of me. He started to run away from my sleeve when my arms got near him. He could be sweet like that sometimes. And smart. He knew what the word potable meant, for example. I couldn't believe that it meant drinkable, because it has the word pot in it, until I looked it up. But I didn't always let him off the hook either. I still admitted that he says really horrible things about people and told him to stop. But I also told him I believe he feels a goodness for others that he doesn't always let show because he is too scared. I have to admit that I was flattered by the call. He wanted comfort from me. Moments like that make you feel needed, you know what I mean? You feel secretly that if somebody could need you like that then maybe you can be loved.

Question

No. It's just that the way I imagined it happening was that it got worse and worse as time went on. He got worse. I would hope that he didn't start out with six year old boys, but that there was some truth to the stories about the prostitutes. The same way all of us do some things we are ashamed of, then feel so ashamed of ourselves that it makes us do some other things we are even more ashamed of. You know, like when you are arguing with somebody and you say something you wish you could take back, but then end up saying something even worse to prove to yourself that there was nothing wrong with what you said in the first place. I do that with my husband all the time. It starts with me asking him why he didn't do this one thing for me and ends with me saying something about how I just don't feel like he does anything at all for me. I would never intentionally want things to get that bad between us. My husband is my best friend, whether I like it or not. My husband is maybe my only friend now. Maybe he got to the point where he was so ashamed of himself being with sixteen year old boys that he began seeing a look of hatred, of disgust towards him, in their eyes. So he had to keep having them younger and younger so he could feel that he was completely in control. He wanted to be around people who couldn't hurt him, people who couldn't reject him because they were completely willing, so to speak. You know, only in the way that six year old boys don't know enough about what's right or wrong to hate you. I think he really just wanted a person's love. He felt he wouldn't be able to actually ever get love, so he had to act it out, you know, go through the physical motions of love. The only way he knew how to act out love was through touch maybe. It's the only way some of us know how to give and take love. But he felt judged being with an adult, so he had to be with children. An adult might look at his body with a grimace, or think about how he didn't do this or that right in bed, you know? I am going to tell you something I have never told anybody. I have myself had fantasies of just pushing my husband's face into my crotch. I sometimes think about what it would be like if I could make him do what I wanted, just like that. He has once pushed my face into his crotch and I didn't say anything about it because of, well, what we were doing at the time…but it still hurt my feelings. I could never do the same thing to him. I would never do that to him. It made me feel weak, and that I couldn't even complain because…

Question

No, I am not defending him. I think he's evil. At least, I think it was evil to do what he did. He had a choice. I think he had a choice. I'm sure. I'm not even one of those people who thinks it's a disease. I don't think he was born sick. I think it gets worse is all, over time. That's what I'm trying to say. That's the point I was trying to make. You have to stop yourself from doing small bad things or else you end up doing big bad things. I mean, I was the only one who knew there was something wrong. I wish I could have done more. There was nothing I could have done. I am only trying to say that sometimes when you are naked with an adult man you feel like you are begging for love just like a child, begging like a child who wants to be good. It might have occurred to him that if he was with a child he could finally feel like a man. But I don't think that's right. I think it's wrong.

Question

Of course, I have been wrong about people before. I do not get any pride out of knowing people well enough to not be surprised by what happened. I just think that all it is… that he was disturbed inside, that's all. He is a disturbed man. But sometimes…

Question

Yes, there are people that I have thought similar things about who didn't end up doing what he did. I don't know, really, what to think about that. I am not trying to claim that there is any rhyme or reason to anything, anything in the world. There are people we see evil in who don't do evil things. That happens. I have disliked good people, and liked bad people. I just feel what I feel, about him, about this situation. We feel what we feel. I felt what I felt at the time.

Question

That's not really true. He wasn't nice to me. He wasn't even at all that decent to me really. He once pushed me down during an argument and said some horrible things that I can't even repeat. It was when we were on vacation together in Thailand, our first year in Seoul, when you say he began doing what he was doing. Yes, I had been drinking and was acting up too, but all I did was throw some sand on his feet and he got really angry and told me to stop. He called me a nasty word. I thought he was being mean so I did it again. I know it was silly of me but I was angry that he was so angry when I was only being myself. He started swearing at me so I tried to walk away. He followed me and we exchanged angry words and he pushed me down. When I tried to get up and push him back, he ran off. No, no, I wouldn't say that I hadn't ever felt hurt by him. All of this affects my life in so many ways I cannot tell you. I cannot begin to explain to you how this has turned my whole world upside down. It is so upsetting to realize that somebody you knew was capable of this. I lie down next to my husband and wonder what he is capable of now. I don't know anybody as well as I know my husband, and I wonder now what even is he really capable of.

Question

Obviously, not as much pain as you felt. I wasn't trying to say that at all. Not as much as you felt, by any means.

Question

You know, I think it's because of Nikita. When I was in the sixth grade there was a girl in my class named Nikita, who nobody liked. And it wasn't without good reason either. She stole. She bullied other children in class. She was very large and dark and loud. One day a girl said that Nikita threatened to beat her up. The teacher asked us if there were any witnesses to this. A lot of children in class raised their hands. I had heard Nikita threaten the girl too, but didn't want to get involved, at first. It seemed obvious that she was in trouble already, she was always in trouble anyway. Then the teacher said that everybody who had heard Nikita make the threat should go to the principal's office as a witness. He asked if there was anybody else who had heard the threat. I raised my hand the second time he asked because I wanted to go to the principal's office too. I wanted to get out of class for a little while. When we got there I heard those kids talk about Nikita and I just felt terrible for her. It occurred to me that the girl who complained was pretty, and white, and small. Nikita was a big girl, and, you know, I'm a big girl myself so I know how it feels. I wanted to take back what I had done. She was in class when he asked us to raise our hands. I knew she saw me. I was scared of her and sad for her at the same time. I just didn't want that to happen again. I didn't want to feel that again. When I was in the fifth grade my teacher asked us to raise our hands if we saw anybody without their hands on their hearts during the flag salute. I knew that Jason hadn't put his hand on his heart, so I raised my hands to let her know. But I had to keep my hands up for a long time because everybody was asking questions about the science fair or something else that was going on. She kept saying I'll get to you, I'll get to you, but by the time she did it had been a long while since the flag salute. I told her that Jason hadn't put his hands on his heart and she just looked at me like I was garbage. She said that's what you wanted to tell me, just incredulous. I shook my head and she just looked away and pretended I wasn't even in the room. I felt so terrible. I felt like a tattle tale when I really was not. I just thought I was following an order. I didn't know why it was important to her that we tell her if somebody hadn't put their hand to their heart. She just wanted us to let her know, so I did. Anyway, that experience too made me scared of telling people things about other people. Sometimes you think back and you feel like that small child again, begging to be loved, repeating in your head I'll be good, I'll be good, I'm sorry.

Question

No, of course it is not the same. I am not saying that. It just might have brought on the same feeling in me. It might have felt the same for me.

Question

There was this one night. We had all come back from the bars very drunk. I didn't want to get a taxi back to my apartment so I stayed at his apartment. We were so drunk that I fell asleep on his twin size bed, next to him, with my coat on. I woke up a little bit before he did. I was parched. The sun had come through the window in the morning and had been shining right in my face for hours. It was a cold night out so he had turned the heat up. I had been sweating in my coat all night. I woke up, then he woke up, we got out of bed and I went home. It isn't such a good memory. I mostly remember that sun beating on my face, not being able to move my arms in that coat on that tiny bed. It's just a memory of him being harmless. You know, his body turned toward a wall so somebody else could fit next to him on a small bed, and just, sleeping.

Question

No, no, not because of that one night on his bed. The only moment I remember ever feeling anything like that for him was the day we were talking about the type of poverty we saw in Asia, that you don't see here, and he brought up that in Thailand some little boys are so hungry that they would sleep with men for money. He told me about a little boy he met in Thailand who was obviously homeless and hungry so he gave him a hundred dollars. Now, of course, I am not sure if he was twisting the story around and there was another reason that he gave the boy so much money. After all, they say that he did start doing what he did when we took that trip to Thailand. Maybe that particular child he didn't make do anything, but then later on he did with another child. Or maybe there were other children he was doing things with at the same time, but not that little boy. I just don't know. But for a moment there, when he was talking about giving that hungry child money, I thought that he would make a good father someday.

Question

I am not trying to do that. I know what happened. I know what you call it when that happens. It was rape. I understand that. I am not saying it was voluntary or anything like that, those kids couldn't have known better. I just think some of those little boys did get money out of it. We don't have to speak about it further, really, I am just saying that if that boy in his story was one of the boys he had been with then maybe he made a lot of money, that his family needed to eat. But I don't think that makes it any more right a thing to do to a child, you know, because they can't choose so easily, or wisely, I mean. A child doesn't know how to make, how to understand, what's happening, or…

Question

I have imagined what it was like for you. You could correct me if I am wrong, but I would imagine that your whole body becomes a stomach. Your whole life suddenly is only this one feeling in your stomach. When I was thirteen this friend of my brother grabbed me and kissed me as I was walking out of the corner store. I couldn't move my arms, and he was shoving his tongue in my mouth. He let go of me finally then turned to my brother and their friends and laughed. They all laughed. I can't even remember what he said to them as he walked away from me. You know how it is, you don't know what's happening to you right away but you know something is wrong because of what is going on in your stomach. There is a taste in my mouth I would like to forget from that day. I'm sure you have tastes you would like to forget from that day with him. I'm just saying we all have more in common than we think. People have more in common than they think they do, don't you think? My husband has done things to me too. I wouldn't say it was rape, but it was something. You know what I mean? He does things, and he is so self absorbed sometimes, that I can't even complain. I am too ashamed after a certain point. I know that's what is so disgusting about the experience, what is most disgusting, that sometimes your body feels a feeling, a tingle, while this person is touching you that you don't even want to touch you but you can't help it. That's why you feel so sick, you realize you can't control your own body's feelings, sensations, you know? You feel a tickle that you wish you weren't feeling, then you get sick. My husband once, while I was crying after a fight, just reached for me and stroked my breasts, pinched my nipples. We had been fighting and I was crying and he just reached for my breasts. He wasn't rough about it or anything, but I felt this sensation that I didn't want to feel at that time. It was the last thing that I wanted to feel. It made me sick. It does something to your mind. You know what I mean? Sometimes he wants me to pretend to be a nurse named Heather. I asked him what he wanted once, thinking that... anyway, he has asked me to pretend to be this Heather before. Could you believe it? He practically had a whole script ready in his head. Heather doesn't wear panties and makes these noises while he is... We all have similar experiences in the end, is what I'm trying to say. We all can understand something of...

Answer

Oh, yes. Yes, of course there is that too to think about. I wasn't trying to say that that wasn't the case. There is definitely that to think about. I wasn't trying to say that.

3 Proses

☆

Gloria Frym

Social Work

Is being homeless your business? If so and you are a U.S. citizen, why not apply for a License to be Poor? To get it, you'll need to complete an application, a short test, and donate a quarter. Or spare change. No one will be denied for lack of funds. Once you pass these simple requirements, you can live and work anywhere, especially outside luxury boutiques, upscale restaurants, start-ups, and high tech campuses, which much to our municipal surprise, persons such as yourself take little advantage. Live/work spaces are in high demand these days! Don't compete with uncertified, toothless thugs, just extend your legitimate ID, your license to ask, your card to kindly extract small amounts of cash money from those who have more than they need, especially in San Francisco where the income disparity may be the greatest on earth. If you sign up for the Workshop, you'll get tips on the best sites and the best strategies. Geography is destiny and beggars must be choosy. Here's a sample of our simple, but important test questions. There are no wrong answers!

Name: _____

Are you a veteran of any war? If so, which one?
[ ] all [ ]some

What is your gender? [ ] male [ ]female [ ] fluid [ ] don't remember
[ ]   housed? [ ] unhoused [ ] semi-housed
[ ]   best place to beg is on the left of a one-way freeway entrance
[ ]   best place to beg is on the right of a one-way freeway entrance

[ ]   best face to have is [ ] a smile [ ] a frown [ ] a scream

[ ]   any combination of the above

[ ]   your signage skills are:
           ( ) excellent to superior
           ( ) fine, legible
           ( ) attended art school
           ( ) studied drone striking with the military
           ( ) calligraphic

[ ]   best place to beg is alone on a dark street so that the rare
driver who spots you will gladly stop

[ ]   best place to beg is while circulating a jazz concert in a public
park with others wearing tee shirts that say "Arise Ye Beggars/Unionize"

[]   best struggle to support is $15 an hour minimum begging wage

[]   best place to beg is by a newspaper kiosk whose owner makes
change

          Having the appropriate equipment for panhandling is
imperative. In this country, no one uses hats anymore to collect
change, unless you've put on an attenuated version of Hamlet in
the Park. But performing is not begging. Performing for money
is payment for services rendered. If you would like a permit for
Performing for Services Rendered, please contact our Rendered

Services Division. Poverty is a much more complex operation due to cause and effect, and thus trying to ameliorate it requires a special license. Street artists have stood still in Las Ramblas of Barcelona in a variety of poses— Golden Man, Silver Ballerina, Statue of Liberty Woman; flamenco dancers have performed in the Praça do Rossio of Lisbon; performers have levitated on the streets of Prague for ages; mimes and puppeteers in Paris, etc., for centuries, performing an important public service that entertains *les enfants* and *les tourists*.

Begging, without offering entertainment in return, however, requires entirely different and highly coordinated skills. You must create signage, you must accost strangers and passersby, you must smile, you must also know how to deal with the inevitable pit bull that accompanies the young runaway. All this, often in rapid succession! During your training, you will learn how to be a mentor to apprentice beggars. We've developed a special federally funded Title 9101112131435x yz11 outreach program for those qualified beggars over 40 to accompany youth beggars. (This will add substantially to your monthly stipend after you acquire your license.) We're very excited about this, as several mayors, governors, and presidents for the last forty years have expressed, at one time or another, enthusiasm, though during their terms of office were too engaged in foreign wars to participate. However, we have recently received both government and private grants to pursue this program and achieved our non-profit status! This means that the monthly income you report to us will be nominally taxed at a small percent and serve to refund new programs for others such as yourself.

We are emphatically committed to persons such as yourselves legally taking from those who have more than enough to finance those who have not enough. Our recognition program will teach you how to assess such persons.

If you want to know who we are, we can assure you who we are not: we are not Communists. We are an anonymous group of individuals, some of whom were once were tooth fairies and who provided their children with a weekly allowance, whether or not they cleaned up their rooms or took out the trash. We believe in a guaranteed annual income for those who want to live modestly, as artists in Ireland can. Is Ireland a Communist country? No sir! You could say we are basically neo-neo-liberals and many of us are on neo-Paleolithic diets. Some of us aren't. Meat does not make us more aggressive. (And btw, we do not believe that all men are testosterone driven, though we do know some and have received substantial donations from those whose down there part has largely driven their existence.)

If you've ever gone hungry to feed your kids, you'll know exactly what we mean. We have long experience visiting developing nations. We have been on cultural missions, brigades, and fact-finding trips. We find their beggars cleverer, on the whole, than those of the United States. For instance, in our recent excursion to Quetzaltenango, Guatemala, we saw no less than five individuals in the streets of this charming city pretending that their legs had been amputated! We saw children under the age of five offering *chicle* on buses from a small dusty box that they fashioned to resemble those of the 1940s. It was similar in beach towns in Mexico; but these children had clearly inherited the *chicle* boxes their mothers before them had used. Begging can be a family business in countries where poverty is inherited. Our NGO has studied gypsies world-wide whose menacing deeply dark eyes promise to hijack wallets from back pockets rather than simply ask for coinage. There's safety in numbers and camaraderie we've only seen in tent cities or refugee camps. We have always been particularly enamored of small slender boys who board local buses to make the rounds of captive audiences. Some sing in high-pitched voices, pre-pubescent and innocent. We scoop them up and teach them how to recognize tourists, because there is no use in asking for money from your own. Education is key! A *campesino* with two chickens stashed in the overhead compartment is unlikely to have any spare cash. We give these boys education which includes lessons in foreign languages of their choice, plus benefits. Of course they're nothing like the street children of Europe who work the crowds with sophisticated psychology. A mixture of guilt and sadness with a dash of amusement arises in individuals. And guilt is precisely what the poor must keep playing on. If you fought in a war and haven't yet obtained proper medical treatment, you're entitled to vets benefits. You're poor and you're going to stay that way, so we urge you to get licensed to be poor. If you work at a minimum wage job, you're poor, and unless a rich aunt you didn't know you had dies and leaves you her paid-up house, you'll stay poor. You know how to work, so work it. If you just got evicted with your four children and your grandfather is in prison, and your mother is dating a guy who is in prison and you don't have a high school diploma, what will you do? No, you need cash. Your once beautiful body can't save you now. You need to get out on the streets and equalize the economy. Your poverty needs to be legitimized. You need to be a card carrying poor person. There are so many people in this country; you're one of them! You're not a religious mendicant! You'll never visit India, but you can imagine the number of successful orphans there, can't you? Many of them are blind and crippled. You aren't. If you were you would be taken care of by the state. With a license to be poor you'll beg better and earn more. Get one today.

Late

In recurring dreams am I late, very late. I can't find parking. In waking life, sometimes I would park in the red to not be late, then rush back to the car and drive off, only to circle the same streets, imagining a space vacated during the previous few moments of rash action. Desperation in those days inevitably involved scarcity, an absolute lack, or an absolute impossibility of arriving on time in the brightly lit world of those dreams, which always occurred long before necessity—that is, months before—which is to say so long before my appointment-- the anxiety of having been chosen among the hundreds of others equally qualified, brought about the fear of inability on all levels. Three or four times I parked successfully, though relatively far away. The walk involved traversing dirt paths, always winding up at a vast intersection of empty lots. I would keep veering to the left or right and suddenly approach a barrio unknown to me. Widows in black shawls rocked on their verandas, fanning themselves in the autumn heat. Men stared at me, as though I were in strange costume, inappropriate to the time and context of the town. Dust gathered and whirled around my naked ankles. I could speak the language but I could not recognize the locale. I walked on and through the foreign landscape. At last I reached a hillside. To climb it or to hike around it pressed heavily on my thoughts. Where would it lead? How would I climb in the shoes I was wearing for work. My sense of direction, poor under ordinary circumstances, failed me entirely. Surely I didn't know the city well, but this new obstacle posed a completely ad hoc spontaneous response. If I could only write the coordinates, consult a map or a native. But I had reached something akin to a tree line—devoid of people, even the last vestiges of wildflowers that sometimes hide behind shrubs still blooming or just blooming in their own spring. The alarm sounded and I woke up. Standing beside the bed whose blankets resembled crumpled papers, my neck and shoulders ached immensely from such tossing and turning during the night.

When I used to park a mile from a university where we both once taught, I would pass Angela Davis walking towards me. Both of us were weighted down by satchels of books. The wind from the bay often blew hard in that treeless suburb, misting the lawns. Often fog shrouded the distant and near view. We would smile at one another in complicity.

Does a dream of being late mean the dreamer would actually like to be late? I once had a friend who was always fastidiously early. Which is as bad as being late because one is not ready to receive an early person. If this friend was late, you knew she wasn't going to be there at all. This was before cell phones. The next morning she'd call with a story: I got on the freeway in the rain, I couldn't see a thing because the windshield wiper on my side stopped working. I kept trying to crane my neck to look out but my breath fogged up the windows. Then I couldn't see anything. I panicked. I took the next exit and it led me to somewhere in West Oakland. I stopped in front of a chain link fenced lot with a sign that said, Dick's Foreign Auto Parts. I grabbed my umbrella, got out of the car and it didn't bode well with three Dobermans yowling at the top of their lungs just sensing me on the sidewalk. I looked for an entrance. There was a buzzer above the gate. I buzzed. The Dobermans kept up. An old man in dirty overalls shuffled to the front and asked what the hell I wanted in this storm. We're closed, he growled. It's Sunday. I explained about the windshield wiper and offered him money if he would let me use his phone. Oh yeah, he says, if I let you use the phone, everybody who gets stuck here will want to. Do drivers get stuck here? I asked. All the time, he barked. Please help me, I said, using all my feminine charms. I need a man to fix the wiper. You can't fix a windshield wiper, hon. You got to replace it. How much did you say? I've got $50 on me, I said, and a credit card. He glanced at my Mazda. I might could have the right wiper for you. But you can't use my phone cause it's inside. I don't let customers inside. I don't let anybody inside. I'm late, I cried, I'm late for a wedding. A wedding, he repeated. Life is just one wedding after another then you get funerals. The rain let up a bit. He led me into the lot. There were all kinds of car parts, junk, salvage, organized by make and model. Some large parts like fenders were stuffed into covered bins with signs above them: Toyota Corolla, etc. And shelves with awnings, neatly displaying headlights. Honda Civic, Saab, Acura SX. Tires had a sort of garden of their own, as if they grew in stacks. I was wearing high heels, silk fuchsia high heels and they'd already turned brown in the mud, so I followed the old man as he trekked through his stock. We walked in circles around sheds of brake boots, horn grills, headrests, shocks and struts, belts and hoses, fuel filters, engines, transmissions.

Suddenly, he got breathless. He wheezed and coughed and leaned against a pile of hoods. You okay, I asked. Yep, just need to sit for bit. Let's go over there, he pointed to a sign about a city block away. We reached an out building of interiors. He chose a Mercedes backseat. I don't know why but I remembered that Eichmann worked in a Mercedes factory in Argentina after WW II. I sat with the old man; I offered him a cigarette.

Got kids? he asked. Yes, I said, three boys. I got three girls, he said. We smoked and talked about what they did, who they married, and why. What happened to our spouses. Whether the Raiders had a chance, who would run for president and why and why not. I didn't hear the dogs anymore. After a while, the sun came out. We got up and walked some more. One of my shoes got stuck in the mud and sucked it off my foot. We stopped, he let me lean on him, and he pulled it out for me, wiped it off on his overalls, and helped me put it on again.

Oh, I said, I feel like Cinderella. Yeah, he said. I'm your prince. If you like a prince with terminal cancer. His disclosure startled me. I asked about it and he told me. He was through with treatment. They found out too late and it didn't help anyway. I'm so sorry, I said, shaking my head. Why do you say that, he asked. Why would you be sorry for a complete stranger?

Soon he found the right wiper and installed it on my windshield. When he finished, I looked at my watch and knew the wedding would be over. Well, I said, how much do I owe you? How about ten bucks, he said. I pulled out a twenty. I don't have change, this being Sunday, he said. That's fine, I said. I appreciate your hospitality.

After listening to her story, I finally said, sounds more interesting than the wedding. I left the reception early. She laughed and said, well, I've got a doctor's appointment soon, I don't want to be late. So long.

My friend's story reminded me that I was trained to be on time, even at the expense of the sort of adventure this friend always seemed to get herself into because she was generally early. I am not one to show up all breathy and blown by the wind, no I'm not a blousy type. I walk fast, think fast, my pulse beats fast, maybe too fast.

Nothing in the Bay Area starts on time and generally, there's no excuse for late. Even movies are late. Even jury duty doesn't start on time. No self-respecting New Yorker would put up with it. The mas o menos schedule of public transportation is only on time when you are late. You hear the swoosh of the doors closing and the squeak of the cars departing way up at the top of the escalator you were just about to run down.

No one is in a hurry here. Try calling the police! This area has a lot of freelance workers who apparently work for themselves, not you. Gardeners, handymen, painters, consultants. They arrive when they can, though they always give you a specific time. When I was young, I dated a lawyer who never arrived when he said he would. I would make an elaborate dinner. He was two hours late, ambling in from tennis with his white shirt half unbuttoned.

He never made excuses or told stories, he simply showed up when he did. (Later I'm told, most of his children were born before he reached the hospital.) Out of town guests, unused to his habits, would often demand the meal they'd driven half the day for. By dessert they'd remark, leave him, he won't notice until it's too late.

I have come to an uncertain conclusion: the too early are anxious, fearful of some judgment that they'll be late. What are the late? Do they lose track of time? Is time not built into their human consciousness? This poses deep philosophical perhaps metaphysical questions. Do they not notice time? Do they plan to be on time and then become ensnared, as my friend of the first part of this account, in all the minute aspects of life that can intercede between them and an appointment? Did people in other centuries arrive not just two hours late but two days or two months, given the modes of transport? Those who traversed the great plains and valleys and rivers, hazarding the deeply unfamiliar and unknown, such as local people, highway robbers, wild animals who could not abide them and hijacked their wagons, etc.?

You said you'd be here latest April, she screamed as he cantered up on his faithful steed. It's fucking July!

And what about Odysseus, the most famous of men to arrive home late, late by at least nineteen years, if not twenty. He didn't stop for a few drinks. Late! Penelope might have screeched were it not for Greek decorum. I can't use your late, Mr.! Sorry? I can't use your sorry! My pussy dried up while you were gone! And your dog just dropped dead waiting for you!

Ah, the faithful who wait for the late. Knitting and weaving and sewing and quietly unraveling. The oven at 250 degrees drying out the lasagna. The candles on the table down to a millimeter, wax melted on the damask table cloth we got for our wedding!

There are the nonchalant late and the guilty late. There is tardy, as for class, like fifteen minutes, and late, like missing the first hour.

The early bird, etc., but what advantage in nature is gained by late? There are birds who sing into the late evening, hurry up hurry up get to your perch, good night. . . . .There are certainly late bloomers in the floral world, and angry expectant bees.

To be or not to be late. A calculated risk. Or unbeknownst? Still invoking in the one who waits primal fear, that the person expected at the event--beloved mother father, lover-- will never arrive. Proust's young Marcel forever suffers the pain of waiting for mama to take leave of the guests in the parlor, ascend the stairs, open the door to his room, sit beside his anxious, trembling body, and kiss him goodnight. But it's too late. He never forgives the torment she causes him when she does arrive, oh so inexcusably late. Later, he seeks it out in every love. He creates a Swann who suffers the wanton duplicity of his mistress Odette, then makes him marry her--long after he ceases to love her, she who made him wait an eternity.

Fiction

If you create a man at the door with a gun and he fires at the person behind the door, he's fulfilled his fictive role.

If he fires into a crowd, he's a different character than the one you had in mind. It's worth investigating this character.

If he kills ten people by firing a gun into a crowd, he may be a character in another story. He may loom too large for the story you had in mind. If he kills fifty, he may require an essay.

If another character declares, It's opened my eyes, I want to keep a gun in the house to protect myself and my family, this character needs a course in reasoning.

If this character needs a course in reasoning, you might send him to France to learn pure and applied logic and new depths of deadpan. Or you might want to open a whole new aspect of the narrative featuring this second character.

If it's tempting to create an interlocutor who asks, And what kind of gun would you keep? And if the answer is an AK 47, this character could well belong in another story. This character doesn't work in fiction, only in America.

If the man fires into a classroom where he assassinates the teacher and nearly all the children, then turns the gun on himself after firing several rounds at the police who enter by the same door, you have the beginning of a Great American Novel.

Work

☆

Richard Makin

VII

A PERFECT HALT

August: she seizes the head and carries it off. There's no evidence of her existence before settling beside the lake. The other protagonists may have been right all along, that she is counterfeit, imitatrix.

He was once of singular conviction, the simple idea of some individual thing in the mind — a man of the galley-sheets: evocator, ruthlessly selecting and schematizing his material. At the base of his back, on either side of the spine, he wears two cubes of translucent stone. The crew graved the ship at the shoreline and remained twenty-six days, one for each letter.

'I fear the nostrum you now take may possibly cause you to suffer afresh.'

Origin is early from used, in the sense of our own making, a neutralized hour. If I mistrusted this statement what could I do to undermine it? Set up experiments of my own? What would they prove? Yet, taken together, a walking eclipse. Nothing here is exaggerated. It rains.

Now, this thing of the bridge, poised for combat. . . . Ear the right showing face slightly tilted before a downward strike. It seems paths are prepared to cross, if need be. The tide must ebb when ashes are countersigned.

Unable to decide from which stack to feed, she starves to death. (I forgot to read the instructions.) Just then, way up through the clouds, something like a shoal of herring, soluble fish, a masterstroke: for the ascent the camera had been strapped to a helium balloon. But I don't think I'm going to trust any of these remarks on time; our parents show us how to die soon enough.

The white cloud creeping slowly down the mountainside caused space to stand still, or at least move very slowly. He was executed by 'wearers of gleaming raiment'. Seen in the context of the victim's epoch, his last request was not so far-fetched as it first appeared.

Magnificent ashlars are still visible at the temple platform. Thereupon is placed a limestone object bearing an inscription. A sprig of lithosperm stands like a little tree laden with dead fruit. . . . A sprig of lithosperm stood like a little tree laden with dead sea fruit, for the naked seed clung firm where the flowers had been. The species is endemic to zone three. The species is hermaphrodite and pollinated by 'Insects'. The roots have been chewed with the gums in order to colour the gums red. The flowers have been chewed with the gums in order to colour the gums yellow. She has not named this, she hasn't named anything yet.

We are dissembling. Please note that an informant may be invasive in one area, but not necessarily your neighbourhood. Geologically speaking, the rigid outer layer of the earth consists of the crust and upper mantle. Outside the world the search for an acceptable name continues. (Not 'afterdeck'.) Somewhere imperceptibly he would hear her and somehow reluctantly sun-compelled.

It's dusk on the sixth and his personal revolution is about to fail. Further along the axis another birth is poised. (See ghost sorry of cabin.) Our comrades had orders. Our comrades had orders to keep the guards talking as long as they could: there are exceptionally fine views in the round from this hill fort and suchlike. In ancient times the usual direction of augury was south-southeast. Cook the stones; we're ready.

The reader will have recognized some typical initiatory motifs: the whirlwind, the tree, the hanged man swinging, kicking out. The first guard punches him in the teeth with his fist. It rains, rains incessant. Only the dead could make anyone feel this good.

Imagine a breakdown. Our shadows were thinner than the bodies who cast them, we upon the flint, blue tracery of branches, gold-flecked snails underfoot. No keepsake shall save thee.

A line of blood spatters the flagstone. We entered the cloister in search of two granite monoliths cut from the oldest quarry on the planet, older than dynasty. We left the shade of a terrace overhanging the marsh where smokestacks disgorged.

Faultless horizon, level grey-green sea, a distant mort. More than one vehicle has been found alone in the wilderness, tank dry, blood-smeared cabin empty.

'Listen, do not use a sharp instrument,' she insists. — 'Never use a sharp instrument.'

From then on I was resolved to bludgeon my way through life.

She opens up the head to reveal deep lines scored all over. This head faces south, its right shoulder points toward the east and the left shoulder toward the west. The feet lie beneath the sea; its spine stretches the cord. This makes it look like an old thing.

I was at home writing when I heard the news of his untimely death. When I said I was going to join the search party she said No. Nonetheless, his corpse was found — a torso cum head minus teeth / eye / tongue / ear. Only through such ceaseless labours can an interpreter find a resolution, a painstakingly constructed mosaic composed of minute details.

Witness now his brutal execution in a quarry. Any remaining object must be surrendered to my mind, obeying the summons of recall: white oleander, the turpentine tree. . . . It was the worst of time (which is a space). I can't breathe.

A brand new undertaking: me, rebuilt, neither from the past beneath nor from the past above — the final cut, a full thirty years after the event.

I should never have left the employ of that lakeside manufactory. Your money isn't correct. All I'm left with is a stack of old family snapshots in a mysterious trunk, but around this kernel lies everything I need: unbreakable deposits, mass noun under the tongue, craw chock with feathers. I've tried everything and the handle just came off.

One protagonist hangs from the ceiling by leather straps, quite inconsolable. Look, he's frozen to a slab of ice — mustn't squander these dying traces, only then will your tormentors show any restraint; there's always a song that is related to any given circumstance. (I'm all right at the moment.) Then again, we were in mourning just the other night, weren't we? It's said that with less water, there's more tin. I am chasing the setting sun, an ill-starred project: it would suit them just fine to trap me in the pursuit. There's a whole subtext here about recapturing time in a forest — it's dark, an immeasurable woodland with a man at the centre. Everything is so obvious. I went next door to read my own book, but not for long.

She had marked her advance with a white feather. I had given. Three red-brown chestnuts have been carefully arranged on the table, alongside.

One mother's dead eye, final glimpse in burnished blue steel. It was her first corpse. The tiny cubes resembled phylacteries, whose significance is lost to a chain of causality that vaporizes on waking.

This reinstates us at a threshold. Cast out breath between each signal; some I am resisting, others not. Above the dome of the head, the volving blades of a copter, beneath the foot lady's mantle, weed of dry wasteland. You have no option but to continue north; a fine castle mound lies just beyond, but there's no path. What is your location? I am under a ladder.

Fictive ships, a pierced stone, and another hid his eyes beneath his wing. I proposed a book of days. (What lovely atmosphere, though I can't breathe.) By eight o'clock is the time.

Further up the slope, and he's in bad shape. In art is everything, whereby the highest achievements of utilitarian reason are transfigured into numinous phenomena; no one is laughing. Origin is semi-divine from will plus nous. See, he is shifting again. For him to be at last isolated — identified and cornered — exceptional circumstances are required, such as are met within the narrow confines of our ship.

You should know: it runs on its side, it cannot stand up.

From the viewpoint of geography and natural history, our island is one of the most remarkable in the polar ocean. We all gathered up on deck in a shivering knot; the reactor will surely blow. Our first mate bears the mark of a bite upon his neck — I warrant his days are over, and all the archived flora and fauna he shall take with him when he departs. Thus do the most sorrowful tales descend gently into memory, our most inconstant territory. A green wave froze beneath the prow.

Always seek advice from a professional. I am easily broken or displaced ('mood seemed generally appropriate, but the patient was often labile'). This is self-defeating dialectic: a most significant event befalling the most insignificant member of the crew — I don't want any of this to follow us as we tip beyond the lip of the earth.

Notes are being made toward a short film based on a single page. Its themes include an impossible uniformity of intention, the lineaments of a giant with rictus grin, a sacred place where none can switch allegiance. Wish upon, wish upon: now awake — memories shift and realign.

'I want the surface to resemble latticework of glass.'

Consider, if you please, a semiconductor manufacturing company versus an evil character from Zoroastrian mythology. At the centre of time is an evil sorcerer, an opponent known for killing those who are not able to answer his riddles. This story is elaborated at great length in the mediaeval *How I Lost Everything*.

I said the pilot, where.

Imitatrix is a small species, very elongate air-breathing land, a terrestrial in the family. See, I'm asking questions aplenty now. I once asked her if she would want pipes and tubes put into her body and coming out. A tea made from the leaven is applied externally in the treatment of fevers, accompanied by discharge of spasm.

The species is a paradox; it cannot grow among shades, yet it shuns the light and prefers a well-drained head and suitable acids. The chemical element of atom fifteen is poison. This combustible was first rumoured in two allegorical tales; origin is mid century of another shape, plus manner from to turn. The only way forward is to begin repositioning the objects we've hoarded over the years. The symbol is P. I prefer mist or dry soiling.

The species once had both male and female organs and rolled about the earth between the young planet's peaks and hollows. We are currently updating this episode. A scarlet dye is obtained from the root: right plant, wrong place.

I was once sectioned — an asylum — day by day my identity eroded until I was left with nothing save me. I lost my possessions — my clothes, my books, my manuscripts — until all that remained was unrecognizably me. I beseeched. I yelled and threw things. The corporation had taken over; I cypher.

The sun is setting on the fountains of Rome: a pageant with hautboys, torches, my lost noun of archaic form. The lithosphere comprises a number of plates. He took it out of the sky.

Their condition is one in which certain faecal vessels are suffused with blood and begin to swell. Origin is very still, late from trespass of rose in the sense rose-coloured. Moreover, they were not numerous in the heartlands; greater concentrations lay in the north or in the opencast mines. We went in to change the locks, the cordite. In this province, people carry their ancestors about with them in tiny boxes worn at the base of the spine. Yet this world is full of corrosive forms — two make a pair, lovers oblivious, while others give alternate endings to infinity.

Memory weighed in the balance, she breaks open the skull, eases pressure; human vehicles form the underpinning. Trepanned to within an inch, propped in bed she reads from the book a lengthy quote, and laughs out loud. We laughed. The fault lies with me, the gnawing scraps of recognition.

Unhead.
[*Subdued on a chair. Rest of chamber dark.*]
'Our party was trapped in a death spiral, a wormhole in space. What I say is extinguished before it can flare up; we all slaughter ourselves in different ways, more or less slowly, with more or less kindness. Very often this secret language is actually the animal language or originates in animal cries.'
All the other guards kick him with their feet. It is seven.
[*Reads.*]
'One of life's details that one never forgets — a person who

evokes, especially one who calls up spirits, one who calls troops to arms. Origin is late middle, perhaps from variant of old grave-shore, because the ship would have been run aground. Summon fog into the form of a man — chew glass, spit blood.'

An addictive, of or with respect to the fixed stars (i.e. the constellations, not the sun or planets). Clearly he has access to equipment and books — is working and living on his own consuming his mind, a position of untrusting quiescence?

I overlooked the propane cylinder. Uranus has twenty-seven moons, most of them named.

His flesh bears the track of a scar with purple rim. Maybe we have overlooked. Somehow this is not so effective as the first spell, whose chief ingredient is adipocere (a greyish waxy substance formed by the decomposition of soft tissue in dead bodies subjected to moisture). And he was on his very last journey; the vessel was a migrant carrier. Origin is bent of dialect, by association with raft in the floating mass sense, her body in his mouth.

Gloriana! Her pet monicker was hell.

Short film of a single page. Awake, but slow — panning, scheming: anecdote of cubist spine. Who did attend these occult fictions. (Excise me, forgive me and so forth.) He at once sent his clerks out of the room with instructions to admit no one. A dog is ritually slaughtered on the roof; this act modifies the sound we hear in its wake — blood is allowed to flow down both sides of the shack. The gathered company, quite desperate now, have thrown dice to determine the animal's fate. It was the best of time.

We find ourselves at the intersection of two vaults, a rib along their crossing. And who in his role as sea god had the power of prophecy but would assume different shapes to avoid answering questions? We are developing a three-fibre bundle that will possess capabilities. It was carnage. I am able to distinguish between the natural glow emitted by your organ tissue and the limitless dark surrounding us. Origin is early, on the pattern of words such as dorsal.

Finally, he severed some ancient runes, whose juice smelt of mould and was at the same time aquatic and sepulchral. A modern wall stands on top of the mutilated rampart, the entrance through which is now unidentifiable.

Consider, I beg you, four shadows surrounded by a radiance; I am alert to the gaseous envelope of other stars. The sun's corona is visible only during a total solar eclipse, when it is seen as an irregularly shaped pearly glow surrounding the darkened disc of the moon. He had no possessions to speak of. His flight was madness: burial gifts, gravegas, a woman begging grace, her cerement the colour of damp ash — the reactor, the final rain.

[*Cage. Silence.*]

Neural spoils, the breakage of bonds — in seven days thy fate et cetera. The master of the vessel threatens to destroy a certain city unless a righteous man comes out and solves his riddle.

[*The dark. Five seconds.*]

Last week he lay on his back like a star and kept very still. No one spoke. Such an answer would be an error, for a cockroach or utilitarian citizen cannot discriminate.

Dead side of the street, this; I have expelled all your ideas. Gradually prepare to enter sleep — I'm sure we'll all be less nervous when the interregnum suddenly collapses. You'd better get used to this; I'm not going away. Origin is late from phosphorous.

When I first engaged in this work, I resolved to leave no word or thing unexamined. The narrative is simple enough, illumination of memory from without. (What offers do we offer you today.) I'm pretty sure that my object was once here, right *here*. My greatest fear is the expected.

White phosphorus is a yellow waxy solid which ignites spontaneously in air and glows in the dark. Red phosphorus is a less reactive form used to make matches. Origin is mid-century from overpriced and hallucinating.

Let's accept that they may come at night. We've learned to appreciate divinities for their own sake, their immaculate forgetfulness — come hither to write false, a book of remnants denoting place, a walk along a mountain ridge in a rainstorm. How is it, then, that we can posit an object culled from these presentations?

Me, I'd sacrifice him right away if the choice were mine. I know many fans will disagree, but he is case-hardened, after all — that business with the ceiling and the leather harness that stretched and tore, being unable to support his weight before the earth's pull took over. His visage is not so pretty as it was prior to this ordeal by gravity. For all that, he would not talk under duress. And this brings us to why I am carrying about an admirably polished torso.

A substitute is needed and our story will spill out through his aperture. The exact form of the door varies from genus to genus: it can be tongue-shaped, spoon-shaped or spatula-shaped. The mechanism is totally different, but is vaguely reminiscent of an automated garage door opener. This species is endemic. Origin is jest. Origin is late middle via amulet, from to guard.

He proclaims the cob is now undersea. Upon the deck stands a wayfarer, satellites pulsing in the night sky above the mainsail. Grain is sown in the sunken valleys, where drowned men silt backward into sleep, glacial flowers quivering, massing genuflectors.

She presses firmly at the base of his spine, easing him deeper inside her body. Accept where you are. Consider the unforeseen quotation: would he actively seek out these catastrophes, or encounter them in the course of life as a consequence of unrelated events? Did we at some time become aware of a phenomenon, such as the tolling of a bell in a distant campanile? The lungs and spleen have a blanched appearance, as if overcooked.

Ever extemporaneous, I forgot the question (the correct answer is scar tissue). The flower sought is distinguished from clover by its sickle-shaped pod and short racemes. So what else has been happening all these years? A smokeless explosive has been improvised from nitroglycerine and petroleum jelly; we have exhausted our stockpile of ammunition.

'No longer anything to be done in that direction.'

'I don't know. Go on as you are.'

The gathering of hair in a crab shape has become fashionable once more; our ancestors are drawn down and marshalled into cycles. The enormity of the impending collision of bloodlines has only just struck me. I am dedicating the edible flesh, pieces of mind. The trail peters out.

We're hooked. I also found a collection of love songs in that garret, but nothing seems of consequence the longer we remain. You are what we were not ready for.

A new look. A new range, open fire (exclusion bag compressed). Now cease.

Nicely timed, the nodal point, as it were. To stop, to hollow out a sense of place, unlimited — papers flutter down from the shattered windows, and again, his brutal execution at the quarry. Origin is middling from star plus pierce.

Hand and foot
they are bound
in the same place
father and son
where waves pound
the white fluid cooling rapidly
where trains run the track
linking direction
counterclockwise,
so brace yourself
he hath teeth in his ear.
And.
Apples, some whole
some halved
painted onto
the sky like
flying wallpaper and
everyone looks up
of course.

Trial and motion. I went into battle. Shoes were thieved — in the tale, written on brown wrapping paper — the stretching of the cord. Our crucial error was a multiform taken as a single thing. Yet this is not all: he is manifest as a veil of dust.

The soldier is imprisoned in a tower and his sweetheart speaks to him through a metal grille; the truth is that he descends through the eyes and into the heart. It could be that we're looking for a symmetry that was never here in the first place murmured my maxillofacial surgeon.

King of the Ring

☆

David Miller

My name's Roger. But they call me King.

I came up through the ranks, fair and square: no fixed fights, nothing crooked. Going into boxing was never my idea, mind you. If you must know, I was forced into it. And I resented it: it just seemed cruel, the whole thing.

They put the gloves on me and shoved me into the ring. I'd been made to have sparring sessions beforehand, and I'd been trained not to kick, which is a natural impulse of mine: I was punished whenever I did. So I knew what to do and what not to do. And I was angry. So I fought.

I was angry because I was being made to do this. I was angry because the crowd actually *laughed* when the other fighter hit me in the face at the opening bell. In fact, they laughed as soon as I appeared in the ring, the morons.

I showed them, all right. I took the guy in two rounds. Izzy, his name was. His legs gave way.

The Kid was tougher. But I wore him down eventually. Jab, jab, jab. Feint with the right. Then a left cross to the jaw: I put all my body weight behind it. The fans screamed for the kill, and they got what they wanted.

So it went on. I admit I got disqualified in a couple of fights, for kicking. Couldn't help myself. My trainers punished me afterwards, cruelly. I won most of my bouts, though, and my reputation gained momentum.

They – my manager and my trainers – kept me in luxury, true enough: the best food available; a nice place to hang out and to sleep in; a choice of sexy females. On the other hand, there was the training: roadwork; sparring; punching the bag and the speed ball. I often felt utterly drained.

Then the big chance arrived. They put me up against a guy called Big Tony, whose nickname was Ten Ton Truck, though he was built more like a beer barrel. And he was extremely familiar with just those sorts of barrels: he was well known as a boozer. But he could fight. And he was rated.

'I'll moider ya, ya bum', Big Tony spat out as we received our instructions from the referee. 'Save it for your saloon buddies, fatso', I replied. Only of course I didn't say it out loud. I just gave him a mean look instead.

There was some sort of problem with the bell, so we waited longer than usual to start fighting. I began to reflect. I suppose I've always been a bit aggressive: I'm an Alpha Male, after all. But boxing had been my ruin. I'd become really bad tempered and would pick fights for no reason, even beating up my females.

Then I had a revelation, or at least I guess that's what you'd call it. 'WHAT AM I DOING HERE?' I asked myself. 'Why am I about to fight a beer-swilling blubber guts like Big Tony – no matter if he's famous or not? And for what? For the amusement of the crowd? For my manager's profit? For a nice place to stay, some sexy females, and good tucker?'

I turned and vaulted over the ropes. to the astonishment of everyone. I hopped and hopped, out of the arena, out into the streets. On and on I went.

But I eventually found that I'd been pursued. It took quite a while for them to catch up with me. 'No one double-crosses me, you mangy marsupial!' my manager bellowed. Guns were trained on me. I was surrounded.

'Can this be the end of King Kangaroo?' I thought to myself, just before the guns fired.

Afterword

I have to admit I admire the skill and grace and prowess of Sugar Ray Robinson or Jimmy Carruthers, and the courage of Don Cockell (in his legendary fight with Rocky Marciano). Legends also enter into it: the vivid performances and lives of Stanley Ketchell, Jack Johnson, Jack Dempsey, Harry Greb... And the extraordinary mastery of craft (for that is one thing that boxing involves, at its best) of Joe Louis or Jimmy Wilde.

However, it's a brutal sport without any question, and some of the greatest boxers admitted they never actually enjoyed it as such: Sugar Ray Robinson, notably. Max Baer's tendency to treat it as entertainment and clown around in the ring chimes in with this, I believe.

But this is Roger's story, anyway, and not mine. He's told it as he saw it.

XI City of Nothing
(from *For the Ride*)

☆

Alice Notley

Ones now leave them in walls. Walk on, says Qui, Past the restes of Future --
ones can disregard it, have been through it. L'Allée now passes through
mist, nothing but, though lit sometimes by shafts of the light invokèd
by words -- mechanical, flat and painted. There's really nothing here,

call it City of Nothing, says the One. How far does it extend?
"Far" doesn't make sense here, Qui says, But beneath the ones' feet appear --
See? are squares, are floating. Ones 're making them as ones walk along --

feet feet feet -- palely hued. Is it a map? Is it that the ones can't
exist without configuration, within or without of it --
one -- ones --mind -- it's The Mind, that ones are of. Each, says Qui, One and
    all . . .
One as all or as one. Doing this together, without knowing . . .

feet feet feet, peach, white, beige . . . Look, there are words appearing in the
    squares,
disappearing before one can read them. Must be a way to hold
onto them, as if to remember them. Try to keep hold of them.

One is slid-ing in words, making the squares or rectangles: First it's
snakelike s's -- see the those? ssss -- then become words: Hold 'em!
Where? In mind ones 're in. Make 'em be fixed, ones 're in control, if
all that's here je suis   See? Whose foot's that? France's or Wideset's --

       Je Suis

       I am

       not she

both ones, of those ones, thought it at once, pink, how anomolous

                       anom

                       olous

                       the

                       uni

                       verse

Ones only make it once? make together, thinking this universe

                       olous

                       am

                       cryp-

                       to

Hidden, Je suis caché, One am the One, point making foot words

                         à chaque

                         point . . .

                         no

                         point

Yes that's it, there's no point.

             pedes

             Platonic

             foot

             fool   Look, it says epithesma, brightness, O

can one just have that, such shimmering?

                one

                is

                b

                r

                i

                g

                h

                t

                   hovering goldenness?

Ones speak of it pastly, the lumen gone, now it's internal, France

thou

the

dead

the

thou

the

dead

thou

says. Is the language? What? Whatever . . . Are the ones there yet?

thing

before

think

or

Tired of trying to be. Don't want to read. Ones can sing it to you,
squares call out under foot, Had to make some thing diden cha.
Whoa whoa whoa, in the notes, where the song hides, decadent

deca

dent

inven-

tion.

Look, a whole poem at one's foot, says the One. One has exuded it:

Poem

If One has left everything but a direct quotation from the soul,
   how is it that that is still divided from the One in the grey day of this
      night?

Speak to me while I am unconscious:

Ancient harbor . . . I almost remember the worst of my dreams,
   where the sails are nets. I am supposed to be stable, eternal but I
      grieve

where are my others when there are no survivors, on the shores of
      air?
I can't find thee, you haven't arrived, the flocks of white-winged

moths though I know you live for I do. There is no eternal solace --
only ever the one moment, and I am stable as the center of time, but
in my time I am its tone as well as its rock, fore'er in each e'er

oh, I am a translation as you'd hear. Seeking my true language

help me o dulce medicum, o heart words that are my blood,
understood only by me until now, until this haunted now.

One's secret heart, is breaking one's unsecret one, France says. Her foot:

Poème

Mon histoire, ignoble et tragique
comme le masque d'une femme oubliée
m'échappe. Aucun détail reste
du meurtre sauf ma connaissance
dans l'hôtel de ville, dans l'hôtel
des particules, des opales maux

Buveuse de l'opium de ma mort
je rêve d'une chambre sale et beige
Personne est là, mon corps est là
moi, je suis dehors en nulle part

Qui m'a tué? La drame des hommes
ou quelqu'un. C'est ton monde à toi
où les gens suivent les autres jusqu'àu
moment sanguinaire, ton vrai amour.

Because they have to have it that way, they -- where there's their own story.
If one remembers it'll just be theirs, even if it's in one's head --

ghost head, what does one need dead -- oh it goes on. Have to sing to past . . .
But ones aren't all dead. Oh ones 're dead, if terran nature's dead.

Shaker says, Ones are contextless squiggles. Snakelike lines, Wideset says --

Not afraid to be that. Principle of rebirth: One's a principle?
No, a wild, slithery line of force, cut. Cut from the linear
perception, when ones was somewhere but parenthetical

to l'histoire. Am a snake. Snakes beneath feet. Lines of magical force,
powerful effigy. Am I, is one. Words pour from mouth, perfect
because enacting one, in afterlife. Maybe it's limbo here

or dark matter. It's light, one means there's no light but it's light, or sight --
one continues to see. Let's agree that the past's undetailed shape,
let's read these present poems underfoot, for they're what ones are now.

Shaker reads ground beneath, almost stumbling, falling down on word slab:

Poem

Someone has a container containing a few pearls. Were eyeballs,

One must change again; feels a hardness against the past as it goes,
foot foot on the street of magenta thoughts abloom like witchy gorse . . .

And one is transformed, in a crystal momentary pull, pulled up
into a much larger thought, towering like Aldebaran, dear red --

One is as big and as forgetful as rocks. Speaking tourmalines,
beryl, plagioclase, hemimorphite, cinnabar, "Apache flame" agate;
lunar and solar eclipses; meteor showers; haloes of space dust . . .

Nothing will ever love one again. Struck by lightning, or icebound.
Everything's happening backwards. One started here or always saw it:
I knew there was no way to portray me and I was left primordial.
One knows there is no way to portray one and one is left primordial --
But one is not left. One is articulate finally, articulated.

Is one no longer one who shook Wideset for whatever reason?
The new language can gain by that, beauty, humor, clarity.
Past motivation is of no importance. Shaker says. Not here --
Have been allowed to forget the details of one's transgressions, now

internalized into materials, concrete, for existence --
"energy," might say -- one was a way, now one's a transformed one,
what one is guilty of pastly, a tone, glint in grain of non-atmosphere.
I'm leaving you, me; I've left it all; can't be in that thought again.

When something is over or someone. One emerges from the husk
that's beige, featureless, or is that a simulacrum of my face
on straw, a portrait of some face stuff, as if there had *been* a *face* --
those gross species identificatory apertures one knew?
Those weren't it, one's it, and what one says: localizing for thee
a federation of singular traits, thoughtful, verbal -- unjudged.

Another one's underfoot, Shaker says. Must be thinking, quiet to me:

> Poem

> In this poem there's nothing left but a shape and some microtones
> I, one, am, is, the shadow within as the curlicued notes
> the spiralling flinted sparks of tones word-set-off
> wing round one's purple-grey shoulder forms patching up existence

> so I, one, can speak, sing, call to oneself watching it react, amused.

> The far-hearing ear of my wideset-eyed lover also distinguishes
> these nuances of shadow longings, of unremembered torments of
>> those histories
>>> you were supposed to,
>> one was supposed to go through o mirage of the world in declension
>> at the end

of   the gorge of detailed spaces.

> I walk into their gothic walls. I mean that I, one, dissolved into the
>> brown-black
>>> shifting texture
> of this sound sounding disinterestedly justified or decreed.
> On the other side of your wall I am taken apart, taken apart
> abstractedly anguished in the language of costs -- in this story,
>> though,

one is never lost because one is a note, clear and inked-in black.
   Pedes, one is
calling to one's feet. Take one further on. And on and one, adding or
   losing e
or eeeeee, screeches into bodhisatvahood. Forgetful of all but, vast,

the dimensions of the one most common note, maneuvering sunlike
   around.

```
        m    apart   i              m    apart    i
         y   e     e s            eye   o    o   eye
          m     n    t                  o
          i     m    a                  O
         n           k                 bbbb
    d d  d         e n n               |||||||||
       a             a                 aaaaaa
       a             a                 cccccc
       a             a                 kkkkkk
       a             a                 rrrrrr
       a             a                 eeeee
      ffff          ffff               ddddd
      f f f         f f f                      following myself
      f f f         f f f
```

```
    ffffffffffff            ffffffffffff
```

on the other side of the wall I am taken apart, taken apart

And waltz with me to thy voice, Wideset says. Can one dance in this world --
oh later but not now. Is one in pair? Why bother now if one
doesn't repopulate this space that way? Oh mind is one's lover!
One's never been in love, Wideset's kid says. Will one not be like that?
But one remembers love. Love's existing. It is what the ones are,
it is the same as to be -- to be love -- the ones are so social,

kill out of love, killing relational. Maybe chaos is love.
Thou're too young to know, know to speak thus, Wideset says, and One says,
Differences between the ones are gone now. Only the ones, and what
ones are is in the air between, among, ones know all the same things,
same words and ones are still differently configured, ones are stars

each -- same light -- not same one. Not same at all. One's name is One, the
    One,
since first entr'ing the glyph, embarked in ark, debarking into ville.
This is way that it is. Contain back together and rain sep'rate.

From Wideset's kid's right foot the following appears in rectangle:

Poem

One with no future speaks as one wishes after all
Shock of no childhood -- do amoebas have one -- but
know the new beings, les mots. One's visage colors of the creepiest
universe imaginable. Or the funniest. But not the sexiest,
"I would like that she love me." Why? One's already old . . .

Fox become vox, denuntio, extravagance of heart deleted
pas de coeur, pas de hardhearted. One is haunted:
former fundamentals crash in headwinds ghost-limned
(drawn with phosphorescent dotted lines): touch and feel me Why

And I don't have to be a generation.

Novator, novatrix, and if one who renews refuses
gender? My name is ending refused . . . Novatendre. Or
nubigenum, born of a cloud. Glyphigenum, born of a glyph

and of Wideset: Or of One, the glyph's first thinker. But I
was never born. I have always been. Exactly at the right time.

One's excited to be, Wideset's kid goes on. So many words in one,
new surges without legend finally: at the end of the street,
deserted quarter foot says sadness, means exhilaration.

France's kid: Yes for one, body of words -- for if one's slow, now *not*.
Now nothing but the words the ones all know. Flourishing, electric.
Best, ones not care what's said -- what's said or how -- gentle rains, no
    memoire,
que'st-ce c'est le pleuvoir? Why mark one's path with fake memory?
Le pouvoir, ça c'est moi. Power's this one, identity's power . . .

retard eyes of cloud, the nebulous stars that brought ones here.
Just to be able to say that, those words. That's worth being. One's mine,

then, heart suspended in space, justly words -- playing the dulcimer
in a lemon grove -- ones don't have those things: who ever had a thing?

Cypresses, eglantine, whistle anciently these old words that are ones,
don't have senses, objects. One has the mind, retard holds, divine.

Any driven animal

☆

Denise Riley

Anonymous animal of the yellow hide,

scat – go figure out the curio of why

your louring passions stump about for more,

lowing that they'd get filleted per usual,

their dewlaps swaying to some charmer's wind

then eyeballed by the taxidermist. Lighter

to wear a dress of feathers and eat berries,

slice dapper arcs of wingtip self-sufficing,

spiral above the leaves, rattle the heather.

But no, your portly body's earthed, perplexed –

tramples at night to know itself unsexed.

Null Set

☆

Robert Kelly

1.
Three poems
dream-given
three shapes
but not one
word inside them.

2.
Should I architect
a house with no
one in it,
shelves, shelves?

3.
Mention *things*
and bring *children* in,
the old formula
hardly ever fails.

4.
Or be an Indian
Hindu or Huron,
smile at the edges,
ever be Other.

5.
But I was Greek
to begin with,
a loop of red
string round
a marble thigh
slips to the ground,
one age is done.

6.
Lost my language
on Mulholland Drive
swept clean by vista
night outstretched
over sparkling orgasms
all the faraways
having fun, I loved
that city when I was free
o memory is seafoam
a miracle of loss.

7.
Revise at leisure,
scrape your own
screams out of the scrawl.
The folk-soul still speaks
but most of us are mixlings
German Celts or Slavic Jews
we have so many angels—
wise folk hearken to them all.

8.
An ant walks on my desk
to tell me things that dream forgot.
Go somewhere and be quick about it,
prompt fruit, literate tree,
subway to the sun.

9.
Book without a title—
hard to get a handle on the sky.

See, already the breath comes back
that was once sent out to pray or persuade.

10.
So what was it like to be him
when he went to church or drank his kvas
or faced the firing squad or washed his hair?
What is it really like to be anybody,
man or woman, shark or savior, you?

11.
That might be
enough to know.
Nice weather today
grass quiet.
I dreamed the Met
was passing
or I passed it, museum
not the opera, façade alone,
outside only, not the stuff
inside, those gorgeous
words in that sprawling
stone sentence. But the sun
was shining, sure, what more
could any decent person ask?

12.
The shapes fill up
with meaning.
The red twine
slithers to the ground.
The leg is bare,
the culture is old
again, the stone.
Fold the image
carefully and fold
again. Put it
in your pocket—
I love that phrase.

13.
Weather is the
longest-running
Broadway musical.

14.
Take the little magnet
off the door of the fridge
and listen to it reverently—
love life of a magnet!
All the iron in the galaxy
is mine, mine, mine!

15.
That is, if you like music.
Someone said the bishop and his wife
ate ice cream cones by the river,
music kept them busy
blocking the sound but the words
came through the taste
butterscotch and caramel
until the music finally

drove thinking out. Except
how come chocolate ice cream
never tastes like chocolate chocolate?

16.
As usual
we turn
to the river
for answers
because water
always yields
holy information
we seem to need.
Come live with me
it says, come home
and live content
in this flowing
landscape bright
with no explanation.

'Solarpoetics,' (concluded) 16-26

☆

Rochelle Owens

16
Reading a word does not depend on the number
of letters it contains

*

The letter P periodic orbital
biological compulsion
like taste and thirst
and in your

Mammalian brain

Lovely the pastoral scene
a graphic design
green the volcanic hills
the story

Of the shepherdess

In elaborate lettering
heat cold wind water
a flow of menstrual
blood

17
The stereotype of a lone researcher
in a secluded lab — a science fiction trope

*

The letter Q a quartet
in three dimensional space
the butcher baker shepherdess
a solitary workwoman

Ravenous her lidless eye

Counting letters spelling
m e l l i f e r o u s the animal flesh
the flow of hormonal
forces

Blood in blood out

From A to Z a set of skills
body of data data
of body gut head tail
o b l i t e r a t e d

18
An experiment designed to control the brain
— movements of limbs with colored lights

*

The letter R under a red
violet light an unknown figure

crouches over the
earth

Where the air smells of poisoned rain

An unknown figure digs rows
of small holes the temperature
of human skin folds
in the ground

The root of love

Blood in blood out
folds in the ground from front
to back from back to
front

19
Electrical pokes regulate balance direction
currents moving neuron to neuron

*

The letter S serpentine
the organ of sight a pair of spherical
bodies in an orbit of the skull
the eyes

Nomads wanderers

Take one step after
the other here where you walk
bones push to the
surface

A snarl of fibrous hairs drifting

In circles chasms and fissures
in the earth holes gaps in a sequence

of events laid down and eroded
away

20
Begin with a few humble ingredients rice flour
fruit and flowers

*

The letter T near a tank
with a spigot stands the baker
collecting words batter
crumbs

Black mold burnt rolls

Dead white the bakers lips
on his tongue a metallic
taste more water
in the loaf

Less flour used

The story of the baker
A set of skills in sequential order
from A to Z   O wicked
world

21
All words may be reproduced stored in a retrieval system
or transmitted in any form or by any means

*

The letter U numberless
tree stumps mark a sequence
of events rows of
holes

Absence of a picture

A story of the solitary
workwoman long ago an hour ago
only a minute strolling in
autumnal leaves

Drifting in circles

And in your mammalian brain
lovely the pastoral scene
grain grape bread
wine

22
Colors forms movement all together an astonishing
neurological image

*

The letter V gouged
into a stone floor blood pushing
to the surface zones of
inclusion exclusion

Here where archeologists

Observe dimensions between
victim and executioner a gap a fissure
a hole that engulfs and
consumes

Here where historians

Pouring coffee organize
body of data data of body piles
of charred human and animal
bones

23
Evolution is smart clean clear and simple
hungry or thirsty eat or drink

*

The letter W when your
eyes move the reading brain
the act of reading how tightly
the letters hold you

Wind heat cold drought

Hot exuberant the butcher's
pleasure cutting deboning grinding
salt for the stew salt
for the bread

Sings the poet maudite

From point A to Z a set of skills
in sequential order blood
and mud chemical
molecular

24
With sophisticated equipment scientists scrutinize
minutiae gathering information

*

The letter X
marks an unknown figure
behind an electric
fence

Patterns of animus

A skeletal frame
crouches over the earth
fingers spreading apart across
t h e r u i n s c a p e

Hidden among geometric forms
a single bloodstained feather
long ago an hour ago
only a minute

25
The two cortex regions operate independently
of each other independent yet intertwined

*

The letter Y yellow
sulfurous a plume of smoke
work is a binding
obligation

Looking to earn extra cash

Take one step after
the other under an occult sky
the hand of the butcher
lops off

Diseased parts

Slapping flying insects insects
far and near hair and nails in the feces
vulnerable flesh-eater spiritual
carnivore

26
Ever-pinging networks twenty-six letters of the alphabet
asterik to zero hour

*

The letter Z a sound
of a buzz saw strange scars
on the sea bed patterns
of animus

Written words lit up

Hidden zigzags
burned buried premonitions
take one step after
the other

Out of the hole of Baudelaire

When I in my youth
strolled in a blue wool dress
I strolled in a circle
of blue

Inside the Cello

☆

George Economou

1/

Stavros, i' vorrei che tu e Luis ed io
could find ourselves enchanted
together inside an enormous cello
immersed in its numinous music
to sustain us against the pinch of sorrow
to come in Poussin's shepherds' quizzing
the tomb that's signed Et in Arcadia ego.
Read right "Even in Arcady am I"
or wrong "I lived in Arcady also"
it sets a fine modulation from one key
of grief to another from memento
to remembrance in a final conflation
of how brief it is and so long tomorrow.

2/

Ξέρεις τί άτιμο είναι το κρίκ αυτό
a treacherous creek my father called it
the one named Hound for its driving flow
that could have drowned and haled away
Daphnis down the cascading undertow
of Love into Hades in time uncontained
and place omnipresent because long ago
has nowhere to go but the here and now.
So the Fates still snip the threads of a callow
boy or girl as readily as of one the Muses love
and Hound will drag them down into zero
again and again from any and everywhere
we leaf and then leave incommunicado.

3/

Now the Seine's flow sous le pont Mirabeau
floods out of control dimly unveiling
a sign for this time Maxime in Aleppo ego
read in splayed infant bodies washed ashore
read right reads wrong right down to its marrow.
An idyll whatever that is this isn't
but a short sweet spot a fateful sparrow
flies through from one dark night into another
only one fleet spot of light just one though
cures for this inborn incongruous term
have been prescribed through divine placebo.
Better this patchy light of Arcady
our intermezzo inside the cello.

*

NOTES

The first line of "Inside the Cello" borrows that of Dante's *Rime* 52, "Guido,
i'vorrei che tu e Lapo ed io," in which he wishes that he and his poet
friends, Guido Cavalcanti and Lapo Gianni, could be magically carried off
with their respective ladies to speak of love forever. I have substituted the

names of two friends of my own for whose presence with me I once wished at a performance of the Philadelphia Orchestra in Verizon Hall, whose design emulates the interior of a cello. The reference to Nicolas Poussin's famous painting in the Louvre, "The Arcadian Shepherds or Et in Arcadia Ego" (c. 1640), and the two contrary readings of its Latin phrase allude to the French artist's unconcealed drawing upon an earlier work by Giovanni Francesco Guercino (1621-23) in which two shepherds are confronted with a large, gruesome skull resting on an old piece of masonry upon which the words "Et in Arcadia Ego" have been engraved. A stark *memento mori*, the elliptical construction in Latin read correctly means "Even in Arcady am I," identifying Death as its pronoun referent, if not as its speaker as well. By recomposing the scene with the addition of a third shepherd and a young shepherdess contemplating the same Latin expression inscribed this time on the tombstone of one departed from this life, Poussin modulates the encounter with Death from one which delivers the message "think upon your end" to one which leads to a meditative encounter with the idea of mortality, in short, from a harsh moralism to an elegiac reflection. As a consequence of his revised version of the encounter, Poussin altered, if not forced, a new and more apt though mistranslated version of the Latin phrase, "I lived in Arcady also." Grammatically wrong, it is reasonably and dramatically right in its reconstructed context. (You can read all about it in Erwin Panofsky's study, "*Et in Arcadia Ego*: Poussin and the Elegiac Tradition.")

The first line (in Greek) of the second part, explained in the following line, is a recalled remark by my father after one of his fishing trips, literally, "You know what a treacherous creek that is," referring to Hound Creek in Cascade County, Montana, a new world addition to the waters of the underworld of antiquity and their guardian hound Cerberus

And the first line of the third part, in which the order of the two halves of the first line of Guillaume Apollinaire's "chanson triste," *Le pont Mirabeau*, have been switched in order to maintain the controlling signature rhyme of lament.

3 Poems

☆

Laurie Duggan

Blue Hills 84

this garden, like the house
resists its environment

the uninviting neatness
of pond and low hedges

nothing to step out into
save these signifiers

fake patio, fake patio

concrete imitates stone

imported figurines
guard the mantlepiece

fake is as real as it gets

Blue Hills 81

a change to hit this afternoon
maybe thunder

and then we go
Tropical Skiing

or drinking
on Nicholson Street

the steady roll of dark clouds
south of here

a baroque backdrop
to the city

Blue Hills 86

                                        a rectangle of sky
lights the kitchen bench

shadows of screeching corellas
cross this space

a cat perched on the coffee machine, stares
toward the front door, another,
eyes closed, faces north

                    hieratic

they are the gods of this household

                        the cat makes the man

A Suite of Dances

☆

Mark Weiss

A Suite of Dances IV: Chicken Dance

How the bones express themselves after all these years.
How the flesh-cloaked emerge from hiding.

It was all goyim before Abraham, even he. Come,
I will wash your feet, come
I will kill the calf.
I will give you
meat and fat.

Doe-like she approaches
on wary feet.

Come, let us disembark!

"Bark! bark!"
the brain echoes.

Oh how fragile
blah blah blah.

Infested with chickens.
The sacred fowl.
The scavenger.

The inhibitions of savages.

This which would have been a wing
is now an arm.

How you get there's
the thing.

Throw shoes at it.

Test with your fingers the mystery of threeness.

"If she have nice breasts let her bow more deeply."

A history of subordination of self
to the larger sound.
Out of the many,
a great noise
wakes the sun.

The least whisper, like smoke drifting
from a pile of leaves.

What's almost lost is the ingenuity of the poor,
a withy knotted,
or a spoon whittled into a frantic interlocking,
at the dangerous edge
where beasts meet.

HELEN

The extension of leg or glance,
or maybe it was laughter caused the
            deaths of thousands and the end
of it.

NUNAVIT

At noon a nun arrived in Nunavit,
the landscape as white as her habit,
            inhabited
by folk who grease themselves
with fat. "Who," she thought,
"could imagine such happiness?"

ETYMOLOGY

Musta bin some guy
had a horse
named Charlie or some Charlie
had a horse
uno u otro eine
oder die andere
so as to demonstrate
the pastness of past.

He was a good horse
was Charlie
while he lasted.

Nat lot let me
married married lemme
la main qui manque de

Stratified as a stack of liqueurs before tilting an elbow.

The familiar sand
the glint of mica.

Looking to make of language a haven.
Conquest by the latest dance craze.

Placate and replicate.

Cluck cluck.
Do nothing.

On the lam.
In the wind.

Readjusting to the direction of water.

Oh schist oh dolomite,
the shriek of stones,
the billions of us tearing down,
building.
Hollowed, winnowed, flattened.

Canada goose, in for a landing
on a filthy ditch beside the highway.

A dwarf too tall for the circus.

Shards of the painted window that once
transfigured light.
See how it scatters gems that when one bends to find them
disappear,
and seen again when one ceases gathering.
Over and over, until worn out by the dumb wonder of it.

Imagine a gestural language, ephemeral as dancing.

Intention.
Draws a bead on.

On the bench at the end of the line
where the wretched wash up.

Judge where the ball's
going as the wind
twists it.

Not the dance, she dreams, but its preparation.

Bend bend bend to her sorrow.

A Suite of Dances V: The Bear's Harvest

Surrounded by dancers, he thinks,
my daughter was one of these. The pull
of gravity on flesh, is it a question of denying temptation?

A lifelong exploration of ways to strap shoes to feet,
that a certain movement
suggests a time, and a kind of travel.

                    LACONIC

                    Soft-spoken as a trained
                    killer in a place where killing
                    is "normal."

                    I dreamt I dwelt in the land of...

                    Olives, and things made of olives.

                    Where once a tree arched o'er the flood.

The fish once caught, strung, and then,
a net to sleep in.
Call it the golden age, the gilded cage.

Clings to her granddaughter as to a flower.

"Age makes a lie of everything."
What else to hold to.

We have three rivers,
and a fourth
in paradise.

Let me not put foot to.

Easy, she thinks,
to mistake a man
for hunger.

A dance begun with imitation.
Let us become the deer to summon meat.
Let us become the goddess.

They imagine animals dancing and invent
the step of the deer
and the lope of the wolf behind them.
Prey and predator.
Loved and lover.
Later they wear the parts not eaten.

In the version of the pastoral
where god is a shepherd,
who's to condemn the wolves?

Greasy weeds through the cracked sidewalk beside the oily river.
Try not to breathe,
try not to drink. At night
the constant flame of the burn-off
announces the cracking plant.
Nature or nurture?

Shoes?

Permission to play with each other's toes?

Parade across the screen
as if beaten. How hard a life,
so that we say
a quick death.
What needs to be done.
What needs to be *done*.
Become in old age a seat by the fire.

One toe the other's comfort.
Saved the world!
The goodest boy that is!

Christ inspects the cross with a craftsman's eye.
Give unto Caesar
if the wage is right. Not the best,
he thinks, but close enough.

Hell of a way for a Jew to die, though.

Joseph serves his purpose
and disappears.
Famous in his generation.
A name and a tomb.

The plane of the foot
the plane of the ground
a film of moisture.

What can be put together can be torn asunder.

"My father was the kind of man everybody standing around laughing
he poke his head in everybody stop laughing. He wasn't a big man,
but he had that way about him."
Bearish, I crash through the undergrowth for a berry.

The shepherd eats lamb chops.

Last night's scavenger,
bent double, each movement a torment,
picking through garbage for bottles and cans and a crust of bread.

By the all-night joint where the taxistas eat,
a scattering of chicken. Thrown out
for the cats, or as lagniappe for misery?

On my street the homeless inhabit the benches beneath the trees.
The one
who claims that the crease in his head is an axe-blow
becomes belligerent if not greeted, invisible,
as he's mostly been.
The toll of the street upon him.

Someone's hair gets lots of attention all the way down to below her
          waist.
Morning and evening stroke upon stroke.
I am lovely it whispers I will always be lovely.

PRO PATRIA

My allegiance pledged
again and again to the vernacular. It's
          the sound itself
defines the boundaries, its absence
exile.

When I was a boy I'd scratch words
into the pavement while the dog
strained at the leash.

Poor dog poor dog.
Among the lost.

Different qualities of crosses, for instance,
the one on the left amateur work, while mine–
did they give me the best because I'm a carpenter?

A well-tuned voice and a story
well-rehearsed.

Miraculous survivor of this or that elder from the time of
"we didn't have those then."

Organs refurbished, good as new.

On such a day
as if the world beyond my eyes
were the blond waitress on tip toes.

Rare to stand flat-footed,
poised as we always are for flight.

One doesn't like to think of the last of anything.

One can offend a dog's sense of what's appropriate.

                    LAST HARVEST

                    Soon enough the air will crisp
                    and the leaves fall. But tonight–
                    pasta! pesto!

                    "Digestion doth make cowards of us
                              all." Off
                    to the near woods,
                    despite the moisture. One more
                    graybeard
                    on the mountain.

Gauging the ball
in a high wind.
Drifts.
Gets under it.

Changed the teeth but not the mouth.

I think of my ex,
each morning remaking herself.
So the question she asks:
"is it always make-believe?"
Imprinted on her shirt: "Less
is enough."

Is there music?
Can you sing it?
Here in the grateful air
the grated air
the gravid air
the rainy snare
the brawny flare
noisy noisy.

Even stature a matter of heels. So,
barefoot   naked
reduced from what she thought to be.

from *Matrix*

☆

David Miller

5.

man becomes boy
becomes bishop

he's enclosed
in scarlet & gold cardboard

he officiates
at three music stands

he recites then intones

energetically he
flaps his cardboard wings

amidst pandaemonium
a

language of light
& darkness

....

photograph into drawing into poem
black grey white

she collapsed in the street
– hunger –

& so flee
to another poverty

time? a
narrow

escape

time – time itself
the impossible a necessity

kingfisher gull cormorant heron
sun lake lake sun

6.

cypresses & clear lakes
the brochures said & showed

& so it was
& mountains yes mountains

artworks followed brochures
following photographs or paintings

dumb witnessing
that doesn't & can't speak

....

kingfisher
plunges his beak

splashingly & precisely
framed by two

moments of flight

image image image
poetic & deadly

if you say he writes
then he'll write no more

death has no
favourites

unlike water
– only witnesses

7.

every time you pass
through a doorway

each moment at
or through a doorway

white black black white

we came to the kissing gate
& of course we kissed

dark to bright
a doorway a

book running
water &

feathers feathers feathers
– snare roll after snare roll

lake sun moon stars
in shatters

....

dunnock splashing frenetically
in the bird bath but

the water now frozen
ice disk thrown into bushes

& now night slow night

no night one said
ever night another

bird bird bird
what the language

isn't asking us
are we now being asked?

8.

no wish to write with a quill
or replicate the colours

the colours non-colours

ink & Chinese brushes
bought in a Chinese supermarket

in Gerrard Street
c. 1973

....

warned by a dream
the white parrot kept to the house

when it was brought outside
a hawk flew down to attack

'peck its leg!' you called
& the parrot did

& the hawk
released it

bitter O bitter joy

9.

famed Filipino artist living in London
– just back from Maoist China c.1972

everything there a spectacle a happening

he accosted me in a Soho bookshop
talking about ancient Chinese poetry

I accompanied him to a health food restaurant
where he added cottage cheese to his soup

....

he stitches
we sew

handkerchief
or hat

or else a shelter
tipi or hut

heavy rain
as I write

not a bead curtain
not a curtain

not beads
not

in dream I held the woman's slit throat together

3 from *Barcelona*

☆

Simon Marsh

6/sis

if infinity is circular
nature's law triangulates
& all things are square
then why did I dream
that huge black dot
& a smudge of red cupcakes?
this elastic hotel pillow
remembers my head
so in a sense I wake
preserved in you
later on we breakfasted
on shredded ham tyres
the colour of ageless
incendiaries

7/set

light wells mean
so much to me
I'd never seen
strawberry custard
cavity wall
insulation
or the inflatable
ribs of cetaceans
in circular light
you walked me
to the house
of bones & yawns
barely a stone
pond's throw
from water lilies
in bloom

8/vuit

we sought afternoons
of shaded release
the seamless drift
of late mornings
& night's granular space
you have *pulpo gallego*
a handful of thrown salt
& beer close to frozen
we can eat & drink
when the hell we like

Moustache

☆

Michael Rothenberg

All it takes is a squirrel in the garden
        to set the dogs off

                Or that oak tree
stricken with sudden death

        falling in the forest at 2am
The startled mist

and full moon glow conjure a white night
on St. Petersburg ghost walk

  with the mustachioed Russian doctor
  who foretold my mother's death

Groggy and disoriented
                We are citizens of hell

The giant slab of concrete
        lowered over the casket

slows the resurrection
and prevents pillaging

The rat skeleton under the house
Ants that carry flesh away

The carcass stench that rises
through the floorboards

In the summer
when the contractor comes to excavate

a new leach line in the rocky ground,
the buried dog

makes a sudden appearance
Now the septic system barks and growls

Ceaseless flea scratchings and urinations
erupt in a drug induced twilight

I can't sleep or stay awake
Wild dogs run through dream fields

Insomnia and restless legs
Tectonic electricity quakes

and twitches through my canine heart
Tossing in my bed

a fanged demon issues an alien cry
as common as poetry.

January 21, 2016

4 Poems

☆

Burt Kimmelman

Threesome

The day you
were born I
heard your cry.

Day's End, Summer

Lace blossom,
the bee rests
upside down.

Sky

Wings apart,
the bird floats
above trees.

Marriage

Making love,
sorrows and
joys are one.

Chikushi School of Poetry

☆

Jesse Glass

Round-faced men & women
huddled here
brushing the Chinese characters
with ink of iron & crushed beetles
on precious Chinese paper,
by open oil lamps, crept
into each other's arms
& untied silk robes to mingle lice
translucent as their skins;
men wearing starched hats
herbs under tongues to sweeten breath
women stinking of incense & open thighs
moan into each other's mouths
as the cold wind rattled the walls
& the guards outside twanged their bows on the hour
to keep the falling stars at bay
& mountain wolves howled their own extinction.

Now only rusted, galvanized sheds,
rice fields lapped in fog

for as far as I can see
from this platform
of decaying concrete--
a late Kyushu train
made Tengu by distance
lights up the tracks
dividing the crickets
from their songs.

Ice Queen

1.

Ice Queen
your crystal cheek
stacked on weeping
needles--

My brow's inverted
in your belly.
Polar Lady
split your
wine glass womb

so these raw hands
may stretch
their thumbs

to loose the
valves of
sardonyx
& thunder--

For here
The rain
pits
every
flow

as wolves lap fog
from rivers
in a thaw.

2.

You, grave
Willendorf (=light as pimpernel
tumble
down my pores—

Slow
my snows until I lean:
one crystal-work
of silver
spirals.

3.

Your daughters are
sharp witches
who crowd my winter
lashes
I glamour
them, they flash
one shard of Venus
each, before
they glyph
the frozen ground.

4.

Here
we are fruitful
as specters (kept
apart in lucent curves.) Release
us, Regina. Let
us float over
cliffs into rime-scurfed
seas. Bevels promise
hope, mirrors frame
Despair, Holbein's skull
domes Truth. From your Palace
a 5-stringed lute
plays the same
the same
the same eight
notes.

5.

Step forward
Stoic Lady
rock your glaciers
of concern
to the sound of sledgehammers
breaking caskets
unravel the cold
as the ghaita
screams like a goat
giving birth
& sing
from both sides of your mouth
of mortal lives &
narrow lives; of the intricate
shuttle strung between
your fingers.
Sing the Mothers as
they weave the first
white seeds into matter
for yours is a brittle sword
fallen from the stars
to gash a tyrant
or a lamb. & Yours
is the cry that powers
each hidden squall,
each thickening of ice.

4 from
Field Recordings

☆

Joe Milazzo

You feel like a chump if you purchase
something, and a sucker
still if you don't.

"You're fucked."

Which is to say, saying
anything could cost
you your throat.

Shame is an edge long
on the unused, a convex
leering that tells you
how much
you love taking it.

Playing to the people
still finding their seats,
the diva shivers

a note whole. A velocity
in the gloom corrects its pitch.
Listening makes its way

around near-bone and hair.
Listening segments and picks, the citrous
response to tumors of static consequence

governable—so-called—by thumb. The requests
the diva auditions are the anthems
she's long-practiced

at recanting. Listening belongs
where the brightest pretending
used to patina. Now the subtones

funnel: an unbending dance.
The tincture never matches the taste
when lips spout so much wax

all over this repertoire of transmission.
Ushered to velveteen
reservation, what hush troubles

abutting knees? Trust,
its toughness roughly unpeeled,
can never worry us.

Verbs that echo being:
in the chambers of
a general insecurity,
we can't recall who locked
the doors, but the only identity
that matters is beyond
our acknowledgment.

We are to be
the counseled.

"Avoid."
No. No.

Make this waste
prosthetic. All assertion
stresses what is counter
in its melody. All dissent
presses its gaping
fractures into what
walls still pen between
these suites and some arena.

What we
could have
predicted

was only
ever history,
the second

skin of its
terrible
library

— dust —
slick
again.

An Ongoing Narrative
with David Antin's Remains

☆

Norman Weinstein

not maudlin saying, his remains come to 7.9 linear feet, 19 boxes
of papers recording tapes disks at the Getty, never been there to
surface mine mime evidence, tho learn now that a letter of mine
(undated) sits in Box 28 but David's correspondence & mine goes
on beyond walls, in motion keyboarding thinking aloud green fleece
sweatshirt sleeve brushing keyboard shirt my wife Mary's birthday
gift surprise with quote printed on front unsolicited review from David
of otherwise ignored book of my prose poems, "Quirky & Elegant in
the Great Vernacular" & when worn shopping strangers at checkout
inevitably ask where one can be gotten with clever they call it motto,
instead of wearing heart on sleeve book review covers heart, that
everyday surrealism that David talks so serenely baroquely about
at "Symposium on Surrealism" in Santa Monica 1994 on a panel
with Jerome Rothenberg & Will Alexander & moderated really
jocularly contained by organizer Douglas Messerli where David
sashays around academic conventions of discussing surrealism in
SoCa public forum interrupting proceedings in kochleffel Yiddish
meaning stirring the pot full-tilt or just starting to rev playing scales
as Coltrane plays them weighing how long any present makes a
present gift hearty broth kettle drops steam invisible only empty 19

boxes, where is he, missing David, he's on a shift sweat stained alive in its folds coming to surrealists he's telling us that they had to get beyond the gag then curse Marjorie reminding that Parkinsons gradually torturously cuts off his talk his talk poems silently crackling vocal, sunset, grief but was that diagnosis a false narrative he keeps transforming if only in unlocking an image of 19 boxes pretending to store his remains he's alive on a sweatshirt on websites in skywriting however banal exhaust spray marketing stream scheme not his rational review to critique terms of your specialists medical diagnosis a renewed Socratic fare well but not that since he keeps dialogue present when you read his talk poems spaces between persons becomes clouds Aristophanic cloud comedy he's in clouds if not in Getty he's in mock-narrative of Seder multiple choice chance rigged questions for each child's supposed proclivity he wouldn't buy that he's unhinging images of whatever constellates on his dinner plate, indecorous egg wobbles knowingly nudging him to absorb nutrients when swallowing Chinese water torture, yet narrative he sez stands for stands up for a desiring subject and I'm desiring to keep conversation with David going in spite of illusion that 19 archival boxes contain character essence they don't they're terminals switching routes of his how-to- transform desires leaving material traceries track re pairs, he's with me in Hudson Valley college classroom, he's approaching podium, sez with Houdini's "look ma no hands" gesture trickster's no tricks up sleeves but in mouth "I didn't bring any books" naturally tho 8 students attending squirm & hour later asks for questions they're so stunned shy around, & walk him to white rented Ford four door compass mobile, we're meeting for first last time, he's with skeleton key to every door of storied self in present you know that present that dying only temporarily takes over, like a violent cabbie comes back for inflated tip there's no present beyond the present gift exchange David, eternity unchains narrative toll booth lanes fan out as Khrushchev pate out car window shines, let's hear soon his remains, rearrange letters give me that starting shot words toppling moving boxes word keeping ball, rolling

Against First Love

☆

Pierre Joris

1. There is no first love, as there is no last love. All loves are first loves, because love is a fall, & the Fall is always unique, always original, always one. It takes the breath away and rebirthes you. You are new now, in love, for the first time, again and again. You fall and when you get up again, wake up again, you are new, ready for the first time. My first love will be tomorrow's love, what my eye falls on as I wake up. After the absence of myself in sleep, coming to life as I open my eyes, it will fall on you and I will fall in love for the first time, again and again, with the one I have lived with for 28 years now.

2. But first I have to love myself, i.e. come to myself as I emerge from sleep. Then I can turn toward you. First love is always oneself. Or needs to be. How else to be in the world. Love yourself as you would love your neighbor. Turn that christian maxime on its head. You cannot love another unless you know how to love yourself. Unless you do love yourself. You have to live inside yourself until you die. You better love what you live in or you are in trouble or worse — dead alreday.

3. Nor, finally, is first love the mother: you cannot give a number
to what is unconditional & of another nature as a first love. The
dependence is so total that it is only after severance, after learning
to walk and feed and love yourself that you can turn back and learn
to love what was there *ab initio*, from before the start, what comes
before the number one, unnumbered, or maybe love degree zero.
Last week I sat on my mother's grave and wept, not about her
or about me or about my loss of her, but about the firmness and
flimsiness, the flimsy firmness and firm flimsiness of the chain of
Being stretching back way before my mother and on beyond me, my
wife and my son. Not tears of love or of love lost, but tears of awe at
a universe that is what it is.

4. "Paul confirmă că va face amor propriu eu Ciuci." "Paul confirms
that he will make self-love with Ciuci." This is the first line in Paul
Celan's prose work, *Microliths*, & opens a little surreal exchange
called *Cărtica de seară /Little Evening Book* consisting in a collation
of some forty puns and aphoristic notations in Romanian by Paul
Celan and his friend Petre Solomon. Ciuci is Corina Marcovici, a
friend (love? lover?) of Celan's. The line is a pun in that inserting
an empty space or line break, (i.e. separating) the Romanian term
"amor-propriu" (or the French amour-propre) and by adding the
verb "face"/"to make," the word "amor" get's a sexual connotation,
wonderfully doubling back on the "proprietary," the "proper" in both
its references as to what belongs to one, what one owns, via the
latin "proprius," and to what is "proper," i.e. French, "propre," clean,
tidy, neat, honest, the way it should be. Of course, "amour-propre,"
which usually has an ever-so-slight to majorly negative intimation,
while usually translating as self-esteem, quickly and easily becomes
pride and *Ehrgeiz*. Another compound term for the same concept
using the "self" as place to start from is "self-regard," which brings
in the gaze, the loving gaze directed at the self, oneself. Or is the
negative connection with the concept of amour-propre, literally "self-
love," due exactly to that notion of self-regard, of the gaze that rests
on oneself?

5. And so the time has come to retell the myth of Narcissus. But
as I have Ingeborg Bachmann say in a play, "why believe myths of
old? They are just stories told." Wouldn't it be more useful to rewrite

them? Make up another, a new story, subvert the old one. Here's how Wikipedia flatly sums up the story: "Narcissus was a hunter from Thespiae in Boeotia who was known for his beauty... He was proud, in that he disdained those who loved him. Nemesis noticed this behavior and attracted Narcissus to a pool, where he saw his own reflection in the water and fell in love with it, not realizing it was merely an image. Unable to leave the beauty of his reflection, Narcissus lost his will to live. He stared at his reflection until he died." In the Greek story the baddie is Narcissus, a good hunter and provider, but isn't it in fact Nemesis, that inescapable bitch that wants to stop the hunter in his tracks, wants to be a better man-hunter & lays a trap. A trap, by the way, I don't believe a hunter like Narcissus could have fallen into because any woodsman would have crossed rivers and sat by pools & would have observed his own features any number of times, scanning the surface of water for fish or movement upstream, whatever. And if Narcissus didn't know his own beauty before looking into Nemesis's pond, how could he have been proud and disdainful? This is an untrustworthy tale. Deep down I suspect it to be a tale about how the human as free nomad is fooled into becoming sedentary and how that sedentarization makes him fall in love with — not himself, but an image of himself. Mimesis, the Greeks called it, and it rhymes with Nemesis. We know what followed upon this sedentarization — it led us to our present anthropocene, where humanity, still navel-gazing is awaiting its end. Nemesis in fact comes later, comes now, as we have to face up to Gaia.

6. How do you learn self-love? You cannot make love (which is the active way of loving) to someone else before you know how to make love to yourself first. And obviously that's what you do, what we all do first. Look in the mirror, even though there really is no *stade du miroir*, because if that was the only way we could learn to recognize ourselves as entities, as objects-in-the-mirror-with-a-subject[me-me-me]-looking-at-me-the-object, no blind person could know themselves, could have an existence, could have language, could have (self-)love. Lay low, Lacan! No, we learn to fall in love when we learn the body, our body, not when we see it in the mirror as a semblance, but when our hands explore it and feel the wetness of the inside of the mouth, feel the beating of the heart,

an artery pulsing at the wrist, the strange warmth and attraction of our genitalia? And when you realize that you can feel this again and again, every day, every morning on waking up, then you'll have discovered the true first love — the one you need to anchor to before you even try to move out into the world and touch someone else.

7. "Une main branle, l'autre écrit," writes Pierre Guyotat, and connects two essentials: love of self and creation of something new — without any need, really, to go all old-fashioned Freudian and identify pen and ink with phallos and sperm. Where would that leave woman? And yet, beyond the "scandale" of Guyotat's line (and marvelous oeuvre!), there is something here worth pursuing: could the real first love be masturbation? Why not? As Woody Allen says: "Don't knock masturbation. It's sex with someone you love very much." It may even be that it is how you discover that you love yourself, or *can* love yourself! There are Darwinian versions for this thesis, my favorite one being the comedian Lily Tomlin's explanation: "We have reason to believe that man first walked upright to free his hands for masturbation." So I'm joking about masturbation? Maybe because it is still one of rare semi-taboo subjects. But is is a "poesis," a making, an imaginative adventure as much as a physical one and a place to learn love.

8. But isn't first love really the first major achievement, the first thing you made that differentiates you yourself (ah! so already again self-love?) from the repetitious humanity you see around you & don't love. That first thing made that wasn't a thing found, that wasn't already there, that you brought into the world? But isn't that love or pride? Self-love, amor(-)propriu? In my case, who had wanted to be a writer from the word go, (which word?, but a word, to begin a book with, maybe the word "go" would have been the best start ever, maybe my next book will start with the word "go"!) it must therefore be my first book. But looking back now, roughly 60 of those items later, what I remember is pleasure, yes, & pride, yes, p & p, pipi, pipi de chat, in fact a barely acknowledged feeling of let-down: so *this* is *it*? This is your first book, the thing you have been waiting for all these years? These measly forty mimeographed & stapled pages? Yes, I love the fact that I did it, that someone thought well enough of

my writing to publish it, but, lawdy lawd, that's, yes, indeed, self-love again and now with the book here comes post-coïtal sadness, and I ...none the wiser. Get on with it, write the next book, it will be your next first love & will let you down just as certainly...

How I Became César Aira

☆

Gregg Biglieri

STAR-CROSSED

Reading in a foreign language allows us to substitute a cluster of words rather than a single equivalent word (to patch in the meaning as one patches in the sound from another *source*) and thus we get a better sense of how it is constructed because we too are involved in the process of constructing what it is we're reading and what the author is doing. At times, it feels as if we're in the process of making a model (or assembling one) but we don't quite know *what* it is, though we trust that we will at least make something based on our hands-on approach as to *how* this object was created in the first place (its originally imagined construction now reconstructed outside its imaginary). And sometimes we produce monstrosities that in no way resemble the original.

I am reminded of the time this handyman came to replace the faucet on the sink. After unwrapping the package and removing the new parts from the box, the next thing he did was take the instructions and throw them in the trash. When I questioned him about this procedure, he said, "What are they going to tell me? I already know how the parts go together." As I watched him go about his work, I saw that he was thinking with his hands and shifting parts around as if they formed a more commonplace version of a Rubik's cube, and he was gaining knowledge about how the mechanism worked by maneuvering the parts in his hands, taking mental snapshots with his eyes and comparing them to some internal picture of how such devices must function. The point here is that when we're involved in the process of translation, we get a better picture of how things work and the mental picture or sense of what the text is about hovers in the background as we are learning and gaining knowledge of how things work by manipulating the actual words rather than relying on the abstraction of printed instructions or subordinating this manual task to the sense or meaning of these ideas or to the content that is being conveyed. In the end, we want the mechanism to function properly, we want the water to flow, and we get a better sense of this by figuring out how the mechanism works. And then, less stuck on efficiency and more alert to effectiveness, we simply want to wash our hands.

STARKIST

I keep thinking of those model-making kits for airplanes that my oldest brother used to labor over. Everything has already been prepared so that you must meticulously follow the precise instructions in the proper sequence in order to reproduce the intended object. (Here, the origin is *not* the goal.) The goal is to recreate a perfect replica that looks like what it was meant to look like. ("Starkist doesn't want tuna with good taste; Starkist wants tuna that tastes good.") I never had the patience of my older brother. I was fascinated by the sheer plasticity of the parts, each separate piece hanging suspended like a bulb from a thin gray tube waiting to be twisted off and then glued in its proper place. I liked the materiality of the plastic and couldn't tell the difference between the parts that were meant to be part of the finished model and those leftover bits of plastic that were meant to be superfluous.

(Years later in college at some kind of group retreat we were given exercises or tests in the form of games that were supposed to teach,

I imagine, the business skills of planning and production. We were given instructions on how to put together some simple construction made of paper and then given time to perfect the process. The next step was to estimate how many of these objects we could make over the course of a given time period. We were asked to write down on a piece of paper the number of objects we thought we could produce over a ten-minute period. Given my inability to fashion even one of these objects (my manual dexterity being barely adequate), I had written "zero" on the piece of paper. My feeling was that since I knew I couldn't produce even one object properly, I had successfully estimated my production capacity and thus my business acumen. Of course, I was thrown out of the game.)

I wasn't really interested in Lego either, since it seemed that you needed to imagine in advance the thing that you wanted to build and then execute that plan. I had no plan and I also might have had suspicions that there was some particular type of imagination that was called for and I knew that I didn't have whatever that was. I would just connect the little blocks randomly based on some chance pattern of colors and create an agglomeration of blocks that most often resembled blobs (monsters) rather than any recognizable object. It should also be said that even I was not satisfied with the results. It is interesting how in writing about this I can also redirect the sense of my own inability to recreate recognizable objects into a justification for my own failures, mistakes, etc. What is striking to me is just how unclear my own sense of imagination was (and is) if "having an imagination" means being able to envision a viable, workable object and then to set about executing a plan to bring it to fruition (bring it into being).

If I were making a model, every time I looked back at the picture of the actual *thing* I was supposedly trying to make, I only noted the flaws in my own attempt to create a likeness and thus the comparison between what my hands, smudged and sticky with glue, were working on and the photographic image of the completed object served as an index to my own lack of manual dexterity and artistic skill.

(Why are all these images of my artistic inability floating to the surface now? I remember one day in fourth grade when the traveling violin teacher auditioned students scouting for rudimentary skills and my inability to even hold the violin securely beneath my chin. Even through all the years that I played the clarinet I knew I didn't play well; I knew whatever modicum of ability I had only came from practice and memorization rather than talent. Perhaps I am trying by contrast to show that I was acutely aware of talents that I didn't possess; I knew about them by marking my distance from ever achieving them.)

My brothers and teachers always used to make fun of how large and awkward my handwriting was. The shape of the letters distorted beyond all measure. I could again produce a justification (or self-deception) in that I had an aversion to keeping my letters inside the horizontal green lines, with the middle line dotted to mark the difference between the lower-case and capital letters. I remember how my handwriting was unfavorably compared to that of one of my brothers who wrote in a smooth flowing cursive script that even I recognized as far superior to my sequence of oblong marks, with *a*'s and *b*'s looking like whales disconsolately beached on the lines of the page. I remember that one of our family activities was listening to Bill Cosby's comedy records on weekend nights. There is one story in which he reenacts his own version of writing his gigantically misshapen letters and having to ask for a new sheet of paper after having penciled in only a few letters. There must have been some extra laughter here as everyone recognized that the truth of his story by pointing to my own awkward penmanship.

One of the few art projects that I thought of as a masterpiece was my "painting" of a man's head that I later thought of as a portrait of Van Gogh, perhaps because of the pointy, bearded chin. The head was out of all proportion to any sense of human scale, nor did it even show the barest amount of symmetry. What was striking to me was how that head emerged and took shape on the paper. We must have been having some creative period in school and were encouraged to try something new. The point (doubly literally) is that this "painting" was composed entirely of dots that gradually emerged into the sense of a face, perhaps my first encounter with the technique of pointillism (had we been shown Seurat's famous painting *La Grande Jatte*?). The point (doubly literally) is that I think I was able to perform this exercise because it was an inversion of connect the dots or paint-by-number. There was no specific order or procedure to follow. It was all about a composition of random dots randomly taking shape before my eyes, and before my mind could sense what that constellation of dots would turn into. I had no picture in my mind, only a sense of making dots in ink. Thirty years later, shortly after my mother's death, sorting through a collection of things she'd kept from our school years, I saw once more that early pointillist portrait and perhaps began to think not just about connecting the dots but how the dots connected even without me.

IT TOOK ME TWENTY YEARS TO SMILE

I remember reading *Six Memos for the Next Millennium* back in 1988 or 1989 and being fascinated by the clarity and precision of Calvino's prose as he traced the sturdy skeleton of the imagination. I especially recall the anecdote about Guido Cavalcanti from the note on "Lightness," where Guido leaps among the tombstones. Twenty years later, as I was reading *The Decameron* in the summer looking for selections to use for a Humanities class, I came across the story in which Guido leaps among the tombstones: "that with his gravity he has the secret of lightness." And I smiled.

GERHARD RICHTER

I have a 9x6 postcard of Gerhard Richter's *Two Candles* (*Zwei Kerzen*). I love how still it is and how it is still there. Sometimes when I whisk past it I hear it fall and hit the floor, so its edges are a bit dented. It always makes me smile when I bend down to pick it up and glance again at the twin flames of those candles and see that they have not been blown out. How something so still, still moves.

JASPER

"it's not gold, it's jasper."

I must have been a little kid once. I picked up a rock in the front yard and became fascinated by how its typical "rockness" seemed veined with a strange purple color. Like veins of microscopic, frozen lightning. If "architecture is frozen music," then poetry (is) rocks. Pygmalion's statue becomes flesh and blood as its marble veins become real veins that carry real blood. As in Ovid's lines, the stories describe the transformation of the real into something else— rocks become human and humans become rocks (There... is there an Echo in her(e)). I remember showing that rock to a friend of my mother's who happened to be an elementary school teacher (Mrs. Paddock). After bending down to come to my level, she told me that this rock was called "jasper." Something happened at that moment; something clicked. I was suddenly more fascinated by the sound of the word than I had been by the color of the rock. I no longer needed the rock because I now had the word and could carry it with me (in my veins) everywhere. I could simply subvocalize "jasper" and immediately see the purple veins in the rock, silently caress them with my tongue. I thought, then, that words are real things, as now I know that words are people, too.

SECRET STRAWBERRY

As I was glancing at my hurriedly transcribed notes penciled in on the inside cover of Aira's *How I Became a Nun*, I thought I read "secret strawberry" instead of what I gradually came to see was actually "secret/transparency." This could be explained by my hastily scratched handwriting which, upon an even closer look, reveals that I had actually scribbled "secret/transpary"—the "*n*" oddly tilting into the "*s*" to form a kind of "*w*." Perhaps I was also thinking of that fateful strawberry ice-cream in Aira's *How I Became a Nun*. Or one of my endless parade of titles for an essay on Aira, such as "Oscar Wilde's Strawberry Ice-Cream: How the Reality of the Story Becomes the Story of Reality in Aira's *How I Became a Nun*." But was I thinking what I was seeing or seeing what I was thinking? How

could this scribbled sequence lead to a misunderstanding that then
activated my involuntary memory so that I remembered once again
the "real" source—the "secret strawberry" from my reading of Alberto
Savinio's piece entitled "Antonio Stradivari" in his collection *Operatic
Lives*?

> In 1874, with the 'Delfino' in mind, Charles Reade wrote
> in the *Pall Mall Gazette* that, in his opinion, the height of
> beauty was the effect of light and shadow produced when
> the velvety outline of a red Stradivarius becomes rounded,
> and the varnish on the bottom wears away in the shape of a
> vague triangle. We, looking at that faded triangle, recall the
> celebrated jaws that have pressed, suffered, and agonized
> above the Stradivarius violin; the adorable little jaw of a
> young lady violinist, on which the burning contact left a light
> strawberry-colored mark. (93)

"RELOJITOS DE FUEGO"

This might be one reason for my not being capable of being a
translator. I keep seeing *aguja* (needle) in *agujero*—not to mention
águila (eagle). And then I think of "eagle-eyed" (also via Kenneth
Koch's reading of Keats's "On First Looking into Chapman's Homer"
(*Making Your Own Days* 104-5) in relation to the "eye of the needle"
(biblical reference or not). For *agujero*, the dictionary provides *hole*
(general) and pincushion (sewing). So it is a *hole* and translates
as "gap" which, in reverse translation comes out as "*vacío*" or
"*hueco*." In Spanish, "eagle-eyed" is an idiomatic expression that
means "*tener ojos de lince*," or to have the eyes of a lynx, to be
"lynx-eyed." This makes me think or hear (and which comes first,
hearing or thinking, or is that the simultaneity of the pun?)—that
instantaneous surprise of insight, to hear this about seeing.

I keep thinking of not only the things we miss, but of the things we
see because when we are translating between languages we always
see literally and think of words as literal objects, as crunchy as they
are sculpted. For instance, when I read "*flor de piel*" in Spanish,
my first thought is to imagine the skin of a flower before I recognize

it as an idiomatic expression. Here, "*flor*" means "surface," rather than flower. And the expression "*a flor de*" means "*a nivel de*," which means "level or flush with" or "on the surface"; on edge, or with raw emotion. And this makes me think of another idiom, "*al pie de la letra*," which means "exactly, or to the letter." Of course, I see "at the foot of the letter" and even think of the foot in the skin's flower, "*pie*" in "*piel*." Another translation would be *verbatim*: "in exactly the same words that were used originally"; thus, literally. This is how I literally imagine the literal. I see myself standing at the foot of a letter as if it were the gigantic fragment of Constantine's foot on display outside the Capitoline museum in Rome.

Thinking is what happens while you're thinking of something else. There's still electricity—even if it just seems like static—that spark of intelligence. For instance, every time I hear someone say, "for instance" (and even when I say it), I immediately translate it to, or hear it as, "four-inch dance." This simple, almost consciously unconscious mishearing provokes a smile and yet it also stimulates me to keep thinking because of the pleasure it gives, no matter how insignificant. Now I am thinking of the expression "*relojitos de fuego*" after seeing it used in Aira's *Cómo Me Reí*: "los sapos glotones se pasaban la noche soltando bocinazos, las chicharras competían en dar cuerda a sus sonoros relojitos de fuego..." (70). In my mind, I translate it literally (but is translation ever literal in the sense of being denotative and stable?) as "little clocks of fire." Even though I know that it is probably an idiomatic expression which means something else, that doesn't affect this moment that occurs between recognition and misrecognition, between understanding and misunderstanding, a kind of productive misunderstanding or creative mishearing which provokes thinking and writing, and prompts us to value that misperception as a kind of perception and not let its senses, and our own, settle prematurely on a single sense, as in this is what it means. After further searching into the "*relojitos de fuego*," I found that there isn't an idiomatic expression it corresponds to, and it appears Aira was using the phrase as a metaphor to describe the sounds of the crickets ticking like little clocks of fire, providing a visual equivalent for a sonic occurrence. I did find a reference in the Spanish Wikipedia to the "*reloj de fuego*," which is an instrument that measures time in relation to the velocity of the consumption of a comestible. It shows a picture of an ancient Chinese Fire Clock, that measures time by the burning of candles.

CLOCKBUG

Perhaps it was just a coincidence that I was reading Kobo Abe's *The Ark Sakura* at this time, in which we find a reference to the *eupcaccia*, or clockbug. This might bring me round to the etymology of "frivolous" once again. I was pleased to see that the clockbug has its own Wikipedia entry: "The clockbug, or eupcaccia, is a fictional insect created by Japanese writer Kobo Abe in his novel, *The Ark Sakura*. The clockbug is an insect species whose legs have atrophied, mobility being unnecessary for its existence since it lives by consuming its own feces, merely by using its antennae to rotate in a counter-clockwise fashion, continuously manifesting a circular trail of excretion and ingestion. The organism's slow, metabolic rate allows time for nutrients in its feces to be replenished by bacterial action. It eats from dawn to dusk and sleeps through the night, and since it is heliotropic—with its head always pointed toward the sun—it also functions as a timepiece. The clockbug's variant name *eupcaccia*, suggests a combination of the prefix *eu-*, meaning *good* and the Italian word *caccia* meaning *hunt*, in other words, *good hunting*. The name also suggests a combination of *caccia* and *eupeptic*, meaning having good digestion and cheerful, optimistic."

I'd like to address this without being told that my method appears to be that of a dog that is chasing its own tail. Perhaps more like a playful version of the Ouroboros.

LA CIGÜEÑA

Se escribe siempre, incluso cuando no se escribe (Aira, *Copi* 53)

In the anecdote of the stork, retold in Aira's book on Copi, the mysterious origin of the sounds heard in the night is only resolved when, in the light of day, the farmer's tracks can be seen to trace the dotted outline of a stork (*cigüeña* echoing "*siguiente*"), his footsteps having punched holes in the snow, forming that dotted line on which it would be superfluous to add the writer's signature.

> ¿Conocen la historia de la cigüeña? Es un cuento del folklore europeo: a la medianoche el campesino oye ruidos, sale a ver, camina sobre la nieve, del establo al molino, una vuelta por el corral, etcétera, y no descubre al intruso. Pero a la mañana siguiente se asoma por la ventana y lo ve: sus propias huellas en la nieve habían dibujado una cigüeña. (*Copi* 96)

> [Do you know the story of the stork? It is a tale form European folklore: at midnight a farmer hears noises, he goes out to see, walks around on the snow, from the stable to the mill, a quick turn through the corral, et cetera, and he can't find the intruder. But the following morning he sticks his head out the window and he sees it: his own footprints in the snow had traced the outline of a stork.]

I'm trying to get at why Aira provokes and disturbs readers by his frivolity (a lightness which they see as frivolous, inconsequential, or trivial), as if he were manipulating them so that they would inevitably fall into traps he hasn't really set for them in the first place. One problem is that "culinary" readers ("Starkist wants tuna that tastes good"), like Sancho Panza, always want the answer to the riddle *first* (this insight comes from Viktor Shklovsky). They want to know that the intruder was a stork without having to "suffer through" the retelling of the anecdote, so that they can end this play (because Aira is just "playing" with their minds), take their deflated ball and go home. The problem with this approach is that it goes against the anecdote of storytelling as such by misreading what it reads rather than experiencing all the possibilities implied by reading its own misreadings. You can't read Aira by trying to trace a single line from beginning to end because there are so many twists and turns, misdirections, and contingencies; you have to walk around quite a bit without knowing where you're going and not knowing until you've stopped reading what kind of pattern you've traced in your wandering. For Aira, "the origin is the goal": "And what could be more common than the act of beginning again? It was being repeated all the time. What else could really be repeated? In the beginning was Repetition, and only there" (*An Episode in the Life of a Landscape Painter* 82). On one level, the anecdote of the stork is about the act of writing and the emphasis on process should alert us to the fact that the farmer's aimless wandering is more important than any eventual conclusion he may never arrive at. He never really arrives anywhere, seems to go in circles, and doesn't discover the "source" of the mysterious sounds that have awoken him in the middle of the night. Even when he sees the outline the next morning in the clear light of day, he never actually sees the stork and can only reconstruct what's happened by writing ... in the clear light of day, the next morning. Aira writes the process by trial and error; he documents his own experience of process in the very process of his writing (fleeing forward, into the unknown in search of the new—Aira cues Baudelaire here—never looking back, an anti-Orpheus: "A ruse against Orphic disobedience: obliterate all that lies behind. There was no point in turning around anymore" (*Episode* 24)). He doesn't know where his own narrative is going much less where it will end, so that the key to this anecdote (Aira's version of the riddle of the sphinx?) is not in the answer to the riddle but in the questions posed by the riddle's construction. The lazy reader can say that he now knows "the answer" and can go on to criticize the writer for his silly sallies through the snow. This reader thinks he knows what it's about because he tells himself that the footprints in the snow formed the shape of a stork and so the writing is "about" a stork. But, first of all, it's not about a literal stork but the outline of a stork created by a series of footprints made by someone who has no idea where he is going in the first place (or the last place). Second, what about the fact that the stork as *cigüeña* sounds so close to *siguiente* (following), which underscores Aira's methodology again (*huida hacia adelante,* or flight forward), the creature that follows the creature that one is following *is* the work in progress. Third, what about the stork as that creature who is said to deliver babies (see Joe Stork in *Krazy Kat*)? Where do babies come from? Here, we might see the stork as an allegory of the anecdote of the stork (an allegory of itself) in that it is *delivering* its message or answer in the form of a question (mark?) contained in and by its own form. Because what we really want to know is what happened, what actions took place in order to produce the "baby," what play, what untwisting of plots, what transparencies of denouement, what exchanges of gender and genre—not simply that the stork brought the baby and dumped it in the reader's lap. Yes, the answer to the riddle of the mysterious noises is the stork, but the real question concerns the construction of the story as a series of flights, sallies, retreats, feints and fakes, with no destination in mind (and no direction home) whose "origin is the goal," the flight and frivolity of the process of writing itself.

A PORTRAIT OF THE ARTIST AS A YOUNG NUN

Now at least I can come clean about chapter seven of *How I Became a Nun* because it's the key to my whole reading of the novella, not just as the allegory of Aira as writer (*A Portrait of the Artist as a Young Nun*—the title for the American movie would probably be *Young Nuns*), but as the relationship between the child and her mother through their mutual listening to serial stories and how that stimulates and encourages her to think up stories about classmates (simulations?) and to imagine alternative histories of their symptoms which suspiciously relate to problems of "reading" that recall her own inability to *read* rather than to *see* words as drawings and relate them to sexual graffiti, and also to understanding that insults somehow all have to do with one's mother. The other revelation, the reason that I initially told you that this book was my own autobiography, was for the shock effect, of course, but it also recalled my own experience of being in a classroom in Australia when I was almost seven years old and still didn't know how to read but could fake it by memorizing entire books that my mother had the patience to hear me 'read' out loud to her—for example, *The Littlest Rabbit*—and then being embarrassed in that class when called upon to read and, not being able to, kept silent and had that silence interpreted as resistance to authority which led to, at that time, the acceptable punishment of holding out the back of one's hands to be smacked by the teacher's ruler. I will always remember that it was a bit later in our three-month stay in Australia (autumn of 1967), the day I "learned" to read, which was more like an instantaneous sensation that all the meaningless ciphers somehow instantly arranged themselves into patterns and constellations, which took place between floors in an elevator while going up to our apartment in Melbourne so that when the doors opened on our floor I turned to my mother and told her I could read and then was running ahead of her because I couldn't wait to prove it to her, and to myself. I saw the words in my head first before seeing them on paper. So, it's important, too, that the beginning of those stories for the writer are the serials heard on the radio and thus imagined and visualized not as words written and seen but as words *heard* that sets up a new paradigm of a writer's initiation into print. And then the sequence (the serial poem) that continues in *Ghosts* and the exchange of ghost stories that all take different narrative turns and recall the Patri's dream section which takes place in her head perhaps spurred on by what she read just before she fell asleep, which is a long discourse on architecture but still, at another level, a story of writing and a sense of place *in time* and not just space. And then we see that architecture is relevant but so is the sense that writing is itself the unbuilt architecture and the unbuilt is related to the creative impulse (or that blue streak I am streaking through here) which manages to assemble disparate thoughts and stories into a semblance of verisimilitude, but really is a construction of words on paper (see Salvador Plascencia, *The People of Paper*). I hope this explains why I was so drawn to chapter seven of Aira's *How I Became a Nun*.

READER UNDO CÉSAR

In those very moments when you get ahead of yourself I find that you are beside me because I am beside myself and I feel like the roadrunner who always seems so far ahead of the coyote that he has always already arrived at the destination before the coyote has even begun to move. But this may be subject to reversal, as in the case of the tortoise and the hare (*la liebre*, which I prefer as jackrabbit rather than hare, because I remember seeing them leap more than run across the headlights of our car going back to our house in Greenbrae after having dined at Sabella's Italian restaurant where we could watch the lobsters propelling themselves slowly and I remember wondering about those rubber bands on their claws and thinking that it must be difficult for them to hold a pencil and write about their own experiences of seeing diners stare at them and wondering why I identified with them more than with the people walking around them, perhaps as a premonition that foreign languages would be important to me and that I would one day describe reading in a foreign language as swimming in a dark aquarium), and the coyote, like the tortoise, might in the long run pass the hare (by the skin of its teeth), asymptomatically and asymptotically, just at the moment before the cloud he's standing on disappears and we catch the quizzical look in his eye before he ends up at the bottom of a canyon, the moment of impact shrouded in a cloud of dust, curiously mirroring the actual floating cloud that he had just been standing on before his precipitous fall.

REMAKING THE READYMADE

Yesterday I thought I had an idea about the readymade that went beyond my mere playing around with a title like "Remaking the Readymade," but I somehow lost it or it simply slipped my mind. As is my usual modus operandi, I tried to retrace my steps logically (though, were my original steps logical?) to somehow magically incant (decant? descant?) the idea, to get it to spontaneously pop up in my head again. I went back to the bookcase where I'd just collected and sorted through four or five books by Alberto Savinio and I leafed through them once more to see if something would stir my memory. But, really, how can you recall something that happened spontaneously, or recreate the conditions for the possibility of cloning a misplaced cell (a lost cell or soul), out of the blue, into another surprise (to splice a sequence of DNA into another near miss)? Perhaps this replicates a version of Proust's voluntary versus involuntary memory. Let's agree not to disagree.

Then I glanced at another book I'd picked up earlier because of a footnote that mentioned Daniel Spoerri in Craig Dworkin's *No Medium* (which is itself an excellent medium for reflection). Then it struck me that I'd thumbed through my copy of *An Anecdoted Topography of Chance*, so I picked it up again and flicked through the pages until I saw the entry that I'd lit upon before—entry 63, Roll of Scotch tape—but nothing struck me (even that tape didn't stick) at

the moment (except for the words "used up" and "surprised").
But then I remembered walking back toward my desk, perhaps
thinking of another idea concerning transparent tape and the concept
of transparency in Aira's work—how the tape could hold something
together but since it's transparent you could see through it to the
jagged edges of the paper that had been jury-rigged or jigsawed
back to together. And what if this tape were also a kind of recording
tape that preserved (corralled) one's stray thoughts to remind one
of them (like magic) or simply to remember the fact that you'd
forgotten, but not *what* you'd forgotten. And what if that transparent
tape had something to do with the allegory of writing in Aira's work,
that this allegory was not hidden, opaque or obscure, but showed
through its own transparency to an idea of allegory that is always
there—simply that writing is always about something else.

At this point I was a bit frustrated because I had forgotten the
"original" idea, but I was also thinking of how Aira links the concept
of forgetting to invention in his book on Copi (of keeping the writing
moving forward despite all obstacles: "*El olvido es el imperativo
de seguir adelante*" (33) [Forgetting is the imperative of moving
forward]) and also where he mentions that anecdote about the
man who invented an alloy of rubber of graphite that allows one
to write and erase at the same time: "*La memoria es el acto de
pederla, el borrado. Como aquel inventor que pasó cuarenta años
perfeccionando una aleación de grafito y goma, para lograr un lápiz
que escribiera y borrara a la vez*" (33) [Memory is the act of losing it,
erasure. Like that inventor who spent forty years perfecting an alloy
of graphite and rubber to produce a pencil that would be able to
write and erase at the same time].

So, despite the frustration and as if to please myself in
compensation, I thought of something (I remembered something
else) from a conversation I'd had with a friend some two days before
when he mentioned that he was going to put out a record on vinyl of
a female harpist and how she had to drive to all her performances.
I had this image of her driving around towing a trailer attached to
the back of her car containing only her harp as if it were a horse
in a horse trailer. I don't know why this reminded me being in our
family station wagon on the highway when I was little and being

fascinated at how still the horses were in their trailers as we drove past them on our way to Clear Lake, their stately heads (I imagined) and whimsical wisps of their tails twitching, belying the speed of the vehicles in which they rode. I must have been thinking of the "cheval" from *A Town Called Panic*.

(And now, as I write this, I'm remembering those nights when we were driving back across the Golden Gate Bridge from San Francisco to Marin, lying down and looking backward, up through the swirling fog and yellow lights toward the erector set towers in a mismatch or wash of memory, where the towers reach into space and everything appears upside down as the car moves forward, and I am looking back, through the window of the station wagon as the fog trails plumes of smoke, at the frozen breath exhaled by a monster)

So, though still a little miffed about losing the "original" idea ("in the forest losing the trees" (Zukofsky)) I also smiled ("*sonrisa seria*") because it made me think of how I like to say that you never really forget an idea, it will come back when you least expect it (smile! you're on candid camera). So I was poking fun at myself for trying to reenact the "chance" circumstances in order to reproduce the original idea which was just a momentary slip and probably not as profound as I was coming to think of it, or as I had originally thought of it in the first place (see Joe Brainard's "Art"), except for the fact that the more time I spent trying to remember the more it inverted the whole project or invested it with more meaning than it perhaps ever called for, if only for the colossal waste of time.

The next morning I decided to think of something else, so I put on an unmastered version of a CD my friend was going to release by the Argentinean composer Federico Durand, called *El idioma de las luciérnagas*. As I was walking back to my desk I heard the first strains of sound and I immediately (simultaneously) realized two things—first, that I had been listening to these initial sounds yesterday at exactly the moment when I had had that idea about the readymades and, second, that that idea popped into my head again precisely because the sounds reminded me of the sounds I was hearing when I had first thought of the idea—the hint of wind chimes—which prompted a link to the Orphic lyre and the Aeolian harp (harp!), but as if someone were "playing" them. And yet, how can someone *play* the wind chimes, aren't they "played" by the wind that passes through them; how can you "play" a musical box, don't you just lift the lacquered wood cover of the box and listen to the music; how *can* you play the wind chimes—but it's about listening, no? You can learn to hear moments of sound and try to capture them or at least "play along" with them in midflight of mind, so too with the readymade—it's already there (already ready—¡que listas son!) just waiting to be noticed and recorded for what it is— and it isn't what it is until you hear it. The readymade is already made, yes, but it's still ready to be turned into something else by tuning into something else, your ears like two dolphins swimming in tandem. So, how do you "play" the wind chimes, how do you use genre conventions to create something new out of something that's already been done? How can you remake a readymade? Well, you need to be ready (prepared as in prepared music; present in the sense of being there for the other; procedure as in previous to the process). And you need to see and to read the word "read" in ready, to see that reading is like swimming in the seas of language (your eyes like two dolphins swimming in tandem), plotting a course of sentences, grooving along the waves' grooves, and at a certain point—surprise!—the flip of a switch—and reading becomes writing. If writing is remaking what you've already read, then reading is a readymade and writing is perceiving that it is what it is and also that it isn't what it is until you read it. What could it be? It is what it could be, taken out of context (like the ragged edges of a jury-rigged, jigsawed quotation) and put into writing. Reading is writing from the margins, in the margins, and through the margins until the book becomes the cook and the cookbook is a readymade and the recipes a manual of procedures and each attempt (essay) will be a unique instance (instant) a new soufflé (a new shuffle), *A Bout de Souffle* (*Breathless*), and when you are ready, ("you just might find...") that when you hear the wind you too can chime in ("...you get what you need"). I was lost until I found sound. Or sound found me.

THE BIRTH OF METAPHOR

When I was a kid we used to get all of our electronics through my great uncle Attilio (Uncle Til—my mother called him "Uncle Tonoose") who seemed to know everybody and worked as a salesman at Ayoob Bros. Television & Appliances in San Francisco. We had an old black and white Packard that was our own "kids' TV" in the playroom.

(Perhaps someday I'll say more about how we watched sci-fi stuff— *Star Trek, Lost in Space, Outer Limits, The Twilight Zone* and local programs on UHF like *Creature Features* and *Captain Satellite*—on this old TV with a fuzzy picture and snow that made all of the images we watched on it as unbelievable, unrealistic and ghostly as they should have been. That TV was the medium and the mode of both transmission and interference and never let us forget that we were tuning into another world via the twisted antennae of rabbit ears. We were never fooled by brilliant HD pictures that would have intruded upon our sense of unreality.)

The stories we heard of Til were things such as that he was a pretty good catcher and played for a time with the San Francisco Seals Baseball Club. We knew that we got our tickets to Giants' games through him—seriously, Box 1A, seats 1-4. Where we could almost reach out and touch "Giants"—Mays, McCovey and Marichal (imagine the feeling of seeing that high leg kick coming right at you?)—dressed as we were in our mini-versions of unofficial Giants uniforms. I remember thinking that this control tower in the parking lot at Candlestick was where the Giants announcers called the game. It didn't matter that my brothers laughed at this or that I couldn't have explained how the announcers could have called the game from a booth in the parking lot where they wouldn't have been able to even *see* the game. Whenever Til called on the phone to talk to my father, all that anyone who answered the phone ever heard was, "Eddy there?"

One of the radios we got through Til was a medium-sized console that my dad kept in the den. Needless to say, we rarely used this radio, and only could when my dad wasn't home. On nights when he was working at home, we could hear him behind the closed door of his den speaking into his Dictaphone (I always remember being fascinated at hearing his cadence and wondering why he would say the word "period" so often). I remember one evening in particular, and I have been remembering it through the years, perhaps simply because I keep remembering it. These were the days when designers thought of stereo equipment more as furniture than as technological devices. This particular console looked like a laminated fake wood double cube a little bigger than a bread box. You had to push in on each half of the box to release the spring catch of each half box which folded out into the left and right speakers. The display on the radio dial was fancier than that of an average radio and had a cool phosphorescent green light that backlit the numbers. I remember one particular evening being in the den by myself and turning on the radio to listen to the Giants game (because I had two older brothers it became necessary for us to have our own transistor radios so that we didn't have to listen to the game or be told what was happening secondhand by a brother who held a transistor against his ear to hog the feed and hide it from your hearing, making you dependent on hearing it through him rather than discovering the details on your own). I remember this particular evening because it was getting dark and yet I didn't want to turn the lights on because it was I was mesmerized by that green light on the dial and wanted to keep that secret (transparency) feeling secret for as long as possible. The Giants were playing the Cardinals and the game must have been in St. Louis because back then the Giants home games started at 8:00PM. I was sitting cross-legged on the floor in the growing dark and listening to Lon Simmons give the recap of the last half inning—runs, hits, errors—when I heard him say, "The Giants trail the Cardinals 5-3." And this is moment that I am calling "The Birth of Metaphor."

Metaphors do not put an image in your head or place a picture in your mind. You don't see them; if anything, they see you. They see how your mind works with them as if in an instant we suddenly get the nature of speed. Faster than the speed of light that you couldn't see anyway. Even if the green electric light, fizzed and phosphorescent, bled across the dial, that's not what makes you see or think you see. The fact of the Giants trailing the Cardinals just comes—it doesn't push some kind of button and make a "jungle" metaphor appear as if called out of the nethersphere by a genie. The room is getting dark and you don't want to turn the lights on because you might disturb the dusk that imagination comes to trust as its secret realism. The trail goes from eyes to mind and what you "see" is that you're moving through a different kind of dark that's not subject to visual enhancement or limitation. You realize that you're the one *doing* the thinking by moving through your mind, following a trail you are leaving behind and you can only make it out because you made it, even as it left you trailing behind yourself. They key is that once you set the scenario in motion it takes off on its own—it doesn't "play" out but leads you on a trail into the unknown and you don't know where you're going which is not a metaphor for birth, creativity or originality—just your imagination coming to grips with the birth of metaphor like Botticelli's Venus on a half-shell—a point where it becomes art that has no shelf life because its half-life is as infinite as its other half. Say the sea spray's *sillage*—you trail in its wake, you wake to trail it, you sleep in its wake, your dream makes the wake that trails after it. Memories wake up inside the sleep of metaphors—who's to say what's dreaming?—memories wake to dream again as metaphors. Or do metaphors dream of being memories. As a friend of mine once wrote, "WAKE SPEED, where 'wake' is a verb." Even if we drop the metaphor, we only wake in its wake.

MOEBIUS-DICK

It's about writing, not being a writer. That's the ticket. The allegory of writing doesn't explain what happens in the story, but it does allow us to see that there's more to the picture than meets the eye, more than giant blue silkworms and less than the autobiography of the writer; more precisely, as Aira would say, the focus is on the myth of the origin of the writer. Each new story adds a wrinkle to that foundational myth and thus changes it.

I remember an experience of going to *Playland* at the beach in San Francisco. I was younger than my brothers and their friends (as usual & obviously). They had slides and arcade stuff there. One

of the attractions was the "Record Player." When the gates were
opened all the experienced kids raced toward the center of the
record player's slippery, polished wood; a circular object that was
supposed to resemble a vinyl disc. Since I was slow and tentative, I
was forced to find room toward the outer rim of the mass of bodies.
When the disc started to turn and gradually pick up speed those
of us on the outer edge began to be thrown off toward the circular
gutter surrounding the disc. Physics people would know that there's
less spin (though more torque) toward the center and that the further
you move from the center the greater the speed and dizziness
(vertigo). I remember trying to stand up to go toward the exit and the
guy who ran the ride screaming at me because I couldn't tell where I
was going and I kept falling down anyway due to vertigo and the fact
the disc was still spinning even though I was no longer on it.

I once heard David Milch say this when he was talking about his
process: "Melville said that any good poem spins against its drive....
The only truly great scene is actually about the opposite of what it
appears to be about." The original quotation is from Melville's *Battle-
Pieces*. Like any good piece of writing, "It spins against the way it
drives."

HOW LIFE IMITATES AIRA

"*I ran to the living room. In a way I had already imagined the worst,
but one could never have guessed everything. That was due to
simultaneity. The mind was ahead of seeing, seeing was ahead of
the mind, and the two waited for each other to effect a coincidence
that would make time go backwards. But time had passed, and what
I feared most had happened. The window was open, water had
entered. I ran to close it, and a few drops wet my arms.*" (*Artforum*
10)

And then I remembered an idea from last summer or two summers
ago that I snatched out of the ether (and snapped me into it).
Before falling asleep in the afternoon, I was reading the opening
of Aira's novel *Artforum*, that really is about his obsession with
that magazine, in which it recounts a nap that "Aira" was taking

and then he's shaken out of it when he hears a thunderstorm and gradually remembers that since he has left the windows open, living as he does on the upper floors of an apartment building, he slowly becomes conscious of the fact that he needs to get up because the wind and rain will come through and ruin his books and magazines that are lying near the open windows. So, after reading this, I fall asleep. And then, after a brief slip (as opposed to sleep's *full* slip) off toward losing consciousness, I am slowly brought back as I hear the sounds of a thunderstorm and gradually remember that I've left the windows of my third floor apartment open and that I need to drag myself back into consciousness and get up and go close them because I've left piles of books beneath the windows and I don't want them to get wet and ruined. I remember thinking afterwards that Aira had written so much and I had read so many of his books (over one hundred *novelitas* and counting) that I was struck by the fact that if I lived long enough I would have to live through the same events that Aira had written about simply because he had written so much. At a certain point you realize that you can't be Proteus, so you have to become a chameleon. But, too, those who read and love books already live *through* them in the sense of being with them, not alongside but *within*, not just part of life but partial to it— we live through them and they live through us. This is what I wrote down on the nearest writing surface (wherever writing surfaces, a pen opens a new window) available to me at the time last summer (two summers ago?), which happened to be at the bottom of page 135 of a xeroxed copy of Gerald Murnane's *Tamarisk Row* (on the right-hand page—134— is a scribbled note that says *The Act of Killing* and then beneath a solid line, Mike Daisey, *The Agony and Ecstasy of Steve Jobs*):

I was reading Aira
in the rain and it was
raining in the story
as it was dark
and what it was about
was about to be
what comes between
words falling like rain
falling in the book like rain

"LO INCOMPRENSIBLE"

"Todo buena prosa es como nadar bajo el agua y aguantar la respiración." ¿Quién dijo eso? ¿Francis Scott Fitzgerald? ¿En una carta a su hija Scottie? De ser eso cierto, entonces leer esto es como ahogarse... (Rodrigo Fresán, *La parte inventada*)

It was when I was reading César Aira's essay "Lo Incomprensible" that I first came across the quotation from Proust that Aira cites in the midst of validating *not* understanding over understanding: "*Los libros que amamos parecen escritas en una lengua extranjera*" [The books we love seem to have been written in a foreign language]. It reminded me of my fascination with reading Spanish stories that I couldn't quite get, much less really understand. (I wrote a story once in a college Spanish class about a deer approaching a clear pool fringed with reeds. I think I eventually lost that story, but I remember that the whole time I was writing I was thinking that the key was that the description of the pool was really that of an eye, and the whole thing was an allegory. When I think back now I'd like to believe that the allegory wasn't merely mechanical because I was already trying to write in Spanish and thus finding words in another "key" to match a meaning key, thus already switching levels through the medium of a dark aquarium). Reading in a foreign language is like swimming in a dark aquarium.

I was always encouraged to pursue my interest in language. I still recall the feeling I would get when I heard my father talking on the phone to his mother (or Uncle Til) in the "Zeneize" (Genoese) dialect. I'd hear this strange baby-talk music jolted out of phase by occasional English words thrown in like rocks in a stream. I remember Señor Carillo teaching us Spanish songs in the sixth grade ("*Naranja dulce, limón partido, / Dame un abrazo que yo te pido...*"). I loved saying, singing and thinking on the cusp between knowing and not knowing as if not knowing and not understanding were the gateway to some deeper understanding or secret knowledge, or perhaps just something else I'd never thought of before (The New). In middle school I remember Señorita Stillinger and her bubbly, snappy manner and her big yellow pen that hung from a chain around her neck. I remember that she called Sandy

Woodhouse "*Casa de Madera*" and Frank "*Paco.*" In high school
I remember Señor Carrasco, his distinguished aquiline nose and
his sharp, angular precision mirrored by the Spanish memorabilia
discreetly pinned to the walls and by his crisp pronunciation (so
different from Señora Martinez who was Cuban and in whom I first
noticed the different pronunciation as when she said "Cuba" that "*b*"
went from "*b*" to "*v*" and then just disappeared).

I spent the last two years of high school taking advanced Spanish
from Señora Diffley, who was called "Madame Diffley" by her
students in advanced French, but she gave her Spanish students
her secret name—"*La Bruja*" (the witch). She was fluent in both
languages and had lived in many countries as her husband had
served in the diplomatic corps. She was also an accomplished stage
actress and I remember her giving me an improvised lesson in how
to project one's voice on stage by projecting it outward above the
heads of the audience. Later, when I was in college and came back
to visit her, I remember asking her, in the arrogance of youth, why
she had "settled" for teaching high school rather than college where
she could have, I imagined, explored the "deeper profundities" (I
just now recall that she used to grade our papers with two marks,
one for "*Forma*" and one for "*Fondo*" (depth)). I remember not quite
understanding her response to me at that time (not in the way that
I do now). She said that she liked engaging with students before
their minds had hardened, and while they were still just pecking their
way out of their fragile eggshell minds (perhaps I'm post-channeling
The Doors here) and were still open to surprise and wonder and
not interested in developing arguments and hardening/freezing the
quickness of their thoughts into petrified theories and criticism. After
I had finished college and sent my wildebeest of a thesis to her (with
the frightfully ponderous title of "Moby-Dick: The Fateful Weave of
the Text in Flux"; a title only rivaled in the audacity of its tin ear by
a paper I had written on Cubism that I'd called "Melting the Cubes
of Rectangular Emotion"), I recall her note back to me counseling
against the incipient pessimism of the thesis and saying that the
indefinable "whiteness" didn't have to lead to nothingness and death.
I think there was also an allusion to Neruda's *Residencia en al Tierra*
or *Las Alturas de Macchu Picchu*. She was very indulgent of my
whims and let me sit in the corner away from the other students in

the class (another of my habitual "attention getting devices"). There were only five or six students in those classes for my final two years of Spanish. I remember reading *El Gesticulador*, Lorca's *La Casa de Bernarda Alba*, Galdos's *Doña Perfecta*, etc. I remember that she gave me a copy of Elena Garro's *Los Recuerdos del Porvenir,* which I dismissively put aside in favor of Joyce, Kafka, and Dostoevsky. This would have been in the years 1977-8. It wasn't until a couple of years ago that I located some of Garro's novels via Interlibrary Loan and the whole time that I was reading I thought of *"La Bruja"* and of the many gifts and buried treasures she had given us (or had she merely hinted at the possibility of treasures that were always just beyond the threshold of understanding, and that that was the true gift of reading, that real readers read for what they don't know or have forgotten somewhere buried in the coils of their cortex like some impossible core text), as if these books were a series of Aladdin's lamps and whenever we opened them, thought with them and through them, we became genies and mingled spirits once again across the gulfs of time.

I am either getting further and further into this story or memory or making these memories into a story, either burrowing into or spiraling out, burrowing centripetally or spiraling centrifugally, but into or out of what?

I still have my copy of Jorge Luis Borges' *Ficciones* from my senior year Spanish class with Señora Diffley. On the first page of the front matter it's stamped with the words "Language Lab" and "San Rafael" (all this in bright red, stamp pad ink). The word "Language" runs vertically down the page while the word "Lab" runs horizontally taking the same *"L"* from "Language." There is also the stamped image of a bulldog's head because we were the San Rafael High School Bulldogs (If you are interested, I did not "steal this book"; at the end of the year we were given the option of purchasing the copy we used for the course). I love the color of the cover and the simplicity of its design which belies the complexity that is "contained" within its covers (there are times when the cover doesn't camouflage, or is it that the color is the camouflage that makes its simplicity discernible by masking its complexity?). On one line it reads "JORGE LUIS" and on the next "BORGES," followed by a thin horizontal line below which appears the title "FICCIONES." There is a half-inch rectangular border that frames the whole cover, a border within the borders of the book itself (as the cover is a map that brackets the territory of the text). At the base of the cover the publisher's name "EMECÉ" (E^3=mc) appears. All of the writing, including the thin horizontal line and the inner border, is in *white*. I'm intrigued by the title, which is *Ficciones*, not *cuentos, relatos,* or *historias*. I think it gives a better sense of the pure imagination involved in these pages (codes in codex) which really aren't merely stories, tales, histories, nor anything I had ever seen before. All of the lettering on the cover is in white and the cover is smudged and foxed by age to reveal further patches of whiteness beneath—blemishes, marks, blurs—so that it resembles a partially erased chalkboard. Not a blackboard, because the color is light purple or blue, periwinkle or lavender (perhaps an "invisible yet enduring lilac") which seems to prompt a sense of tranquility that is at once strangely natural and clearly unnatural. It's as if the infinity within were partially erased, or that infinity itself mirrored the partially erased imagination.

What I'd been thinking of saying when I started this digression concerned an anecdote that actually happened and meant enough to me that I've continued telling it over the years (it's been exactly forty years now), so that the original has been erased through the series of improvised retellings. The story itself, like Borges' *Ficciones*, is an uncanny palimpsest; what is told or written, now, is both partially erased and partially rewritten.

In the advanced Spanish class we were frequently left to read on our own during the class period. I remember that it was during one such session that I was reading a Borges story (perhaps "Las Ruinas Circulares"). I was patiently, and perhaps too scrupulously, going through the process of "reading" the story by switching back and forth between the text and my Spanish dictionary. This was a painstaking process because there were so many words that I didn't recognize. And then, since I was trying to figure out the meaning of the story and not just the meaning of the words, I ended up looking up words I already knew just to see if I'd perhaps missed something in the definitions the first time around that might somehow have held the key to the mystery. At a certain point during this grueling activity I seemed to notice (carefully ensconced as I was in my favorite corner of the classroom) that someone was looking at me. I had an intuitive sense that it was "*La Bruja*" since the other students were engaged in their own reading just as I was. I began to feel a surge of pride, related to my desire for getting attention being satisfied at that moment, feeling that she must have been so impressed at my dedicated desire to decipher this difficult text as seen in my constantly stopping my reading in mid-sentence to look up yet another obscure word in the dictionary. I felt her get up from her desk and I saw her approach me out of the corner of my eye, but I still did not look up, savoring that delicious sense of attention and feeling that she was going to praise my dedicated and assiduous work. When she was standing next to me (I still hadn't looked up), I felt her reach down with her hand and close the cover of the dictionary I was using at that moment. Then I looked up and she said, "Señor Biglieri, how will you ever come to understand the Spanish soul if you don't immerse yourself in the language, regardless of whether you understand the definition of every word?" Maybe she didn't use those exact words, but that was the gist. And this came to mind while I was reading Aira's essay "*Lo Incomprensible*," where he mentions an anecdote from his own reading of Proust when he was fifteen years old. And this sense of the gist ("*Los libros que amamos parecen escritas en una lengua extranjera*" [The books we love seem to have been written in a foreign language]) struck home in relation to my reading of Borges— what fascinated me most was the mystery of *not* understanding and this would never be dispelled, dissolved, simplified or solved (channeling Coleridge on the secondary imagination: "It dissolves, diffuses, dissipates, in order to re-create")—each separate fiction a miniature archaic torso of Apollo, or the colossal fragment of Constantine's foot on display outside the Capitoline museum in Rome. And since I was reading these fictions in Spanish, all of this was happening in a foreign language, which magnifies the mystery exponentially. If I had understood his stories, perhaps I would have forgotten them. It was because I couldn't decipher them that I would always return to find more in them and more in me. The spell—to conjure in these fictions the genie from the Aladdin's lamp of the text and never to dispel it by understanding it—to nudge open the door to infinity and get lost there in gardens of gloss (as in those other "imaginary gardens with real toads"). I would never stop glossing no matter where I looked, no matter how far I wandered in my own labyrinths, in search of lost time.

"Only a language experiment:"

a Few Reflections on Translating the 1855 "Song of Myself" into French

☆

Éric Athenot

Prelude: why translate the 1855 *Leaves*?

Whitman's poetry has mostly circulated outside the US in the form of the so-called "Deathbed edition," published in 1891-1892. It came with a special mention from the author on the copyright page that it should be regarded as "[his] concluding words," closing a poetic career which had occupied him on and off for the past thirty-seven years.[1] The complete Deathbed has been translated twice into French. First came the sedate but pioneering translation by Léon Bazalgette (1873-1928), in 1909. Bazalgette, friends with several European men of letters—among whom Stefan Zweig—, was a noted Whitman enthusiast and propagator. Not content with publishing the first-ever complete Deathbed in French, he released a two-volume panegyric of the poet, grandly entitled Le *"Poème-Évangile" de Walt Whitman*—a straightforward allusion to Whitman's "Starting from Paumanok," in

---

1 Whitman's recommendation is the following: "As there are now several editions of L. of G., I wish to say that I prefer and recommend this present one, complete, for future printings, if there shoudl be any; a copy and fac-simile, indeed, of the text of these 438 pages. The subsequent adjusting interval which is so important to form'd and launch'd work, books especially, has pass'd; and waiting till fully after that, I have given (pages 423-438) my concluding words."
(https://whitmanarchive.org/published/LG/1891/images/leaf006v.html)

which the speaker states his ambition to write "the poem-evangel of comrades, and of love".[2] This particular translation, although immensely instrumental in disseminating Whitman across Europe and beyond, was very early on criticized for the propensity shown by its author systematically to censor any remotely homoerotic allusion or imagery.[3] Such an attitude is precisely what Zweig emphasized approvingly in the pages he devoted to Bazalgette in his memoir, *The World of Yesterday*:

> My friend of friends was Léon Bazalgette, whose name is improperly omitted from most accounts of modern French literature, in which it stood for something exceptional, namely that he exclusively employed his creative energy in fostering the work of others, and thus saved up his truly amazing intensity for the person he loved. [...] He had devoted ten years to making Walt Whitman known to the French by translating all his poems and by his monumental biography. His life's aim was to carry the intellectual outlook beyond its frontiers, and to make his compatriots more manly and more comradely with this example of a free world-loving man: the best of Frenchmen, he was at the same time a passionate anti-nationalist.[4]

The second, and to this day only alternative French translation of the complete Deathbed was published by Gallimard in 2002. Its author, Jacques Darras (b. 1939), a former university professor, is an untiring promoter of American poetry in France.[5] His translation of *Leaves of Grass,* appearing in the prestigious Poésie/Gallimard collection, occupies an enviable position as the most visible and most affordable collection of Whitman's verse in French. It was preceded by a two-volume selection of poems a decade or so earlier by the same translator but with a different publisher, Grasset. The two are still available commercially, and the link between them is far from

2 Walt Whitman. *Leaves of Grass* (edited by Sculley Bradley and Harold W. Blodgett). New York: W. W. Norton & Company, 1973, p. 19.
3 Pages 115-156 of Betsy Erkkila's *Whitman Among the French: Poet and Myth* (Princeton: Princeton University Press, 1980) offer a thorough analysis of—among others—Paul Claudel's and André Gide's response to Bazalgette's "heterosexualizing" of Whitman's poems.
4 Zweig, Stefan [1943]. *The World of Yesterday*. London: Viking Press, 1945, p. 136.
5 A complete bibliography of Jacques Darras can be found at http://www.jacquesdarras.com/biobibliographie/bibliographie

obvious, with the Grasset edition having finally evolved to offer the complete Deathbed. What is apparent to the careful reader, however, is the liberties taken by Darras with the original in both editions as is his refusal to accept the limits imposed by Whitman's lexicon and the meanings particular words in this lexicon may have had in the 19th century. This sometimes makes for arresting options. It often leaves the present writer perplexed if not downright unimpressed at carelessness posing as invention.

A reader not familiar with the lengthy evolution of Whitman's poetry collection could quite justifiably wonder why anyone would want to translate the first of the six successive editions. Most scholars and Whitman afficionados, in the US and abroad, will nevertheless admit to some degree of fascination with the 1855 edition. No one has articulated my own reasons for preferring the first edition above all others more convincingly and elegantly than J. M. Coetzee:

> The rule of thumb in the scholarly world is to take an author's last revision, his or her last word, as definitive. But there are exceptions, cases where the critical consensus is that the late revision is inferior to or even traduces the original. Thus we tend to read the 1805 version of Wordsworth's autobiographical poem *The Prelude* in preference to the 1850 revision. In much the same way, one might argue in favor of reading Whitman's early poems in their first published form, since his tendency after 1865 was to revise in the direction of the "poetic" (i.e., the Tennysonian) in the hope of winning a wider readership.[6]

To my eyes, one of the most distinctive and endearing features of the 1855, besides being a beautiful artefact,[7] is precisely—to rephrase Coetzee's judgment—its "unpoetic" audacity. Unpoetic, indeed, the book seemed to most of its contemporary readers, just as unpoetic enough, apparently, were Emily Dickinson's poems to justify a thorough rewriting by her first editors. As regards Whitman's unpoeticity, the reviews of the 1855 *Leaves*, even when negative, register some of the spell it still casts on its readers more than one hundred years on.

6 Coetzee, J.M., "Love and Walt Whitman", *The New York Review of Books*, Sept. 22, 2005, Vol. 52, N°14
(http://www.nybooks.com/articles/2005/09/22/love-and-walt-whitman/)
7 A complete electronic edition of the 1855 edition with page images can be accessed on the irreplaceable Walt Whitman Archive at
https://whitmanarchive.org/published/LG/1855/whole.html

Called an "odd genius" by Charles A. Dana writing in the 23 July, 1855, New York *Daily Tribune*, labeled a "monster" by Rufus W. Griswold in the 10 November, 1855, edition of *The Criterion*, Whitman had penned a "curious and lawless collection of poems" according to Charles Eliot Norton writing in the September, 1855, edition of *Putnam's Magazine*. Looking back on his poetic career, the poet famously remarked to his confidante Horace Traubel that *Leaves of Grass* was "only a language experiment, [...] an attempt to give the spirit, the body, the man, new words, new potentialities of speech."[8] And this is precisely the language-oriented character of the 1855 which drew me to attempt the first translation into French.

The foreignness of Whitman

During the eighteen months I spent working on the translation of the 1855 *Leaves* I complied with no particular theoretical principles. Having carried out the exercise myself on a few occasions, I was only too keenly conscious of how easy and frequently pointless it can be to write a critique of other people's translations (this made me aware of the fact that the reservations voiced above about the complete translations of the Deathbed edition reflect my own sensibility and probably my own limitations too as a reader and as a Whitman scholar). Having taught Whitman at university for half a decade by the time I endeavored to try my hand at translating the 1855 *Leaves*, one thing had progressively dawned on me: nowhere in the various translations available on the market did I "hear" what I imagined to be Whitman's French voice. I had gradually internalized a voice which had some degree of ponderousness, was not averse to quicksilver changes of tone and register, spoke in a kind of endless flow, while striving to mesmerize its audience into more or less full adhesion. I use the word "audience" on purpose, as I felt that what I missed most in the existing French translations of Whitman was precisely their lack of a consistent vocal dimension, a tone-deafness to the kind of sermon-like cadences and imagery which David H. Reynolds has so convincingly identified as one of the pillars of 19th-century literary imagination.[9] Whitman's own cherished "vocalism"—rooted in his love

8 Horace, Traubel [1987]. Foreword to "An American Primer," in Whitman, Walt. *An American Primer*. Stevens Point: Holy Cow! Press, pp. viii-ix.
9 See David H. Reynolds. *Beneath the American Renaissance* (Oxford: Oxford University Press, 1988), p. 21: "The new popular sermons were filled with unusual images

of Italian opera—makes for a poetry that is begging to be performed, to be read out by and grounded in a speaking body, making "voice" not just the usual topos of literary criticism but calling on the human vocal cords as an organ active in the production of poetic meaning and playing a key part towards sharing this elusive meaning with the audience through the corresponding sense—hearing. The concluding lines of later poem entitled "Vocalism," for that matter, call for a voice "which has the quality to strike and to unclose," a voice "which has the quality to bring forth what lies slumbering forever ready in all words." (Whitman 1973, 384) If translation can be approached as performance[10] then performing Whitman's poetry meant for me to take into account the specificity of Whitman's idiom and syntax, its sermon-like periods, the particularity of its lexicon and the high/low register and make it performable, i.e., find the middle ground between the American-language original and a French version that, to my ears at least, would, while read out by a French performer, sound naturally French while retaining its unmistakable Whitmanian ring.

These feelings led me to try and work in keeping with what Antoine Berman—a French post-Benjaminian translation studies theorist—termed "the experience of the foreign." What I felt while translating the 1855 *Leaves* was the absolute need to keep true to what he calls "the strangeness of the foreign work."[11] Such a strangeness implied in this case being attuned to the numerous particular features of the original and their uncongeniality vis-à-vis the French language. To my mind, trying to make those features heard in the target language and acceptable to the readers of that language was not just to be regarded as an illustration of the faithfulness which any translator is too frequently and too routinely asked to demonstrate in his/her translation. Berman's "experience of the foreign" implies that the target language in which a translation is being carried out must strive to welcome as best it can features from the source language. After all, he reminds his reader, these features confer a given text its

that showed the 19th-century religionist search for poetic alternatives to doctrine. These images, however, were unpremeditated, unrestrained. This combination of artifice and artlessness was noticed by the major authors."

10 Among the many scholarly books and articles devoted to the matter, I would just like to point out the introduction to *Theatre Translation in Performance* (Silvia Bigliazzi, Peter Kofler and Paola Ambrosi, eds.). New York: Routledge, 2013, p. 3), in which "the ideas of translation and performance" are analyzed as "coterminous," translation being viewed "*as* performance" (emphasis in the original).

11 Antoine Berman [1984]. *The Experience of the Foreign: Culture and Translation in Romantic Germany* (trans. S Heyvaert). Albany: State of New York Press, 1992, p. 5.

actual literary uniqueness within its own culture. In this regard I will go one step further and argue that in Whitman's case, by challenging the translator to make these features amenable to his/her language, the features making his poetry unique within his own culture should actually be relied on to guide him/her on the road to experiment with his/her own language.

Most of Whitman's many rhetorical devices, as I have already hinted, happen to be highly uncongenial to the French language and recur at regular intervals in the 1855 version of "Song of Myself." These features impact the complex transaction between the poem's *I* and *you* carried out throughout the poem, and they reveal with what care Whitman crafted his verse, a care which is too often downplayed and which may at times appear absent from his later creations. As far as I am concerned, the freedom supposedly inherent in Whitman's free verse[12] does not stand the test of close reading and calls for a translator who is sensitive to the precarious balance—what is frequently referred in the poems to as the "tally"—Whitman keeps between the micro- and the macrostructures.

I will start with the most minimal micro-structures to be found in the 1855 "Song of Myself," the two personal pronouns acting as the poem's protagonist/antagonist—*I* and *you*. A reader not familiar with romance languages may wonder what is so difficult about translating these two pronouns. *I* would logically be rendered as *je* and *you*—well this is where trouble begins. Not only are both pronouns gendered in French but the second can also be numbered, depending on whether it refers to one person or several people. I hope to show that, except for a handful of cases, that was not the problem. *You* also implies a concern with register which English-languages users are usually unaware of: in the case of an individual *you* is the poem's speaker addressing this individual formally (*vous*) or informally (*tu*)? The translator has to choose. And I will claim that in this particular case, this choice felt—and still feels to me as I write these words—as a defeat. I chose *tu* (which is more intimate and more immediate) but still resent having had to make a choice and not leave this option as open as in the original.

As for *I*. The various titles given to the poem can be relied on to decide that its protagonist is male. While untitled in the 1855 edition,

---

12 Donald D. Kummings, in *A Companion to Walt Whitman* (Malden, MA: Wiley-Black-well, 2009, p. 383) writes that the "long line captures the expansive freedom of Whitman's poetic style and evokes his vision of an expansive American culture."

the poem was printed as "Poem of Walt Whitman, an American" in the second, pared down to just "Walt Whitman" in the third before receiving the splendid title by which it has been known since 1881— "Song of Myself." This poem does not shy from stressing the *I*'s manly features, particularly in the famous section narrating a scene of lovemaking in the June grass, now section 5 in the final version of the poem. Whereas the "vampiric"[13] partner is not gendered and may or may not be the soul, the concluding lines of the section make no mystery that *I* is male since the elusive *you* "reached till you felt my beard, and reached till you held my feet."[14]

Yet believing this male *I* to be Walt Whitman is to take a huge leap, which I am not sure a close reading of the poem would confirm. As a matter of fact, something usually unaccounted for happens to the *I* in one of the poem's key sections, which I will quote fully now:

> Walt Whitman, an American, one of the roughs, a kosmos,
> Disorderly fleshy and sensual . . . . eating, drinking and breeding,
> No sentimentalist . . . .no stander above men and women or part from
> them . . . . no more modest than immodest. (Whitman 2008, 94)

One might be forgiven for rushing to the conclusion that this "Walt Whitman"—who as an individual did not yet exist, as the copyright title page reminds us[15]—is to be equated with the poem's ubiquitous *I*. Yet one should note that precisely as the name appears so is the *I* notable for its absence from the lines. Added to the numerous dots printed in succession—a feature which Whitman unwisely removed from the second edition onwards—the disappearance of the *I* may be read as an invitation among others not to read these lines literally, not to make ours the facile assumption that *I* = "Walt Whitman" = the flesh-and-blood originator of the poem who had not yet chosen for himself this nom de plume.

I will deal with Whitman's present participles shortly, which I chose, for reasons I will explain later, *never* to render as present

13 I borrowed this adjective from Ed Folsom's introduction to the section available at https://iwp.uiowa.edu/whitmanweb/en/writings/song-of-myself/section-5
14 Walt Whitman. *Leaves of Grass* (Éric Athenot, trans.). Paris: Éditions José Corti, 2008, p. 58.
15 The copyright page reads as follows: "Entered according to Act of Congress in the year 1855, by WALTER WHITMAN, in the Clerk's office of the District Court of the United States for the Southern District of New York." (cf. https://whitmanarchive.org/published/LG/figures/ppp.00271.009.jpg). "Walter Whitman" was also the correspondent to whom Emerson sent his famous letter of appreciation.

participles in French. When it comes to this particular passage, however, they happen here to enable the lines to sway between two poles, the first and the third singular persons, making it possible to read "Walt Whitman" both as the first-person speaker of the verse and its third-person subject-matter. The challenge in French was to find verbs which would accommodate a form that could be construed in either person. The French version runs as follows:

> Walt Whitman, américain, dur à cuire, kosmos,
> Charnel et sensuel jusqu'au désordre . . . . mange trinque copule,
> Pas sentimental pour deux sous . . . . pas du genre à se tenir
>   au-dessus des hommes et des femmes ni à part d'eux . . . . ni
>   pudique ni impudique. (Whitman 2008, 95)

The only verb group making it possible in French to link each verb to a first- or third-person indifferently is the first group, i.e. verbs ending with an "e" in both first and third persons. That was easy to do for "eating" and "breeding." The former I translated as "mange" (which can come either after the first or the third person), and for the latter I decided to pun, thanks to the verb "copuler," which means to "have sex," but through which I hoped to hint at the noun "copule" ("copula"), the arch-example of which in English if the verb *be*, slippery identity being exactly what I tried to foreground in translating these lines. "Standing" comes in my translation with the reflexive pronoun "se," bending the passage toward the third person. As for "drinking," it took me three printings of my translation to settle on a solution which makes the lines slightly more colloquial than I wanted them originally to be but "boire"— the verb I first used—has one form for the first person—"bois"—and one for the third—"boit," and I therefore belatedly resolved to do away with it. "Trinquer" comes from the German *trinken* and derives from the same proto-Germanic etymon, *drenkan*. I resigned myself to use it once I had decided that keeping the first/third-person ambiguity was more important to me than adhering to one fixed meaning or register, despite the risk of making the lines sound slightly more informal and festive than they may sound in the original ("trinquer" indeed is closer to "toast" or "drink to something" than to the more neutral "drink"). The way I chose to translate this passage acknowledges my perception of the poem's *I* as being polymorphous and striving to occupy as much of the whole pronominal spectrum as possible, being both *I* and *he*—the aptest confirmation of this being when Whitman condenses the *I* + *he* + present participle triad into "I am he attesting sympathy"[16] (Whitman 2008, 92).

The more obvious pronominal dialogue occurring in the 1855 "Song of Myself" is, of course, that between the *I* and the *you*. For that matter, the whole poem can be read as forming an arc from its first word—*I*—to its last—*you*. As I hinted earlier, this, for me, may be where translating this poem proved most slippery and self-defeating. This, still in keeping with Berman's call for the translator to cultivate the "strangeness of the foreign" in the target language, led me to make choices as to the translation of the English *you* which impacted on how the lines themselves would unfold. I will use the poem's opening as an example:

> I CELEBRATE myself,
> And what I assume you shall assume,
> For every atom belonging to me as good belongs to you (Whitman 2008, 50).

My translation runs as follows:

> Je me célèbre moi,
> Et mes vérités seront tes vérités,
> Car tout atome qui m'appartient t'appartient aussi à toi (Whitman 2008, 51).

There are no clues as to the *you*'s gender or whether the *I* is addressing one or several people. I chose to go for the most intimate option, the second-person singular, which denotes singularity and informality—*tu*, here to be found in various guises as *tes, t',* and *toi*.[17] The apparently casual use of the words reveals a very careful ordering on Whitman's part, with the first line being contained between *I* and *myself*, the second having *I* and *you* in perfect symmetry (two words before *I*, two after *you*) and finally, *you* being and having the last word in line 3. French cannot naturally replicate this word order, if only because the

---

16 The edition of the 1844 Webster's dictionary lists four definitions of "sympathy," each relevant to Whitman's strategy: 1) "Fellow feeling;" 2) "An agreement of affections or inclinations;" 3) "In medicine, a correspondence of various parts of the body in similar sensations or affections;" 4) "In natural history, a propension of inanimate things to unite, or to act on each other."

17 The singular pronoun—*yourself*—appears one page later and therefore confirms the fact that the *you* is meant to be addressed at—or at least received by—one addressee.

pronouns, when used as complements, are expected to come before the verb (hence "Je *me* célèbre", and "*t'*appartient"). I felt it necessary to emphasize these pronouns by doubling them (hence the use of "moi," in line 1, and "toi," in line 3). I adopted the exact same strategy for the poem's concluding line—"I stop some where waiting for you (Whitman 2008, 170) by doubling the final pronoun ("Je suis arrêté quelque part et n'attends que *toi*") (Whitman 2008, 171). Only could this doubling of the pronouns enable me to keep the progression from the *I* to the *you*, which I see as giving the poem its thrust and making the *I*—and the *Myself* of the title—vehicles for identification and final appropriation by its readers. In doing so I was aware of upsetting the lines' verbal economy, a notion that is of paramount importance when translating such expansive lines as Whitman's and all the more crucial as translation studies specialists usually estimate word-count increase from English to French at between 10 and 20%.[18]

On being economical

In trying to be true to what I perceived to be Whitman's pronominal strategy, I also seized on the expansiveness of his lines in paradoxical fashion. I tried in my translation to work against the received wisdom encapsulated by Kummings' statement quoted earlier. One would, after all, be forgiven for thinking that any translator dealing with such a monumental piece as "Song of Myself" would feel both unconstrained by the length of the lines, their deceivingly apparent explicitness and be liberated by the sheer size of the poem. Most French translators of Whitman's verse seems in that respect to have been oblivious to the poet's description of *Leaves of Grass* as "only a language experiment." The consensus among them seems to have been that syntax and grammar should be treated in a fairly straightforward manner. Present participles call for present participles, and Whitman's trademark repetitions entail straightforward repetitions in French, rendered verbatim. I, for my part, have always felt that the greatest risk run by anyone translating Whitman into French was, while keeping his/her attention focussed on the many stylistic constraints inherent in the poems, fall a prey to the surface boundlessness of the lines. Because French lacks the concision and economy of English, I resolved to be as economical as possible in my rendition of Whitman's

18 See, for example, the chart at
https://www.andiamo.co.uk/resources/expansion-and-contraction-factors.

lines to try and reach some degree of poeticity by not posing as garrulous and slangy in a desperate effort not to make Whitman sound verbose and flat, as he unfortunately does to my ears in most French translations.

In that respect, Derrida's notion of *économie* came in handy to formulate what I was aiming at. In his essay on translation, *Qu'est-ce qu'une tradiction relevante?*, Derrida insists on the notion of quantity.[19] "Translation," he writes, "is always an attempt at appropriating, at importing home, into one's language, in as proper and as relevant as possible a manner, the proper meaning of the original." Economy, he adds, is "a law of quantity: when one discusses economy, one is always discussing a quantity that can be quantified. [...] One counts and accounts for" (Derrida 2005, 15, I translate). Dealing with a poet prone to being verbose and translating into a language requiring between 10 to 20% more words than the original, in order to try and keep clear of the flatness I feared and came to deplore in French translations of Whitman, I soon came to realize that striving to be economical might help me keep the sermonizing lilt I heard in my mind when imagining Whitman in French. Derrida, in a rather unorthodox way, goes so far as to state that économie "is not about counting the number of signs, signifiers or signified, but counting the number of words, the lexical units called "word[s]"" (Derrida 2005, 16). However extreme if not downright unattainable and undesirable such an approach to translation may at first sound, it nevertheless proves extremely valuable in accounting for the constraints that I set myself in translating such a profuse text as the 1855 "Song of Myself."

To go from the *I* to the *you* in the poem any would-be translator is confronted with recurring features that give substance to the sheer size of the poem and often proves wearisome to readers who do not care for Whitman's style. One of these is the ubiquitous reliance on repetition, a writing device central to Whitman's use of parallelism, and one utterly abhorrent to the French language. Translating Whitman's parallelisms verbatim risks making the French version tiresome. The pioneering translation of the deathbed edition of Leaves of Grass carried out by Léon Bazalgette in 1909 does exactly that. It reads today more like stylistic mimicry than outright translation. The second alternative, favored by Jacques Darras, is to play around with the form and frequently jettison it altogether in order to lighten and jazz

19 Jacques Derrida. Qu'es'ce qu'une traduction relevante? Paris: Cahiers de L'Herne, 2005.

things up. While literal translation is often detrimental to poetry—and perhaps not more so than in the case of *Leaves of Grass*—I doubt that Whitman can survive being hip and light-footed. I therefore chose to steer a middle course by keeping the parallelisms while displacing the repeated terms when they occur at a higher frequency than usual, or by making the repetition bear on a different signifier from the one repeated by Whitman, as in the following case:

> Outward and outward and outward and forever outward (Whitman 2008, 156),

which became in French:

> Toujours, toujours et toujours plus loin (Whitman 2008, 157)

the repetition bearing here on "forever" and not "outward."

Another key Whitmanian rhetorical device is the present participle, fortunately less systematic in the 1855 "Song of Myself" than in many later ones, but still present in many places. French does not wear the present participle very handsomely and, where Whitman uses it at great length, I felt it necessary to find an alternative form, as in the following extract:

> Speeding through space.... speeding through heaven and the stars,
> Speeding amid the seven satellites and the broad ring and the
>   diameter of eighty thousand miles,
> Speeding with tailed meteors.... throwing fire-balls like the rest,
> Carrying the crescent child that carries its own full mother in its belly;
> Storming enjoying planning loving cautioning,
> Backing and filling, appearing and disappearing,
> I tread day and night such roads (Whitman 2008, 120).

In this passage, the repetitions are coupled with Whitman's choice trope, i.e., anaphora. My translation reads as follows:

> À toute vitesse je traverse l'espace.... à toute vitesse je traverse le
>   ciel et les étoiles,
> À toute vitesse je vais parmi les sept satellites, le vaste anneau et le
>   diamètre de quatre-vingt mille milles,
> À toute vitesse j'accompagne les météores à queue.... lance des

> boules de feu comme les autres,
> Porte l'enfant-croissant qui porte dans son ventre sa propre mère
>   pleinement formée;
> Je tempête me délecte projette aime avertis,
> Soutiens et remplis, apparais et disparais,
> Voilà les routes que jour et nuit je suis (Whitman 2008, 121)

In this instance I chose to turn the verb "speed" into the periphrasis "à toute vitesse" (literally "at full speed") and to use fully-inflected verbs in the final lines, while dropping the subject almost completely in the last three lines, as Whitman does with his present particles. In order to compensate for the loss of the rhyme-like effect induced by the accumulation of present participles I tried to introduce assonantal and consonantal rhyming echoes within my list of verbs.

Another example where the present participle introduces a rhyme-like effect and a certain semantic ambiguity is the following example:

> In me the caresser of life wherever moving.... backward as well as
>   forward slueing,
> To niches aside and junior bending (Whitman 2008, 70).

In my translation, I tried to keep a vocalic rhyming effect on the last syllable of each line and aimed to mirror the mimetic positioning of the verb "bend" at the end by keeping it there in French, fully conjugated and as oddly archaic as I perceive the original to be:

> Caresseur de la vie où qu'elle aille.... je pivote en arrière comme en
>   avant,
> Vers les moindres recoins écartés je tends (Whitman 2008, 71).

Celebrating contradiction

The 1855 "Song of Myself" is a long poem and as such requires an endless attention to its macro and microstructures. My ambition was not to come out with a self-proclaimed French poem—which would have been illusory—but, to echo Antoine Berman again, with an American poem in French.[20] In the case of the 1855 "Song of Myself," this is

---

20 Berman notes about Pierre Leyris's remarkable translation of Hopkins that admirable as it is, the resulting text is not "a genuine French poem but an English poem in French" (Antoine Berman. *Pour une critique des traductions: John Donne*. Paris: Gallimard, 1995,

somehow rendered easier by Whitman through a plurality of voices, resulting from the poet's desire to impress on the reader the full extent of his poetic skills. This led me to endeavor to remain economical with my signifiers, precisely in an effort to render Whitman's signature stylistic devices.

At the end of the day, and to go back to my initial remark, I will now conclude that in translating Whitman's signature poem I regard my method not different from the method likely to have been adopted by any translator dealing with a short poem written in regular meter. I pruned my lines in order to keep them as compact as possible. This compactness seemed to me to be in keeping with Whitman's avowed reliance on contradiction, not an invitation to chaos and carelessness but a feature firmly kept under control and betraying a perfect sense of continuity and logic from the first line to the last. Hence, when perusing his famous statement on the mattter ("Do I *c*ontradict *m*yself? / Very well . . . . then, I *c*ontradict *m*yself; / I am large . . . . I *c*ontain *m*ultitudes.", my emphasis, Whitman 2008, 168) the final alliterative repetition on *c* and *m* belies the deceitful casualness of the lines while echoing of the very first words of the poem: "I *c*elebrate *m*yself" (Whitman 200, 50). I chose to mimic this alliterative repetition and give it a twist in the resolution:

> Je me contredis?
> Eh bien soit . . . . je me contredis ;
> Je suis vaste . . . . j'ai en moi multitudes. (Whitman 2008, 169).

In the final line, I decided to steer away from Whitman's alliterative strategy in order to introduce a twist, a pun not in the original and probably lost on all my readers but me: « J'ai en moi » (which sounds like "géant moi" or, literally "a giant, I"). Keeping the foreignness of Whitman central to my endeavor emboldened me to play with the poetry and appropriate it in keeping with the call for appropriation I can hear in "Song of Myself," the title this originally untitled poem finally was to take. Thus did I strive to keep true to an ethics of translation that was defined by Antoine Berman as "openness, dialogue, blending, and decentering" (Berman 1984, 16), an ethics of translation which seems to me to be in perfect keeping with Whitman's poetic project in 1855.

---

p. 58, I translate).

Excess—The Factory
by Leslie Kaplan

☆

Ian Brinton

Having spent all her early years cooped up in the Marshalsea debtor's prison near London Bridge Amy Dorrit, nicknamed 'Little Dorrit', is released into the freedom of European travel. After having spent a quarter of a century behind walls and iron bars her father is confronted with a new reality: he has inherited considerable wealth. The family travel to Venice where the young girl leans upon the balcony of her rooms overlooking the canal from which she can "musingly watch its running, as if, in the general vision, it might run dry, and show her the prison again, and herself, and the old room, and the old inmates, and the old visitors: all lasting realities that had never changed." Dickens describes the manner in which her father breaks down at a public dinner as the "broad stairs of his Roman palace were contracted in his failing sight to the narrow stairs of his London prison". It is as if the stain of all those years behind bars forces itself to the surface and the hideous effects of long-term imprisonment re-appear as a reality which has never been escaped. And as if echoing this sense of the inescapability from confinement Maurice Blanchot wrote about Leslie Kaplan's 1982 book-length poem *L'exces-l'usine*:

Other remarkable books have described the work done by a factory and in a factory. But here from the very first words we understand that, if we enter into working in the factory, we will belong henceforth to the immensity of the universe ("the great factory universe"), there will no longer be any other world, there has never been any other: time is finished, succession is abolished, and "things exist together simultaneously". There is no more outside – you think you're getting out? You're not getting out. ("*Vous n'en sortez jamais*")

Being divided into 'Nine Circles' *Excess – The Factory*, in its English translation done by Julie Carr and Jennifer Pap, inevitably calls to mind the structure of Dante's *Inferno* but Kaplan's poem is very different from the schematic world of the Italian poet. In the 'Fourth Circle' Kaplan refers to "Palpable air" and it is that very palpability that also reminds us of Dante: this world possesses a vivid sense of being there. However, the "You" ("*On*" in the original French) which sees itself "endlessly" in Circle Five is there throughout all nine sections of the poem: differentiation according to individual sins does not exist in this dystopian nightmare of the factory. In their Afterword the translators talk about the third-person pronoun designating the subjective presence that moves through the poem. They conclude that to translate "on" as "you" has the advantage of sometimes referring to the self, sometimes to a specific other, and sometimes to anybody:

> "You," then, offers the floating subjectivities of this assemblage of persons made disconnected by the factory system.

The opening lines of the poem emphasise the wisdom and effectiveness of this decision and the first passage, "L'usine, la grande usine univers, celle qui respire pour vous. / Il n'y a pas d'autre air que ce qu'elle pompe, rejette" is soon followed by the uncompromising phrase "On est dedans":

> The great factory, the universe, the one that breathes for you.
> There's no other air but what it pumps, expels.
> You are inside.

With an increasing awareness of claustrophobia the passage on the first page concludes

> No beginning, no end. Things exist together, all at once.

> Inside the factory, you are endlessly doing.

> You are inside, in the factory, the universe, the one that breathes for you.

The protest movements in France in 1968 had led in turn to the strike at the Brandt factory in Lyon where Kaplan was working at the time and she recorded the liberating effect of having the high walls of routine and expectation taken down, even if for only a short time:

> People invite each other to come see their work spaces. Until then, it was not allowed to go into another work area besides your own. For the first time, workers circulate in their factory, which seems extraordinary: the factory belongs to us. Above all, you have the feeling of time.

The sense of removing the prison walls leads to a feeling that "Time becomes a way to meet, and also to imagine." It is perhaps with this in mind that Leslie Kaplan can present us with those moments of connection and tenderness that, as the translators put it, "seem to us to offer, if not a *way out*, at least an alternative reality hovering in the margins":

> You walk with the girl along the edge of the water. The sky is white. Banks, banks of the Seine. You walk together, you talk to each other, while the sky touches the earth, and the water. Benches, a painted snack bar…
> You hold the girl by the arm, you walk…
> You walk. You have an apron, the girl has a smock. The trees are
> detached, stiff and green. The sky hovers.

Threading a path through the nine circles of the poem we are presented with the isolated traces of human lives and these are often presented in a fractured state, a face, a dress, a mouth which is lacking a tooth but through which come words. In the world of Kaplan's factory "You wander in places without names, courtyards, corners, warehouses" but you also sense what she wrote about the central truths of Kafka's world:

> This sentence of Kafka's has always seemed to me to be the very definition of what writing is: "To write is to jump outside the line of the assassins": the assassins, contrary to what one might believe, are those who stay in line, who follow the usual way of things, who repeat and start over again the bad life as it goes.

In that first circle the poet tells us "Words open the infinite" and it is this gesture perhaps which takes us beyond the world of Dickens's *Little Dorrit* where the stain of the Marshalsea prison dries up the canals of Venice for Amy. In the world of Leslie Kaplan's factory

> You advance in a boat, through muddy and narrow streets.

It is in those words "On avance dans une barque" that we see that even if "Vous n'en sortez jamais" there is at least an alternative reality hovering in the margins.

Fifty Shades
of Joseph McElroy

☆

Mike Heppner

For seven years I taught a writing course at Emerson College in
Boston, and during that time I noticed my students rarely wrote
about sex. Not that I especially *wanted* them to—I didn't care, they
could write about whatever they liked, but I found it odd that so
many nineteen and twenty year olds would resist a subject that
must've weighed heavily on their minds outside of class. Some of it
might've been self-consciousness, a reluctance to get too personal
on the page. I could understand wanting to save one's most intimate
work for another stage, although the students weren't hesitant to
explore other personal matters in their stories: rape, drug addiction,
suicide, eating disorders, watching friends and family members die.
They wrote about *wanting* to have sex, but only as a vague and
distant longing.

Joseph McElroy also rarely writes about sex; rather, his
characters are preoccupied with other things: geology, ecology,
space travel, war, globalism, the burden of celebrity, the legacies
handed down from a parent to a child. Many of McElroy's novels
are quest narratives, wherein the protagonist is so focused on his
goal—solving the mystery of a kidnapped boy, tracking the impact of
a subversive, experimental film—that other concerns get brushed to

the margins. One gets the sense McElroy's interests are so varied that the subject of sex, which might dominate another writer's work, simply has to wait its turn. But look closely and one can see how the occasional sexual content in McElroy's fiction amplifies his core humanism. Sex, even masturbation, strengthens and re-centers the individual—even helps *define* her—amid the volatile social tectonics McElroy has spent his career chronicling.

He explores the subject most frankly in 1987's *Women and Men*, set in New York City during the mid-1970s. Any comprehensive statement about McElroy's 1293 page novel is bound to mislead; there's just no way to succinctly express what the book is about without being overly general or leaving too much out. It's even misleading to spotlight those passages that focus on gender roles and sexuality because so much of the book has little to do with either. It's a novel that almost demands a specialized critical approach rather than a holistic one.

If you've never read *Women and Men* and know only one or two things about it, you probably know the book revolves around a man and woman, strangers to each other, who live in the same Manhattan apartment building. The woman is Grace Kimball, who conducts group therapy sessions out of her home. These sessions are called "workshops," and the participants are usually though not exclusively female. Here's Grace herself describing what typically goes on in a session:

Well, in a workshop we do a bit of everything: I'm open: we share sexual information, we talk about Body-Self image, we do some yoga, I demonstrate massage, we explore masturbation, diet, alternative energy-bases for self-love because even in a regular sex life so many women put a man's orgasm first. (*W&M*, 135)

Two things worth pointing out: one, for Grace and her followers, masturbation is only one part of an overall lifestyle that also includes women's health and mindfulness, and two, Grace views masturbation as a political act and an expression of her idiosyncratic brand of feminism. (McElroy partly based the character on Betty Dodson, who lived in the same building as McElroy in the seventies and whose 1974 book *Liberating Masturbation* is considered an urtext to the pro-sex feminist movement.) Grace has sex on her mind, surely, but her project isn't limited to sexual self-exploration; diet is important too, along with hygiene and maintaining digestive regularity. ("Listen, dear, I'm in the middle of an enema, I gotta hang up," she tells a friend casually over the phone.) If there's a common theme, it's a near-obsessive preoccupation with the body: what goes into it and what it puts out. A male friend of Grace's chief acolyte, Maureen, observes of Maureen:

I mean she would talk endlessly about her body, the quality of her gums if she went a day without eating a grapefruit, the number of days she might go without taking a shit, how to brush your teeth (though one day when I thought What the hell, we'll talk about this, then, why she closed the subject as soon as I opened my mouth), the hint of past surplus along her lower back, the exact feel of pubic hair growing back in, how her insteps felt when she came with a man, with a woman, or alone, or—but orgasm was good or better because of how *you* managed things. (*W&M*, 994)

Grace's mission isn't an intellectual one, but physical—and with political implications. One of her earliest acts of personal liberation was discovering she could masturbate in bed next to her sleeping husband without waking him up. Masturbation became her way of declaring her sexual independence from her husband, soon to be ex. It allowed her to avoid the twin traps of placing her husband's sexual needs above her own, and becoming exclusively dependent on a man for sexual gratification. As she later advises another woman, "Your need and his need on separate tracks: that's why you get a hard-on for yourself, honey. Masturbation no obstacle to anything else you *want* to do." It's a message she's passed on to her many followers, sometimes to the detriment of their own marriages. (One character, Marv, seems to blame Grace for encouraging his wife Sue to leave him.)

While men aren't excluded from the workshops, Grace's focus is on building women's confidence in their bodies, often by means of brash rhetoric. Of this, she is unrepentant; when the earlier mentioned Marv accuses her: "You always go too far," her response is, "I try to." There's a bit of the provocateur in her, as evidenced by her self-acknowledged need for attention. Even masturbation is best done in the company of willing co-participants. She writes of one of her few male followers, "I said Cliff better jerk off the way I showed him, preferably *with* someone." There's an implied paradox in the idea of group masturbation, which utilizes a self-absorbed means to express intimacy and openness with another person. Grace takes the personal act of masturbation and turns it into a shared celebration. She writes:

Yes that's how I see myself at eighty, eight-five, ninety-five, a hundred in my wheelchair at the home with all the sisters, we're all in our chairs in front of our TVs, good TV porn funded by a government inspired by the Goddess, a Body-Sex government decentralized all over the land, California, Florida, and here we all are, a bunch of happy old ladies in our wheelchairs, our vibrators plugged in, happily jerking off. (*W&M*, 151)

A classic over-sharer, Grace, who also seems to be an around-the-house nudist, finds clothing oppressive and enjoys the freedom she feels while naked, especially when someone else is there to see her. It's her way of being both candid and confrontational with her body. For Grace, being naked is about personal bravery, an advertisement for her sex-positive lifestyle: "*Naked* was the word to use, proud of warm skin, gone public so you can really work on yourself."

This last phrase asks us to consider masturbation as part of a larger mission, which to Grace it is. Being assertive about one's own sexual autonomy—which in this context means feeling comfortable enough about masturbation to do it in front of other people—is as much an element of a woman's health as diet and exercise; and like diet and exercise, it takes "work." It's a message that resonates with the women in Grace's orbit who view her as providing an alternative to mainstream feminism, which Grace would reject as anti-sex. One woman's experience is typical, and her name is Norma:

She wasn't having anything to drink tonight before going upstairs to the first session of the workshop which was fairly hard to get into. With all those women sitting around on the rug. Letting it hang out. And Norma with them. Naked as they. Rapping. Sharing information, said Grace Kimball. Find out you're like other women, said Grace.

(Not unique, then?) Learn to breathe, said Grace, learn to use a plastic speculum (easy enough) and a standing mirror. Go public. (*W&M*, 525)

Certain phrases start to recur: "Sharing information," "Go(ing) public." "Share" means the women are there to help each other—they bring their individual experiences to the workshop and share them for the benefit of the group; but "information" feels intriguingly non-specific. What *is* this information? The word suggests the concrete and factual, but we don't know exactly what it is. Then there's the idea of "going public." If step one involves covertly masturbating in bed next to your husband, step two means taking sex out of the bedroom, maybe even out of the confines of traditional marriage.

Naturally the husbands of the women in Grace's workshop don't necessarily know what to think of Grace, nor do they entirely approve. (One suspects many men of the times would've wondered if women "sharing information" implied women complaining about *them*.) Norma's husband Gordon feigns indifference, claiming, "… he didn't care one way or the other if she went to the workshop, were all these naked gals in the workshop workshopping, he asked, were they throwing vases on a pottery wheel?" Feeling helpless to intervene—surely things were different in his parents' day!—his only recourses are patronizing jokes and dismissive asides.

In fairness to the guys, Grace's workshops haven't always had a positive influence on the edgy interplay between women and men; Marv's broken marriage to Sue is one example. Maureen's unnamed boyfriend implies a criticism as well, not only of Maureen's exaggerated orgasms at the two workshops he attended, but of the way Grace's advice to Maureen—that Maureen take ownership of her orgasms, in part by practicing masturbation—has resulted in the boyfriend feeling less intimate with her. (Note the boyfriend's sarcastic characterization of Grace as "the Leader"):

But then with me one time she did come, and in all those quick breaths like contraction control, then some soft long breaths even before she let go that last private wonder and laughed and I did, too, but I knew it was real and I had felt it in the muscles of her buttocks that must have been drained of all fatty tissue by lecithin or God knows what recent compound. But it wasn't me supposedly; it was her being (as the Leader said) responsible for her orgasm. (*W&M*, 995)

Maureen's boyfriend (I use the term loosely; it's the seventies, after all) expresses skepticism toward Grace and her sometimes shocking-for-the-sake-of-it provocations. He challenges her, and Grace seems somewhat insecurely inclined to accept his challenge if only to evade deeper scrutiny. There are times when Grace's confidence breaks, and she responds with overcompensations:

I pointed out to Grace Kimball that in wanting to be a "top," a business, a (God! a) vagina that is much more than a subtly hooded cock and its patient balls (lower extension of, i.e., shape of, outer lips) and its claims to ejaculate, and in sashaying around like a boy trying to look like a man or whatever I am trying to say, Grace was further confusing what a woman is. She said I might be right, but so what?, she had seriously considered how she might have a child by Maureen. She laughed, then, and disappeared into her kitchen to bring me some tea. She was talking about the neglected asshole and how she would like to raise its status. She said she felt more comfortable with some gay men than some women she could name. (*W&M*, 1006)

Confronted with a challenge, Grace leaves the room; she concedes the point by minimizing its importance and then uses her characteristic outrageousness to reclaim the upper hand. We don't dislike her for this; it's part of her charm, her tea room repartee. McElroy persuades us that Grace's intentions are good, and that her raunchy sales pitch is simply how she gets her message out. (Again: she *has* to "go too far," because "it's how people know me, it's how I'm public.") Even Maureen's generally oppositional boyfriend is unable to suppress a grudging admiration for her: "Yet the Leader was something else, and I would not pretend to sum her up except that she enjoyed her life enormously and if she, as she used to say in her own famous words, 'ran the fuck' (with whoever), and if it was a little on the Olympic side of lust, she was fun and preferred a long-distance variety of body trips to the usual."

McElroy, whose writing over the years has expressed an occasional but keen interest in Buddhism in particular and Eastern medicine and philosophy in general, sees in Grace's quest for sexual self-fulfillment something akin to meditation. The goal is both individual—sexual liberation and self-expression—and global: a kind of world-wide "coming together" group-conceived by people masturbating in the embracing company of others. Masturbation *is* meditation; the individual's method of stimulating herself, whether with fingers or a vibrator or another implement of choice, is her mantra. When McElroy describes masturbation, he could be describing yin yoga:

Plug in, turn on; the vibrations are light but right, the underground waters are felt faraway and the right hand guides the wave length in its grip toward those faraway waters. Find what is right for you. The soles of your feet together. Let power find *you*, if you have to play hard-to-get. Sometimes she thought there would be peace on earth if we would just learn to breathe. (*W&M*, 160)

By associating masturbation with meditation, McElroy connects Grace's workshops to the novel's broader narrative. He calls many of his chapters "breathers," which together account for nearly two-thirds of the book. These complex, palimpsestic sections—written in the first-person-plural—postulate "angels" as mediating presences between strangers and familiars alike. The characters in McElroy's world inhabit a shared consciousness that stops just short of the tangible. Early in the novel the narrator wonders, "Who is this 'We'? We have but to ask when lo! it curves piecemeal off breakneck into nowhere, we shouldn't have asked. Was it these angel relations trying to change their lives, adopting the local language cum customs? Have we learned to breathe together?" A woman who meditates counts her breaths to keep out unwanted thoughts; for the purpose of meditation, counting breaths is more effective than "thinking about nothing," because a truly empty mind leaves too much space for distractions. Breathing is meditation's basic unit, and whether writing about sex or masturbation, McElroy rarely strays far from the breath. Here's a description of a man (actually Jim Mayn, the novel's other main character) and his wife making love:

Not just that he on his back with his knees V'd out licked her insteps' wrinklable arches while from below her she divided and trained his soft-skinned old beanbag either side of her soft, struck-open breather (take a breather, sweet) while he broke the V of his knees to run his own instep up and down her ribs, pigeon-toeing under onto a softer flesh to the returning touch of separateness, each soft spot of nipple marking his motion. (*W&M*, 1089)

The sexual, meditative breath can be found elsewhere in McElroy's novels. Here's another instance of making love, this time from 1974's *Lookout Cartridge*:

I speak for myself, not for her, though—and for her ribs and a down above the knees and for her fleshly shoulders that are not what you would think from her tense figure clothed, the parts of her body I speak for still speak for themselves, but I can't speak for her, I have her, I breathe with her, have in my hands even what I wouldn't ever want to get at in her, like one of my whole memories I can't divide. (*LC*, 160)

Based on this, we might conclude that when McElroy writes about sex or masturbation, he wants us to keep meditation in the backs of our minds. If one goal of meditation is inner stillness, and if group meditation attempts to globalize the inner stillness of the individual, then masturbation and group masturbation share a similar goal, at least according to believers and practitioners. Here's Grace alone in her "fully mirrored Body Room," on the verge of orgasm; note that her masturbation seems to have an objective beyond simple sexual gratification:

But she didn't quite have it, didn't quite get what it was that came after her—she the future—orgasm peace. Until, coming or on the point of it coming, her softening eyes moistened the tall pier glass (my dear) across the candlelit room, so it was wings taking her away—but her own—one throb, but that didn't quite end—a woman-minute of her constant self: which was not enough… (*W&M*, 162)

These are tricky things to write about without alienating the reader; masturbation is so personal, and Grace's motivations are so eccentric as to be potentially off-putting. Beyond all that, it's simply difficult writing about sex without succumbing to any number of pitfalls. There's the "bad sex writing" that fails because it resorts to cliché, or is too clinical, or pornographic (which has value, but that's another topic). Bad sex writing seems more concerned with accurate reportage than capturing a feeling. In some ways writing about sex is similar to writing about listening to music or eating fine food, other experiences that evade description and can really only be understood firsthand. It's not that it can't be done, but the job must be approached with patience and an awareness that even one's best efforts will come up short, however slightly.

Joseph McElroy, a writer not prone to clichés, tackles the challenge with a uniquely varied approach to language. A lengthy quote from *Women and Men* is helpful here; what we're looking for is not consistency, but a deliberate *inconsistency* of tone. Some of the language is abstract and disorienting, some of it descriptive and concrete, even crude:

The buzz did not let up, someone telling her what she knew with the words all changed into someone's words-to-be, universe-orbit of infinitesimal cunts that hers was if you blew it up to find smaller and smaller stretches—not *her* words, she didn't know these: the buzz loosened into its cycles and met the music from her sound system in this room and the next, and the friendly machine's low song going on as long as she wanted made spaces of a grand cloud that was like her becoming her—and the cloud lost its shivering buzz as she came, and at every spread breath-fork the cloud really got into her and was her, and the tips kept coming, rips of grip in passing, dear, in passing—beyond applause, for who was here to applaud? They made her laugh at herself, this was all there was to it—not even a young male secretary thrown in (she had old friend Cliff anyway). From the interior of her feet haired in the expanding carpet that her heels and toes pressed hard into, crests walked up through her knees, down through her thigh-thighs like a lightness to meet themselves tiding from head and shoulders, scalp and eyeballs, like parts of her that didn't tie off at the end, bunches that, with some rocking happy fuck-ya that she didn't quite put her finger on, didn't end. (*W&M*, 122)

Contrast "spaces of a grand cloud that was like her becoming her" with "some rocking happy fuck-ya that she didn't quite put her finger on." Both describe orgasm, but one is indirect and almost pretty, while the other uses profanity (typically rare in McElroy) and a blocky syntax that feels semi-improvised. The word "cunt" has not only crass but pejorative connotations—it's a word that frequently suggests a violent attitude toward women—but since we're in Grace's point-of-view, we're given to understand that the word derives from her sensibility, the way she talks and thinks. McElroy uses the word because Grace would use it too.

At the moment when the passage seems most directly concerned with orgasm—"the cloud lost its shivering buzz as she came... etc."—the language turns abstract; it's purely emotive, not strictly-speaking "descriptive" at all. The writing both makes and illustrates the point that no one *thinks* their way through an orgasm. But McElroy also captures Grace's sensuality, from the feel of the carpet against her bare feet to her dim awareness of the music playing in the other room. If we're not actually sharing in Grace's orgasm, we're a lot closer to a direct experience than a more literal and conventional description might allow.

McElroy's language to describe sex organs varies as well. It's a decision all writers have to make when describing sex: do I call it a "penis" or a "cock"? "Vagina" or "pussy"? As mentioned earlier, McElroy isn't a writer who generally resorts to profanity, though in the bedroom he's often inclined to speak in the vernacular, as some of the previous quotes have shown; but even there, his approach seems deliberately hard to pin down. Generally speaking, McElroy's preferred substitution for penis is cock, and cunt for vagina; that loaded word again, cunt, which has unpleasant overtones but also a monosyllabic forcefulness that "pussy" lacks. (Arguably, "pussy" isn't much less pejorative than "cunt"—or even "dick" or "cock" for that matter. Why do all substitute words for sex organs sound like insults?)

By using cock and cunt instead of penis and vagina, McElroy avoids preciousness and keeps the writing earthy and real. It's how he stays true to his point-of-view; nowhere in the novel do we get the sense that Grace Kimball lives in a world of penises and vaginas—it's simply not the way she thinks or talks. (The same could be said of other characters in *Women and Men*.) Because profanity is the exception not the norm in McElroy's writing, his occasional coarse language winds up elevating to the level of the rest of his prose, as shown in this example, where he alternates between the high (vagina) and low (cunt) modes:

Vibrators lay like mikes or hair-dryers at two far strategic corners of her Body Room plugged in beside softly overflowing clusters of brown, orange, purple, and gold cushions and ceramic trays she had made—in another kind of workshop once, and painted rainbow vaginas on—which held carved pipes of wax or wood, double-ended for mutual toking, a cock's peeled bulb, a cunt's deepish flower, the chimney-bowl midway between. (*W&M*, 143)

The cumulative effect of McElroy's attention to detail—both emotive and descriptive—brings us uncomfortably close to Grace's undeniably zany world. One frequently laughs at the over-the-topness of it all, which I think is certainly intentional. (Another aspect of McElroy's work that gets frequently overlooked: he's often very funny.) Sex is gloriously dirty: it's fun! His characters come with smiles on their faces. They're loud in bed because they want their neighbors to know what a good time they're having. Sex isn't about power or putting other people down, unless that's your mutual thing. Sex is athletic—it's even a sport. *Who can come the loudest, the longest, the most times?* (Or who just wants to watch?) Orgasms are good for you, just like eating raw vegetables or self-administrating a colonic flush. It's all positive, all life-affirming. Sex can be holy ritual or as impersonal as a handshake, depending on your mood, *your* mood:

(Grace) had designed sessions with fifteen women and men around the edges of her Body Room: fifteen vibrators at once, with Grace in the middle, that's sixteen, until the collective energy rose peacefully from the group, and some people made noise, Cliff always, but not Desmond, who was all legs with thighs of a bike racer and later asked Maureen to tell him her trip again and asked Grace if his fruitarian diet might be why he was ejaculating a foot further than before, beyond the small towels Grace had distributed, beyond the small, woolly rug he himself was on, and onto the free spaces of the brown carpet: Grace said she would have licked it up wet if she had known all that protein was going to waste on her rug. Masturbation opens a menu of lifestyle choices, though the rug *fibers* might be carcinogenic though with months of charge built up from vacuuming. Her neighbors up in the penthouse felt their floors bowing and their roller skates rolling down to all the corners of the house. (*W&M*, 151)

What I love most there—and there's a lot to love—is that Grace hesitates to lick Desmond's semen up from the floor *because she's concerned there might be carcinogens in the rug.*

Though the larger narrative of *Women and Men* spends more time on Grace's male counterpoint, Jim Mayn, Grace's verve and utter lack-of-filter make her the prickly heart of the novel. We learn the squirm-inducing facts from her past, that she was molested both by her uncle and a "friend-of-the-family," and harbored an incestuous attraction to her brother when they were growing up. We see her at her most naked and vulnerable, which also seems to be her sweet spot. Coming down from another orgasm, McElroy writes of a nude and prone Grace, "She arched and farted like Mona Lisa if you really looked at her and moistly for good fruitarian measure." None of this is particularly titillating, because titillation depends on air-brushed fantasy: the idealized woman doesn't let out a fart while trembling in the throes of ecstasy. Nor does the reader come away feeling like a voyeur after watching Grace masturbate and strut about the house naked. She's in charge of how she displays herself to the world: she *wants* you to watch. In the lingo of the times, Grace embodies sex-positive feminism; she's independent, smart, tough, and proud of her body, and she always "runs the fuck."

David Miller,
Spiritual Letters
(Contraband Books 2017)

☆

Keith Jebb

David Miller started writing the prose poetry collage texts of *Spiritual Letters* in 1995, finishing in 2016. Since around 2003, I have been hearing him read them, and been reading them myself in various small press and pamphlet editions as the seven series came out. It has been a long distillation, and perhaps, in a world where concpetual works much longer than this can appear in a matter of a couple of years, an unfashionable one. In certain quarters of the innovative field, you might think words like craft, distillation, accretion have become outmoded. Something similar to the UK academic research notion of 'impact' is abroad. And though I have issues with Kenneth Goldsnith's production of texts that he says need not be read once you've grasped the concept (which is never that trying), I see nothing wrong in this. Except as the only valid strategy.

You could say *Spritual Letters* is a writerly text, rather than a readable 'classic' one—it is genuinely innovative in its construction—but it must be read. And it bears several readings which will generate, performatively, different reading experiences. There are other writers in the broad scene of British Linguistically Innovative Poetry (a descriptive term, coined by Gilbert Adair in 1988, and not a school that anybody actually signed up to) whose work demands a similar reading process: Alan Halsey, Maggie O'Sullivan, Gavin Selerie and Johan de Witt to name a few; but there are some things that are Miller's and Miller's alone. The textual and textural weave of *Spiritual Letters* is quite unlike anything else published in English poetry this century.

In the notes at the end of the volume Miller writes: "'Spiritual Letters' derives much of its inspiration from the Scriptures, especially tracing certain keywords through the Scriptures, using a Biblical concordance" (p.131). Importantly he stresses that the Scriptures here provide "a springboard for the imagination." With that in mind, I'd like to use my own readings of these prose poems to suggest some other senses for the term 'spiritual letters' and the two words that comprise it.

As I just said, these are prose poems, composed by a kind of collage or fold-in technique. The notes list some, but by no means all, of the references and quotations included in the texts. There are personal anecdotes, dreams, stories of friends, biographical incidents from the lives of artists, writers and (mainly jazz) musicians, as well as quotations from and allusions to Scripture (of course), but also other religious material and material from other religions. He has said there is a 'two-sentence' rule in the composition: no one source or anecdote can stretch beyond two consecutive sentences (often it is only one). Though they can return in other prose poems in the same or other series. At least for this reader, it is impossible to trace or identify the action of a single 'keyword' in any one poem. There is a sense of thematic drift, a slow rotation, or slippage from one thread to another:

> Sitting at a small table on the balcony, drinking wine and writing draft after draft by lamplight. More and more incapacitated, his head snapping backwards in spite of himself, the boy was stranded in the waiting room. Having dropped the heap of leaves, the little girl beseeched her sister and parents to help her pick them up again.
>
> (Series 3, p.40)

One thing to notice here is that this form of prose poetry is not the descriptive mode of classic French prose poetry. It is a narrative form, a fractured narrative form. It is no coincidence that Miller edited the anthology *The Alchemist's Mind* (2012), a collection of innovative fiction by innovative poets; he has also written fiction, some of it published in *The Dorothy and Benno Stories* (2005). To explain the relationship between the three sentences quoted above might have one stretching logic to breaking point: could the second two be simulacra for the writer (Miller?) in the first? That would be odd and delimiting. There may be something about control here, and there is a clear juxtaposition between the second two. But it is unlikely that anyone would be able to predict the drift of the next sentence: "You should try writing a novel, he told me;" or the next: "Dear is the honie that is lickt out of thornes," a sentence, not from a religious book, but from Gerard's *Herball*, as the notes tell us.

Within these fractured narratives, it is the emergence of repetition, leitmotifs of all kinds, the re-emergence of kinds of image or event that creates the textures across the letters. And to go back to the question of what those two words 'spiritual' and 'letters' can mean, one thing that keeps coming back at me is the issue of inscription, and how it is handled.

On the very first page: "The sheets of paper blacken" (Series 1, p.13). "Messages disguised as postage stamps" (Series 1 p. 19). "A darkened room: a scribble of red, hypnagogic; pulsating, glowing, hovering over the pile of letters and photographs" (Series 2, p.33). "It was *a map of heaven*, yet one he couldn't follow" (Series 3, p.51). "After his wife's death he went through her diaries, crossing out passage after passage" (Series 4, p.64). "Printed on your postcard, with a schematic drawing of a person: *I'm lost*" (Series 5, p.77). There are numerous other examples of text with some kind of spiritual or prophetic dimension appearing as liminal or under erasure. The message isn't revealed, or is itself a sign of futility.

A similar fate awaits those who claim or aspire to spiritual ascendency:

His efforts at proselytising were hindered by the interpretor appointed to him, alcoholic and uncooperative. *There were two monastery buildings, but no monks lived in them. If a guest monk attempted to stay, the native people would drive him out with fire.*

(Series 5 p.79)

In a sense, this points to one of the most important aspects of *Spiritual Letters*: they are not overtly spiritual, and it takes no deference to religiosity to read them as an atheist or an agnostic. As long as one respects the Other *as such*, as that which is not revealed, as the Beyond that apppears fleetingly, if at all. And of course the most telling home for the Other is other people. With Miller we enter the world of Martin Buber's *I-Thou* relationship, where one can give one's self up to the other in a perfect stranger without even intruding into their life. Or take Emmanual Levinas from *Totality and Infinity*: "The Other precisely *reveals* himself in his alterity not in a shock negating the I, but as a primoridal phenonmenon of gentleness."

Spiritual Letters is a book full of strangers, people whose aloneness is a magnetic force for our compassion. "The woman has entered through the doorway, a metal cup in her hand; her face, through the thin veil, is that of someone still very young and unwilling to believe in her beauty" (Series 1, p.14). There is a patina of sadness, almost regret, to so much of the prose, even when there is humour: "She told me that as a little girl she thought of spiders as her friends and would read stories to them. *Did the other children call you Spider Girl?* I wondered, hoping that they didn't." (Series 6, p.101).

There is a lot more that can, and I believe will, be said about this relatively short compassionate book. How its multi-vocalic arrangments are scored in a way that blends and counterpoints the various voices into something that sings, that isn't 'prosy' in any derogatory sense. How Miller's skill with a relatively open syntax allows us to drift across junctures that would be jarring in less skillful hands. How the range of reference—only hinted at in the fourteen pages of notes—is truly impressive. One could write at least a chapter, probably a book, tracing the links between the Letters and jazz (Miller is a particularly gifted clarinetist) and how jazz influences the form of the texts.

Strangely, for me, writing this comes with almost a sense of bereavement, realising again that there will be no more Spitiual Letters to read. This is important work that links three continents. Miller arrived in London in the early seventies, to become one of the mainstays of the innovative poetry scene in the nineties and since, helping to run, first the Crossing the Line readings, then the Blue Bus series; but along with Lee Harwood and Tom Raworth he took much of his influence from the States, in particular from Robert Lax. His Kater Murr's Press has launched a number of new names in pamphlet form, and he has dozens of credits as a thoughtful, careful editor. But this volume here on my desk is truly something else. Forget concepts: it really needs reading.

Notes on Contributors

Éric Athenot is professor of American literature and translation at Université Paris-Est Créteil. His main field of study is 19th-century American poetry, with a particular interest in the poetry of Walt Whitman, to whom he has devoted numerous articles, one short book (*Walt Whitman: poète-cosmos,* Belin 2002) and whose poetry and prose he translates for Les Éditions Corti. This led him to translate the first edition of *Leaves of Grass* (2008), and a volume comprised of *An American Primer* and *Collect* (2016). He is now working on the translation of the original edition of *Drum-Taps*. In 2018, he co-edited *Walt Whitman and Emily Dickinson: a Colloquy* (The University of Iowa Press). He has also written on contemporary prose writers such a Richard Powers, Rikki Ducornet, Mary Caponegro, and Gary Lutz.

Andrea Augé is an artist and an art director for film and print.

Lori Baker is the author of *The Glass Ocean*, a novel, and of three short story collections, *Crash & Tell, Crazy Water: Six Fictions* and *Scraps*. She lives in Rhode Island with her husband, the poet Gale Nelson.

Gregg Biglieri is the author of several books of poetry, including *Little Richard the Second* (Ugly Duckling Presse 2011), *Sleepy with Democracy* (Cuneiform Press 2006), *I Heart My Zeppelin* (Atticus Finch 2005), and *Reading Keats to Sleep* (Cuneiform Press 2003). He lives in Buffalo.

Ian Brinton's recent publications include a *Selected Poems & Prose of John Riley* and *For the Future, a festschrift for J.H. Prynne* (both from Shearsman Books), a translation of selected poems by Philippe Jaccottet (Oystercatcher Press) and he is working on a selected poems of Douglas Oliver for Shearsman. His translation of Baudelaire's 'Tableaux Parisiens' is due for publication in 2020. He co-edits *Tears in the Fence* and *SNOW* and is involved with the Modern Poetry Archive at the University of Cambridge.

Laurie Duggan, b. Melbourne, later a resident of Sydney Canberra and Brisbane, moved from Australia to Faversham, Kent, UK, in 2006. He has published numerous books of poems the most recent of which are *Selected Poems 1971-2017* (Bristol, Shearsman, 2018), *No Particular Place To Go* (Shearsman, 2017), and a reissue of his first two books as *East and Under the Weather* (Sydney, Puncher & Wattman, 2014). Additionally he has published *Ghost Nation* (Brisbane, University of Queensland Press, 2001), a work about imagined space. In October this year he returned to Australia and now lives once more in Sydney.

George Economou is working on a book of "rough trade" translations (see *Golden Handcuffs Review*, Vol. II, #23 (2017), "Bless thee, Bottom, bless thee! Thou art translated," 35-41) from ancient Greek, Cavafy, and others. He gratefully acknowledges Jerome Rothenberg's previous posting in February this year of his poem in this volume, "Inside the Cello," in *poems and poetics* and *Jacket2*.

Gloria Frym writes poetry and prose. Her most recent book is *The True Patriot,* a collection of proses. Some other books are *The Stage Stop Motel* and *Mind Over Matter.* She is the author of two short story collections—*Distance No Object* and *How I Learned*—as well as many volumes of poetry, including *Homeless at Home*, which won an American Book Award. She lives in Berkeley and is professor of writing and literature at California College of the Arts.

Recent work by **Jesse Glass** featured in John Tranter's *The Journal of Poetics Research*, and *Otoliths*. The books *Still Life With Dragonfly* and *Intonarumori* (Noise Machines) will be published in 2019. Professor Jessica Lewis Luck (California State University San Bernadino) gave presentations this year on Glass' visual poetry at Université Paris, Diderot, and at the PAMLA Conference at Western Washington University, Bellingham.

Mike Heppner is the author of the novels *The Egg Code, Pike's Folly*, and *We Came All This Way*. He is currently finishing a "novel in three novels," *Sitting Next to Strangers*. He lives in the Boston area.

Keith Jebb teaches creative writing at the University of Bedfordshire, England. He has poetry published in various magazines, including *Golden Handcuffs Review* and has two pamphlets with Kater Murr's Press. From 2008 to 2016 he helped run The Blue Bus series of readings in London.

Pierre Joris has moved between Europe, the US & North Africa for more than 50 years now, publishing as many books of poetry, essays, translations and anthologies — most recently, *The Book of U /Le livre des cormorans* (with Nicole Peyrafitte); *The Agony of I.B.* (a play); *An American Suite* (early poems); *Barzakh: Poems 2000-2012;* and *Breathturn into Timestead: The Collected Later Poetry of Paul Celan*. Forthcoming is *Adonis & Pierre Joris: Conversations in the Pyrenees* (Contra Mundum Press) & his translation of *Microliths (Posthumous prose)* by Paul Celan (attem-verlag). When not on the road, he lives in Bay Ridge, Brooklyn, with his wife, multimedia praticienne Nicole Peyrafitte.

Robert Kelly's most recent books are *Calls* (fifth and final volume in a cycle of long poems: *Fire Exit, Uncertainties, The Hexagon* and *Heart Thread*), a collection of shorter poems (*The Secret Name of Now*), and a new sequence, just published, *The Caprices*. A novel, *The Work of the Heart*, is forthcoming from Dr Cicero Books, and *Ten Fairy Tales* (with illustrations by Emma Polyakov) is forthcoming from

McPherson & Co. Kelly teaches in the Written Arts Program at Bard College, and is married to the French translator Charlotte Mandell.

Burt Kimmelman has published seventeen books of poetry and criticism, and more than a hundred articles on literature, art and other matters. His poems are often anthologized and have been featured on National Public Radio. Interviews of him are available in print or online. His ninth collection of poems, *Abandoned Angel* (Marsh Hawk Press), appeared in 2015. A new collection, *Wings Apart*, is due to be published by Dos Madres Press in 2019. He teaches literary and cultural studies at New Jersey Institute of Technology. More about him can be found at BurtKimmelman.com.

Marream Krollos was born and raised in Egypt. She has since lived in many parts of the world, including Denver, where she earned her PhD; and Jeddah, where she taught the only college creative writing class for women in the Kingdom of Saudi Arabia. She is at work on a new novel, and has finished assembling an anthology of writing by her Saudi students. Her collection, *Big City*, was published by FC2. Her novella Stan is forthcoming from Meekling Press. She currently lives in Detroit.

Richard Makin is a writer and artist. He studied painting at the Royal Academy, London. His publications include the books *Mourning* (Equus Press), *Dwelling* (Reality Street), *Forword* (Equipage), and *Universlipre* (Equipage). His *Concussion Protocols* is serialized in Alienist magazine. *Work* is publish in 2019 by Equus Press and *Martian* by *if p then q* in 2020. Richard lives at St Leonards on the south coast of England.

Brian Marley. A novel, *Apropos Jimmy Inkling*, will be published by Grand Iota, an imprint of Reality Street, early in 2019.

Simon Marsh grew up in Margate, England and moved to Milan in 1984. Since 2009 he has lived in Varzi, a small town in the Oltrepò Pavese. His published poetry includes *The Ice Glossaries* (Poetical Histories), *The Vinyl Hat Years* (tack/Many Press), *The Pistol Tree Poems* with Peter Hughes (Shearsman), and *Stanze* (Oystercatcher Press). *Stanze* has been translated into Italian by Riccardo Duranti

(Coazinzola Press). His own translations include "Stanley Kubrick and Me", by Emilio D'Alessandro, with Filippo Ulivieri (Arcade, New York).

Joe Milazzo is the author of the novel *Crepuscule W/ Nellie* and two collections of poetry: *The Habiliments and Of All Places In This Place Of All Places*. He co-edits the online interdisciplinary arts journal *[out of nothing]*, is a Contributing Editor at *Entropy*, and is also the proprietor of Imipolex Press. Joe lives and works in Dallas, TX, and his virtual location is http://www.joe-milazzo.com.

David Miller was born in Melbourne (Australia) in 1950, and has lived in the UK since 1972. His recent publications include *Black, Grey and White: A Book of Visual Sonnets* (Veer Books, 2011), *Reassembling Still: Collected Poems* (Shearsman, 2014) and *Spiritual Letters* (Contraband Books, 2017). He has compiled *British Poetry Magazines 1914-2000: A History and Bibliography of 'Little Magazines'* (with Richard Price, The British Library / Oak Knoll Press, 2006) and edited *The Lariat and Other Writings* by Jaime de Angulo (Counterpoint, 2009) and *The Alchemist's Mind: a book of narrative prose by poets* (Reality Street, 2012). He is also a musician and a member of the Frog Peak Music collective. 'Matrix' is an ongoing sequence of poems; the first four sections appear in the UK magazine *Tears in the Fence* #68, 2018. He describes it as "involving a fairly complex combination of variations, shifts, contrasts, transformations, affirmations and negations".

Alice Notley has published over forty books of poetry, including (most recently) *Benediction, Negativity's Kiss,* and *Certain Magical Acts*. She lives in Paris, France.

Rochelle Owens, a central figure in the international avant-garde is a poet,playwright, translator, editor and video artist. The author of four collections of plays and eighteen books of poetry, including recently *Hermaphropoetics, Drifting Geometries* (Singing Horse Press) and *Out of Ur-- New and Selected Poems* (Shearsman), other poetry collections are *Solitary Workwoman* and *Luca, Discourse on Life and Death* (Junction Press). She is a recipient of five *Village Voice* Obie awards and Honors from the New York Drama Critics Circle and is widely known as one of the most innovative and controversial writers of this century whose groundbreaking work has influenced subsequent experimental poets and playwrights. Since its first publication in 1961, her play "Futz" has become a classic of the American avant-garde theatre and an International success. Her work has been translated into Danish, French, German, Greek, Italian, Japanese, Swedish and Ukrainian.

Denise Riley has written *War in the Nursery: Theories of the Child and Mother* [1983], 'Am I That Name?' Feminism and the Category of 'Women' in *History* [1988], *The Words of Selves: Identification, Solidarity, Irony* (2000), *The Force of Language* (with Jean-Jacques Lecercle; 2004), *Impersonal Passion: Language as Affect* (2005) and *Time Lived, Without Its Flow* [2012]. Her poetry collections include *Marxism for Infants* (1977), *Dry Air* (1985), *Mop Mop Georgette* (1993), *Penguin Modern Poets series 2, vol 10* (with Douglas Oliver and Iain Sinclair; 1996), *Selected Poems* (2000), *Say Something Back* (2016) and *Penguin Modern Poets series 3, vol 6* [with Maggie Nelson and Claudia Rankine; 2017]. She lives in London.

Michael Rothenberg is the editor of BigBridge.org, co-founder of 100 Thousand Poets for Change (www.100tpc.org), and co-founder of Poets In Need, a non-profit 501(c)3, assisting poets in crisis. His most recent books of poetry include *Drawing The Shade* (Dos Madres Press, 2016), *Wake Up and Dream* (MadHat Press, 2017), and a bi-lingual edition of *Indefinite Detention: A Dog Story* (Varasek Ediciones, Madrid, Spain, 2017). He lives in Tallahassee, Florida where he is currently Florida State University Libraries Poet in Residence.

Joanna Ruocco is the author of several books, including, most recently, *The Week* (The Elephants of British Columbia) and *Field Glass* (Sidebrow Books), written with Joanna Howard. She is an assistant professor in the English Department at Wake Forest University and chair of the board of directors of the independent, author-run press Fiction Collective Two.

Norman Weinstein's books include *A Night in Tunisia: Imaginings of Africa in Jazz* as well as the poetry collections *No Wrong Notes* and *Weaving Fire from Water*. He is currently learning weaving with the help of his beloved wife Mary, and seeking a translation partner for a selection of poems by the great Catalan futurist poet Joan Salvat-Papasseit.

Mark Weiss has published ten poetry titles, most recently *As Luck Would Have It* (Shearsman Books, 2015) and *As Landscape* (Chax Press, 2010). *Thirty-Two Short Poems for Bill Bronk, Plus One* appeared as an ebook in 2013 (http://www.argotistonline.co.uk). He edited, with Harry Polkinhorn, *Across the Line / Al otro lado: The Poetry of Baja California* (Junction, 2002), and, with Marc Kaminsky, *Stories as Equipment for Living: Last Talks and Tales of Barbara Myerhoff* (Ann Arbor: University of Michigan Press, 2007). Among his translations are *Stet: Selected Poems of José Kozer* (Junction, 2006); *Cuaderno de San Antonio / The San Antonio Notebook*, by Javier Manríquez (Editorial Praxis, 2004); three books by Gaspar Orozco, *Notas del país de Z* (Universidad Autónoma de Chihuahua, 2009), *Autocinemas* (Chax Press, 2016), and *Memorial de la peonía* (Shearsman Books, 2017); and the ebook *La isla en peso/ The Whole Island*, by Virgilio Piñera (www.shearsman.com, 2010). His bilingual anthology *The Whole Island: Six Decades of Cuban Poetry* was published in 2009 by the University of California Press. He lives at the edge of Manhattan's only forest.

The essential David Bromige

if wants to be
the same as is

Essential Poems of David Bromige

Edited by Jack Krick, Bob Perelman, and Ron Silliman
With an introduction by George Bowering

'Among the three or four most significant writers of his generation.'

— Michael Davidson

"a poet of enormous intellect, humor and innovation who is always shifing out from under the solutions of the last book and posing new questions and linguistic possibilities for a song."

—Kathleen Fraser

Publication date: June 21, 2018
Available through Small Press Distribution

www.newstarbooks.com

CPSIA information can be obtained
at www.ICGtesting.com
Printed in the USA
FFHW021721130119
50164561-55082FF